Drive for Dough

Marj Charlier

SUNACUMEN
PRESS
Colorado Springs, CO

Roslyn

W hat could be better than being alive, young, and healthy at five on a Friday afternoon in summer ... with a bottle of Pinot Grigio open in front of you ... and a dog snoring at your feet?" Lena asked Terry, taking a sip of wine, leaning back, and sighing contentedly on her barstool.

"Not much," Terry answered, reaching into the refrigerator behind the tasting bar of her wine shop and pulling out a plate. "Unless it's having olives, cheese, and salami to go along with it."

She set the antipasto in front of Lena with a flourish and bowed as if she'd performed a fine ballet. "And actually being young."

"Ah, true!" Lena laughed, plucking a slim piece of Manchego from the offering. She sighed again.

The end of the work week was more emotionally disconcerting than she liked to admit. On the plus side, it meant getting out of Seattle, heading over the pass to Terry's wine shop in Roslyn and her condo at the golf resort of Suncadia, and playing some stress-free golf for two days.

On the other hand, it heralded two days of fighting the urge to slip into the desk chair in her condo and clean up some irritating work problem so she wouldn't have to face it when she returned to the office on Monday morning. Staying out of the condo and avoiding the computer was the only way could she keep from violating the summer weekend no-work rule she had mandated for her employees at The Perfect Tee.

"Excuse me, I've got to check on the evening appetizer prep in the kitchen," Terry said, slipping around the end of the bar and disappearing into the back of the ancient tavern that she had reclaimed as a wine bar and craft shop. Lena looked around and admired the job her friend had done in making the place inviting.

After she bought the one-hundred-year-old building, Terry had scraped down the old wooden plank floors and coated them with enough polyurethane to hold up to the road salt customers tracked in on their boots five months of the year. She'd saved most of the old wooden display cases, turning some into wine racks and cleaning up others so that they could hold the quilts, tote bags, and pottery Terry sold for local artists on consignment.

The old town of Roslyn, once the setting for the TV show Northern Exposure, had attracted many artists and crafters to its hodge-podge of miners' cabins and disheveled downtown storefronts in the past decade. It took perseverance like Terry's — and the acceptance of a Spartan, bohemian lifestyle — to live full-time in the tiny town.

Terry's shop was frequently Bounty's and Lena's first stop whenever they drove up the mountain to Suncadia for the weekend. Lena looked down at Bounty, her big yellow mutt curled up against the foot of the bar, contentedly snoozing in a place the dog knew as her third home, after

Lena's loft in Seattle and condo in Suncadia. Lena thought the floor might still smell a bit like Rex.

Rex, Terry's lab, died from plain old age two years before, and Lena and Terry both missed his calm, ruffle-proof demeanor. After Rex died, Lena found Bounty at the animal shelter, and he filled a void for both women. Since then, Bounty was Terry's only option for canine companionship, as her husband, Tom, wasn't crazy about sharing their cabin – let alone their bed – with a big dog.

Lena had named her shepherd-mix Bounty for her heavy, multi-layered fur coat that soaked up Seattle rain as efficiently as her namesake paper towel. The thick coat also produced a bounty of dog-hair-reinforced dust bunnies in the corners and under the furniture in Lena's two small condos, but putting up with the endless shedding was worth it. There was nothing quite like a good long cuddle on the floor with her soft, hairy, sweet canine when she needed unconditional love. Bounty was the pal who demanded neither conversation nor explanation.

Bounty sensed that Lena was looking at her, and the big shepherd lifted her head to gaze back. She blinked and yawned. Lena leaned down with a sliver of salami and gave the mutt a quick scratch behind the ears. Satisfied, Bounty let her heavy head drop back to the floor and closed her eyes.

To be so content herself was Lena's goal. She had started running The Perfect Tee three years earlier, at the end of a long golf-obsessed sabbatical from the working world during which she challenged herself to win the USGA Women's Senior Amateur tournament – and succeeded.

The Perfect Tee was a new challenge, one that required

managing a large team of employees and creating a company strategy. But, unlike golf, it was hard to leave work behind at the end of the day. Given a couple of quiet moments, Lena's mind was likely to wander back to the office and whatever problems were unresolved. Granted, the business, so far, was running well. Sales were increasing, brand recognition was growing, and profitability was within sight. But it seemed to be getting more difficult to keep nagging personnel problems from sabotaging her success.

Terry returned from the kitchen and leaned down to give Bounty a hug. Even though she was fifty — just a couple of years younger than Lena — Terry still wore her dishwater-blonde hair long and loose, and, as she bent down to Bounty, it brushed the floor. The dozen-or-so silver bangles jangled on her wrist. Terry stood up and gathered her unruly mane in her hands, twisting it into a messy knot and securing it with a stick that looked suspiciously like a chopstick from a cheap Chinese restaurant. She hoisted her tiny frame up on a bar stool to join Lena on the customer side of the bar.

Lena often wondered if Terry were thin by genetics or by effort. She seemed to eat plenty in Lena's presence, but never gained weight, in spite of being only five feet tall and post-menopausal. Lena wasn't much bigger, but the twenty pounds she had shed while pursuing her golf championship was sneaking back.

"Is Kim coming up this weekend?" Terry asked, settling down and pouring herself a glass of wine. "I haven't seen him for a couple of months, I think."

"I don't know," Lena shook her head and tucked her short brown hair behind her ears. "It seems that his latest release isn't on schedule, and he may have to work all weekend." Kim, Lena's boyfriend, ran a software team at Microsoft, where there was little consideration of something as radically benevolent as Lena's no-work weekends.

"Bounty and I would love to bring Cali up with us, but Kim misses her too much if I take her along. He's been really close to her ever since Stacy died," Lena said. Kim's wife had died of Parkinson's three years earlier.

Kim's dog, Cali, was a middle-aged mutt, still limber enough to knock around the woods with Bounty, chasing chipmunks and ground squirrels up trees and sniffing petrifying elk and deer poop with a focus that would have cured cancer, had she the right cognitive abilities. Bounty's nose was long and powerfully sensitive, too, but her youthful attention was generally drawn to anything that moved, particularly if it was mammalian and willing to run when chased.

"I can relate," Terry answered after a long enough pause that Lena wasn't sure what she was talking about.

"Relate to what?"

"To the suitability of dogs as surrogate mates." Terry laughed.

"Are things still rocky with Tom?" Lena knew her friend well enough to surmise where she was headed. It sounded like Terry's relationship with her husband was slipping downhill.

"Yeah, when they're not terrible." Terry's tone turned sober. "We probably should have stayed apart back when we split right before we got married. I don't know what possessed me to think that a guy who has a fit over orange bathroom paint would be flexible enough to live with me."

"Perhaps his fit over Rex walking down the aisle with you could have been a clue," Lena suggested.

It was right before Lena had competed in the senior women's tournament that Tom, then Terry's live-in boyfriend, had been noisily ejected from Terry's humble cabin in the middle of the night. It was the culmination of an argument over the paint Terry had chosen for her tiny bathroom that escalated into an examination of everything the two hated about each other.

Eventually, though, they had kissed and made up, and they were married three months later, although Rex's participation in the ceremony had nearly been a deal breaker for Tom. Terry had prevailed, and Rex died in his sleep a week later.

"That's one decision I'm so glad I stuck with," Terry nodded. She frowned, accentuating the fine wrinkles that had sprouted around her eyes over the past couple of years. "If Rex hadn't been there with me, I'd never have forgiven myself."

"So, what's going on now?"

"It's pretty much the usual. You know, control issues. Who I am and what I do," Terry said. "And you know, when it comes right down to it, we don't have that much in common. I mean it's not like we can play golf together like you and Kim or like Carly and Brandt. I do my things, and he does his, and they have nothing to do with each other. I lived by myself for an awfully long time, you know."

"Yup, I do," Lena raised her wine glass signaling agreement, simultaneously signaling her need for a refill. Terry reached behind the bar for the bottle sitting in an ice bucket on the counter.

"I actually feel a bit of your pain," Lena continued. "Kim isn't in my house all of the time these days, but he's there enough that I'm starting to resent it sometimes."

"How's that?"

"It's little stuff. Like he's such a neat freak that I have to fight to keep him from throwing out the newspaper before I get finished reading it. I can't tell you how many times he asked me on Sunday if I was done with the Times yet so he could stick it in the recycling bin."

"Irritating." Terry nodded. "But not a big whoop. It's better than Tom telling me I can't cook bacon in my own kitchen because he doesn't like the way it smells up the house all day."

"Well, that's just stupid," Lena agreed. She lifted her glass for a toast. "Here's to the pleasures of living alone. And bacon!"

Immediately, Lena regretted the comment. It was easy for her to reclaim her condo by making it inconvenient for Kim to stop by in the evening. And, with The Perfect Tee always capable of soaking up more time if she let it, it wasn't hard to avoid his company when she was particularly tired of him. But for Terry, going back to living alone would require divorce, or at least a separation. That was anything but an easy decision or an easy process to get through.

Terry leaned forward and frowned at her wine glass.

"Oh, come on," Lena gently chided her. "It's Friday night. We just said there's not much wrong with this picture. Wine? Summer? The weekend?"

"Yeah, you're right. Let's change the subject," Terry conceded. She leaned back and slapped her hands loudly on the bar, startling Lena. "Your birthday is in August, isn't it?"

"Always has been." Lena laughed. "But it's not a big one this year. Just fifty-three."

"I know, but I was filling out my calendar for the shop the other day, and noticed that, oddly, I have a lack of events in August this year. I was thinking we should block out your birthday weekend and have a Saturday night party here. Would you mind?"

"No, of course not," Lena said. "But I can't imagine enough people would show up to make it a real party. And I wouldn't let you pay for it."

"Well, we've got plenty of time to figure that out," said Terry. "I just wanted to be sure you'd be up for it."

"Why do you want to do that? Couldn't you just schedule a benefit for the Roslyn animal shelter or something?" Lena asked, invoking one of Terry's favorite charities.

Terry pursed her lips and thought about it for a minute. To Lena, it looked like Terry had something other than her birthday on her mind.

"I guess it's because we've started to build a kind of community here — you and me and Brandt and Carly and Ryne and Kim and some others," Terry said, still kneading her eyebrows in thought. "We kind of wander around and see each other when it's convenient, but it seems that — other than me and you — we never commit to get together just for the hell of it."

"Is that true?" Lena asked herself out loud. She tried to think of the last time they had gotten together for a barbeque in someone's yard or planned a get-together more than twenty minutes before converging at the winery or the lodge for drinks. She couldn't think of one. "I guess you're right," she finally concluded. "If I must donate my birthday to the cause, I would be glad to do it. But, again, I'm paying for the wine and food."

"Whatever. We've got three months. Let's not pull out the spreadsheets yet,"Terry teased her friend.

Terry knew that Lena rarely made a decision — about taking a job, throwing a party, or going on vacation — without building a spreadsheet. "But," she interjected, "why do you suggest Ryne? I haven't seen him in more than two years. Is he still in town?"

"Yeah, I saw a story in the Tribune the other day that said he's just finished a book, and a publisher has paid him a nice advance. They didn't say how much of an advance, but these days, I guess any advance for a first novel is unusual."

"Hmmm. I wonder what the novel is about." Lena frowned in concentration.

"Probably about you."Terry laughed. "Or at least you'd like to think so, me thinks," she teased.

Bounty suddenly jumped up and barked a single syllable, his usual warning that strangers were approaching. Lena hushed him and reached down to hold on to his collar in case he decided to personally greet Terry's first customers of the weekend.

"Oops! Time to talk up the Chardonnay sippers,"Terry growled under her breath, rolling her eyes and slipping off her stool. "We'll discuss this later.

Jim

The 2017 Tumble Creek Club Summer Solstice Tournament the next day was the first competition of the year that Lena found time to enter. Even though Lena's game had slipped a notch or two from the scratch golf she played when she won the amateur tournament, her single-digit handicap was still good enough to pretty much guarantee her first-place finishes at the club's events.

It was a blustery cold morning, not unusual – even for late June – on the east side of the Cascades in central Washington, where one summer day could be followed by a winter one without warning. The cold wind overwhelmed the sun's efforts to warm up either the golf course or the golfers. Lena was usually a fair-weather golfer, but given the lack of alternative grown-up activities at Suncadia, she showed up for early-season tournaments dressed in layers, hoping she could shed a jacket or sweatshirt at some point in the round. Playing in so many clothes was difficult, like swinging in a straitjacket.

The wind, however, didn't affect the views, and although she preferred playing Suncadia's Prospector, the course closest to the lodge, for its layout and tree-lined fairways, Tumble Creek, the private golf course across the river, had much better views of the mountains. The dregs of late spring snow still draped the mountain tops with graying, ragged blankets, clearly delineating each narrow range between the golf course and the jagged peaks of the Cascade divide.

When she played golf, Lena had to remind herself to stop every now and then and take in the view. She believed that the scenery was one of the reasons she played the sport, but she often returned home after a challenging round and realized that she hadn't looked up all day at the clouds or the mountains.

A few minutes after they were supposed to tee off, Wade, the club pro, gathered the competitors on the practice green to give them instructions for the day. It was typical: these events never started on time, although the ten-minute delay wasn't going to make much difference at the end of June, when the daylight stretched over nearly seventeen hours. It was far more irritating in the fall when a late start and slow play pushed the final holes of a round into twilight.

Lucky for Lena, Wade had grouped players with similar handicaps together, so she wouldn't have to play with beginners. Over the past four years since she started working seriously on her game, she'd honed a lot of skills on the course, but one of them wasn't patience.

Contrary to its usual pattern, the wind died down by mid-day, and the air warmed up considerably. By the time Lena's foursome finished the front nine and stopped at the clubhouse, she already had shed her winter golf gloves and her jacket.

"This is more like it," she said, back into the cart after the bathroom break. She pulled her sweatshirt over her head, and raked her fingers through her short hair to restore some order to its chaos before replacing her visor.

"Yeah, finally," agreed Kate, slipping back behind the wheel of the golf cart they shared, jiggling the ice in her fresh screwdriver before setting it in her cup-holder and driving up to the tenth hole. "I hate having to drink coffee to warm up on the golf course."

Lena appreciated Kate's casual attitude toward the game, an approach that made room for on-course alcohol consumption, a few swear words, and some catty remarks about other players. Another thing Lena liked about Kate was how her score never affected her — good or bad. She took the capriciousness of the game in stride and remembered it was a game, not a job. Too many people took it more seriously than they should, especially given their skill level.

"Do you know Jim Treacher?" Kate asked, surprising Lena with the sudden change in subject.

"Yeah," Lena paused, wondering how much she should reveal about her uncomfortable run-in with the ex-banker three years before. Without knowing why Kate was asking, she was loath to say much. "We met a couple of years ago at Prospector, but I haven't seen him since then. Why do you ask?"

"Oh, he's my neighbor. I saw him this morning, and he asked if you were playing today."

Shit. Lena hadn't thought about Jim for a long time, and the middle of a competitive round wasn't the time to revisit what happened. Especially when she was about to tee off on the short tenth hole, a must-make birdie for her.

The easy, downhill par-four was particularly suited to Lena's drive. If she could post a three on this hole, it would give her a bit of a cushion as they reached the harder holes on the back and her nemesis, the thirteenth, with its tee-shot over a deep, brush-filled ravine.

"What did you tell him?"

"That we were playing together."

Lena was glad she hadn't seen Jim at the pre-tourney group meeting with Wade. It would not have been a good way to start her round. She let out a deep sigh.

Relieved that the group ahead of them had cleared the fairway, Lena jumped up, grabbed her driver. She took a couple of extra practice swings to clear her head and concentrate on her shot. Her drive was nearly perfect, and, aided by the downhill slope, it didn't hit ground until after it slipped to the right of the bunkers in front of the green, bounced slightly left and came to rest on the fringe in front of the putting surface.

Kate took a hint from Lena's silence and didn't bring Jim up again on the back nine.

Two hours later, milling around the patio behind the clubhouse, awaiting the simple ceremony where she'd get her trophy for first place, Lena chatted amiably with the club members she hadn't seen since the fall. They were either eager to hear how her game was holding up, or at least pretended that they were. Perhaps, some of the most competitive among them were secretly hoping to discover that she'd lost her game now that she was back working full time in Seattle.

The cheap loudspeaker set up in the corner of the patio crackled, signaling the start of the awards ceremony, and

Lena returned to the table she shared with the rest of her foursome. She was reaching the end of her rope – both in terms of patience and energy – and was looking forward to getting home to Bounty and her quiet condo for a nap. The group hooted and clapped for the men's winners and then for the women's division runners-up. Finally, it was her turn.

"And, women's first place, gross, goes to – who would have doubted it? – our own USGA champion, Lena Bettencourt!" Wade announced in an exaggerated announcer voice, holding out the trophy as the big finale to his awards ceremony. Clapping and a couple of wolf whistles accompanied Lena as she walked up and accepted the small crystal vase.

"Speech! Speech!" someone yelled from the back. It sounded like Jim. Lena kept her eyes down, waved off the request, and returned to her table. Before she sat down, she looked around to confirm her suspicion.

She didn't have to look far, as a tall, gray-haired man approached with a big grin and his arms outstretched for an obligatory hug. The last time she'd seen Jim, she was pushing her chair back at the restaurant where he'd made a pass at her. She'd run out of the restaurant, feeling naïve and gullible for believing he cared about her golf dreams and her career, and realizing at the end that he was simply looking for an affair. She heard a year later that his wife had finally divorced him, supposedly not for philandering – or intent to philander – but because she wanted to move back to the East Coast where she'd grown up and enjoyed the kind of patrician social status about which heavily Democratic Seattle didn't care very much.

Lena dodged the hug by stepping slightly behind Kate and quickly introducing her other playing partners, Jan and Elysse. He graciously shook their hands before he leaned over and gave Kate a quick peck on the cheek. Lena's three playing partners looked expectantly at the good-looking, aging banker, waiting to hear what he had to say.

"You were terrific as always," Jim addressed Lena warmly. "I watched you come in on eighteen. There probably aren't three other women here who can par that hole," he said of the long, challenging, uphill par-four finishing hole. "How far did you hit that drive?"

"Maybe 260?" chimed in Elysse, smiling at Jim and then looking to Lena for confirmation. Elysse was recently single, and her solicitous tone was transparent; the banker represented potential. Everyone at the club knew everyone else's business, even if they'd never formally met. Word of Jim's divorce had reached her as well.

"Yeah. Probably," Lena said. She paused to give herself time to see how much of her anger persisted. Somewhat surprised, she realized much of her ire was gone.

"How did you play?" she asked, advancing a conversation with the man she very willingly would have strangled three years before.

"As usual. Good shots, bad shots."

"That's golf!" inserted Elysse, a little too eagerly. Jim looked over his wire-rimmed glasses at the redhead and dismissed her with a blink. Lena felt a little sorry for Elysse — but a little embarrassed for her at the same time.

"Do you want to join us?" Lena asked Jim, pointing to an empty chair next to Elysse.

"Nah. But I'd love to catch up sometime. Can we play

golf one of these days? I always get inspiration from playing with great golfers."

Lena glanced around at the expectant faces of the women at her table. Elysse met her eyes and then looked down, acknowledging regret that her game didn't measure up to Lena's, and she was unlikely to get invited to share a cart with Jim.

"I don't know, Jim," Lena said. "I am not up here very often anymore, given my work schedule. But I think Elysse would love to join you."

Jim looked from Lena to Elysse and back again.

"Okay," he said. "I will let this go for now, but I'm not giving up. We will play together."

Jim turned to Elysse and smiled. "I will give you a call. You can tell Lena what she's missing later."

The Perfect Tee

Lena had no experience at being a top executive when she took the job running The Perfect Tee. She had chafed at the bit for a chance to show she could be a leader – not just an implementer; not just someone else's tool; not just a lackey for top management. She had applied for top positions in management at TrueWeb, the last place she worked before taking her sabbatical, but she was always passed over for someone with "more experience."

"How am I supposed to get more experience if I never get a chance to do the job?" Lena asked TrueWeb's CEO after one of her rejections.

"I think it's not just experience," he answered, looking away from her to reveal that he had trouble giving bad news to employees. He continued slowly, as if he thought Lena would accept his criticism better if she had more time to absorb it.

"I don't think you have the social skills for management," he said, and paused. Then: "You're too much of a lone ranger." Another long pause. "And you don't have the technical skills or technology savvy people expect of top executives in this industry."

Lena was shocked at the blunt, negative critique. She

had received high marks on every one of her performance evaluations over the years; no one had ever criticized her "skills" or "savvy." No, she didn't have an engineering degree; not everyone who worked in high tech needed one. Yes, she knew that her "soft" skills – communication, negotiation, diplomacy – were not valued as highly as an ability to write computer code. Supposedly, that was why she was paid so much less. And, yes, she'd often been told that she should work harder to be part of the team, but given the sole-contributor roles she held, a lot of teamwork wasn't necessary, or at times possible.

"What am I supposed to do then?" she asked the CEO. "How am I supposed to get out of the rut of these support roles I've been playing? Do I have to be a speechwriter forever?"

It wasn't that Lena didn't like writing speeches, helping the company articulate its strategy, and shining a bright light on its performance. But after doing it for a few years, she recognized it as a dead-end career.

"Be happy with what you are," her CEO responded, Zen-like and out of character for the straight-talking, demanding executive he always had been.

Astounded, Lena laughed in response, knowing that it probably wasn't the most professional way to react. But it was either laugh or cry, and when he joined her in chuckling at the inanity of his advice, she slipped away and closed her office door behind her. *So, this is it,* she thought, waiting for her anger to dissipate. *This is as far as I get.*

Not long after that, Lena and her direct boss, an insecure and meddling vice president, got in an argument, and Lena spouted out what she'd been thinking – but not saying – about the woman for a long time: that she was incompetent. Lena didn't regret having said it, even though it seemed to prove the CEO's point about her lack of potential as a "company man." She was "let go" from TrueWeb two weeks later.

That was followed by six months of futile job-hunting, complicated by her age – nearly fifty at the time – and by the recession. With little hope of rewarding work, Lena gave up and decided to work on her golf game for eighteen months. She won the USGA senior women's title she had set as her goal, and then accepted the job at The Perfect Tee.

Sarah, a former co-worker at TrueWeb, had founded The Perfect Tee, and secured funding from four venture capitalists who invested in Seattle start-ups. The Perfect Tee sold golf clothing for women online. Recognizing that not all size ten skorts, shorts, or shirts fit the same, Sarah hired software developers to create a set of online retail tools that would take a woman's own precise body measurements and marry them with clothing manufacturers' specs to help her find the brands that would fit her best. It increased satisfaction and reduced returns, which increased repeat sales and cut down on costs.

Shortly after the company launched its website, Sarah decided to retire and focus on her family instead of the business. Lena had always supported Sarah's own efforts to rise through the ranks at TrueWeb, and Sarah paid her back by hiring her as the first outside CEO at The Perfect Tee. This gave Lena the chance to prove herself capable of being the boss – not just taking orders – and proving the CEO at TrueWeb wrong about her.

Now, though, her leadership was facing its first serious

challenges. The toughest one was managing her two top software developers: Ken, who was in charge of the software that ran their corporate financial, legal and HR systems; and Taylor, who ran the search engine and retail website. They had started to quarrel over little things, and the squabble threatened to reverse the progress she had made in building a cohesive team over two years. Lena figured that she had less than a year to pull them back together before she started losing good employees.

Ken didn't get along well with Lena either. He seemed to fancy himself her rival, or at least her adversary, although she didn't think she'd ever given him a reason for it. But he wore his disrespect for her on his sleeve. He clearly thought little of her managerial experience, which she could understand – she was new to this CEO role – but he frequently made a point of bringing up her lack of technology training and experience, which she felt was irrelevant. Running an online retail business did not require her to know how to write the code that translated a customer's search criteria into a purchase. The CEO at General Motors didn't have to know how to bolt a fender onto a car frame, did she?

But in the tech world, this was not uncommon. Ever since Microsoft, Apple, Google, Facebook and Amazon had turned nerds into multi-billionaires, Seattle and San Francisco had become nerd-joke-free zones – places where computer techs, electrical engineers, software engineers, code writers, and others of their ilk roamed the halls of business, not only with impunity, but with an aura of gods. The geekier they were, the safer they were. The geekier, the more revered. The more video games and tech devices they played with, the higher their status.

Lena respected these guys. Who could argue with the success of Bill Gates, Steve Jobs, Mark Zuckerman, and Jeff Bezos? But did it mean every techie was a genius or that their skills were the only valuable ones left in business?

Apparently Ken thought so, and he seemed to be maniacally focused on making that point. The first six months of her reign at The Perfect Tee wasn't so bad. But once she had started to get some credit for the company's progress from the venture capitalists who funded the company, Ken turned difficult. Lena thought he was getting a fine salary, his share of the credit for their success, and a responsible portion of the company's investment in R&D, but apparently he didn't.

"I don't expect you to understand this" he frequently said in front of other staffers and executives, often turning to them with a wink as he belittled her technical expertise.

I'm big enough to overlook this behavior, Lena thought at first. He'll come around.

He didn't come around, and to make matters worse, he clearly had Blake on his side. Blake, the leader of the four VCs who had put up most of the capital to start The Perfect Tee, had been unenthusiastic about hiring her when Sarah recommended her for the job as CEO. He'd gone along with the others in approving her appointment, but he had continued to be argumentative and condescending. As long as she was producing results, though, his attitude had little impact on the other VCs.

Despite her problems with Ken, Lena didn't want to fire him. It would have made things even more difficult with Blake, and firing a high-level employee always caused serious disruption in a company as small as The Perfect Tee.

So, she tolerated his attitude and looked for other ways to help calm the turbulent employee-seas around them, like announcing all employees would have Friday afternoons off with pay through the summer months. Half-day Fridays had spread across most of the high-tech companies in the Pacific Northwest that The Perfect Tee competed with for talent, so it wasn't a tough decision.

The timing couldn't have been better for Lena, herself. Summer had returned to the Pacific Northwest, and it was time to play more golf. Being a successful business leader was important. But it wasn't everything.

Schmoozing

One of the benefits of being the CEO of an online women's golf clothing retailer was free entry to golf tournaments and invitations to the hospitality tents that dotted the periphery of the tournament courses. Too busy to travel to most tournaments, Lena had rarely taken advantage of the invitations. But the opportunity to watch a senior men's tournament at a private course just east of Seattle, gave her a chance to cash in on one of the perks of her position.

Lena had played the course at the invitation of the club pro, one of hundreds of nice offers she'd received right after winning the USGA tournament, and found it one of the toughest she'd ever played around Seattle. She played with a couple of members on a cold May morning, and she never felt comfortable with them. They watched her every move, as if they were trying to figure out how such a short, unprepossessing older woman could have won a national tournament. Perhaps she had some trick that charmed the ball into the hole.

Watching other people play the course was more fun, especially when the golfers were the down-to-earth older men with expanding waistlines on the Champion's Tour, not the young, flashy, freakishly talented and fit twenty-some-things that dominated the regular PGA Tour.

Lena felt pleasantly excited as she pulled into the grassy spill-over parking for the practice round of the event and made a mental note of landmarks that would help her find her way back to her aging Prius later that afternoon. She showed her credentials at the gate, and walked the course backwards from the eighteenth hole to the first, stretching the five-mile walk out to three hours, stopping to watch some drives, some approach shots, and some putts along the way. Finally, on the tee box of the first hole, she tried to wend her way through a thick crowd to get a glimpse of Freddie Couples, a Seattle native and local favorite, as he was teeing off. It was impossible to get close enough, though, even at a practice round, and Lena finally decided that it wasn't worth the effort.

Ready for a drink, Lena pulled the zipper of her quar-ter-zip golf polo up a couple of teeth above her cleavage for an appropriately professional look, and approached the gate-keeper who was taking names at the entrance to the tent of Cutter & Buck, one of the brands she carried on her website.

"Lena Bettencourt," she said, wondering if he would recognize her name, and if that would trigger a nod of re-spect from the young man. She never knew who would recognize her as a women's senior champion or as CEO of The Perfect Tee.

The preppy youngster – his crystal clear complex-ion and perfectly symmetrical face clearly the result of a union of two very pretty people – didn't appear to care. He checked her off on his clipboard and nodded, stepping back to let her into the stuffy enclosure.

Schmoozing at events had certainly become easier for Lena following her senior women's victory and after she had lost twenty pounds in the effort. She looked fit and healthy, an attractive, athletic woman in her early fifties — or maybe even younger. On top of that, her confidence had risen now that she was running her own company, not just playing mouthpiece for some CEO.

Slipping through the crowd to reach the stand-up bar at the back of the tent, Lena bumped into a tall young woman in a slim skirt and a sweater, the low v-neck revealing a smooth décolletage unmolested by sun spots or wrinkles that would come with a couple more decades of life. A little wine splashed out of the woman's glass, and she frowned at Lena.

"Please be careful, honey," she admonished Lena condescendingly, looking down from her six-inch-high-heel-enhanced-height and snottily turning back to the bevy of not-as-young men gathered around her.

Lena cringed. Ever since she had turned fifty, she noticed how young waitresses and clerks started to call her "honey." It pissed her off. At first she protested, but after a year, she had given up. They saw her as a pitiable senior citizen, and the more she protested, the more they pitied her. Of course, more years in age was a gift, not a curse. The young woman was guaranteed only the thirty or so years she'd lived so far; she might get hit by a bus tomorrow. Lena, however, had nearly bagged fifty-three.

"What do you have for white wine?" Lena asked the bartender.

"Chardonnay," he answered lifting an opened bottle as proof.

"Of course," Lena groaned. And she knew it would be a cheap, cloying, over-oaked California Chardonnay. Not that any Chardonnay was going to be her choice, but at least some Washington wineries knew how to make a wine without hitting you over the head with oak and vanilla, and the French still handled the grape respectfully. Subtlety was a winemakers' art, and, in her opinion, as long as the Californians had been at it, they'd never gotten the hang of it.

"I'll just take a cranberry vodka," she decided. "Tall."

Walking away from the bar with her drink, Lena noted that all the women in the tent were young — very young — while the men ranged in age from barely-able-to drink to twenty years her senior. That didn't surprise her; she'd been to enough golf events. She stood off in the corner by the bar in the back of the tent and watched the slow morphing of groups as people moved in and out of conversations.

Nothing interesting was catching her eye. Each tall, thin female clothing rep was surrounded by at least two and as many as five men, who hung on every utterance of their female cohort, or stared, fixated on their high cheekbones, perky breasts, and massive white teeth. How did it happen that these gorgeous women looked exactly the same? It was like that on the Golf Channel, too; with very few exceptions, the female anchors were tall, blond and pretty to a fault, while the male anchors looked like average schmucks you'd find on your local municipal course—guys she'd probably like.

Lena felt guilty. It was stereotyping. Just because the reps were young and beautiful, she assumed that their heads were empty and that the men surrounding them were only attracted to their bright smiles and large breasts.

Lena shook her head. She really didn't care. Did she crave the lust and reverence radiating from the guys' faces as they stared at the pretty specimens next to them? No! Oh yuck. Seriously. Yuck. She shivered, shaking off the thought.

Was it only her age and looks that separated her from these women or was there something more basic – a choice of what they wanted from life, what they wanted to accomplish, who they wanted to be? Even when she was young and could have made up her wrinkle-free face, highlighted and sculpted her hair, and displayed perfect cleavage, she didn't do it. She wasn't as tall as they were, but six-inch heels would have taken care of that. But she never wanted to be one of them.

"Hey, aren't you Lena Bettencourt?" A voice pulled Lena out of her reverie. She struggled a bit to abandon her thoughts and shift her focus to the man who had been standing right in front of her.

"Oh. Yes. I guess." Lena shook her head as if coming out of a deep sleep. The walk around the course had been good physical therapy. After a nice long hike, she often slipped into a pleasant nap on the couch in Suncadia. "I mean, yes, I'm Lena. Who are you?"

"Sorry. I didn't mean to wake you up." The man laughed.

"I guess I was napping. Walking eighteen holes will do that to you." She smiled, sticking out her hand for a shake.

"I'm George Tatlinger."

"Lena. But I guess you know that."

"I met you once after your big win at an event at Puetz Golf on Aurora. Do you remember?"

"Oh, gosh!" Lena shook her head. The evening at Puetz, one of a chain of golf stores in Seattle, had blurred and merged in her memory with the dozen other appearances that local businesses had paid her small stipends to attend. She had won as an amateur, but with no intention of ever competing in an amateur event again, she took advantage of her fifteen minutes of fame, and made a little money at PR events before she landed the job at The Perfect Tee.

"I remember the event, but George, I met so damn many people over those few months after the tournament," she said by way of apology. "I have to say, I can't even re-member all the events, let alone all of the nice people I met. So, forgive me. What did we talk about?"

"I think we talked about your victory."

"That must have been nice for me!" Lena laughed. "It's pretty cool to get to spend all night talking about yourself."

"It seemed to be the subject of the night." George nod-ded, as if he understood her embarrassment at the narcis-sism.

"Yeah, but what should we have talked about?" Lena warmed to his casual demeanor. He had a typically reced-ing hairline for men of a certain age, slight jowls that soft-ened his jaw line, and a little pudginess around the waist. Lena could relate to all of that, if in her own feminine way. Like her, he was dressed nicely in grown-up, muted golf attire – no plaids, no madras, no pink.

"I actually have a business idea I wanted to talk to you about that night, and it's bugged me ever since that I didn't get a chance."

"Really. Wasn't that two years ago?"

"Yup. And the good thing is that my project has been

proceeding, and now I have a much better idea of what I want to do with it."

"What is it?"

"Well, first let me say that when I saw you at Puetz, you weren't running the Perfect Tee yet."

"Oh, you know about that."

"Sure. Who doesn't?"

Lena imagined there were thousands of people — actually hundreds of thousands of people — in Seattle who didn't, but there was no reason to argue the point.

"Then, why is it important to your project that I'm at The Perfect Tee?" she asked.

"Well, let me back up," George said. "When I met you, I could see that you weren't just a good golfer but you were also articulate, and it seemed like you had a good head for business."

Lena was slightly embarrassed by the flattery, but let him continue uncensored.

"I was working on a concept that I thought might have market appeal," George explained, "but I needed someone who could both help me come up with some capital to invest in development and then move onto creating the marketing strategy and manufacturing deals."

"Whew! That's quite a mouthful! Do you think we could sit down?" Lena asked, suddenly feeling light-headed. She wanted to focus on what George had to say, but the heat of the tent and the good walk of the afternoon were getting in her way.

"Oh, gosh, I'm sorry," George stuttered. "Here, let's grab a table. I should have been more considerate. I should have -- "

"Oh, no. I'm not a wilting flower or something," she interrupted. "I've just been traveling a lot lately, and I'm a bit out of shape. You know. Airplanes. Meetings. Restaurants."

They pulled out wooden folding chairs and set their drinks down on the tiny table between them. Lena let out a contended sigh and sunk into her seat.

"God that feels good. My feet were starting to kill me." She laughed, hoping she didn't sound as old to George as she sounded to herself.

"Me, too," said George. But he was eager to continue his story. "So let me cut to the chase. Have you ever lost a Pro V1 in three inches of rough and been furious when you couldn't find it?"

"Oh, duh!" Lena exclaimed with a smile. "Who hasn't?"

"Well, I've got the solution. But, again, let me back up."

His story was taking on the shape of one of those crime novels that starts at the end – with the murder – and works backwards to put the focus on the why, not the what. She didn't mind. George was pleasant and engaging. And now that she was sitting down and her drink was still half full, she was willing to let him tell his story however it pleased him.

"Sure. Go ahead," she assured him.

"Well, I am the CEO of a small tech company in Everett. We make RFID tags for clothing." George motioned toward the racks of clothing at one side of the tent. "Cutter & Buck is a customer."

"RFID tags – the inventory chips, right?"

"Right. Radio frequency ID chips, usually used to control inventory. But obviously, RFID chips can be used to locate anything. Even golf balls."

"Ahhh," Lena nodded. His stuttering narrative was

starting to make sense. "Haven't other people tried to do this before? I'm thinking of a company that came out with a big bang in, like, 2005 or something, and then disappeared. They'd invented some kind of radar device in golf balls that emitted some signal. Nobody I know ever saw one of their devices or their balls."

"You're right. The problem is that it sounds simple, but it's actually not. An RFID chip is lightweight and fairly inexpensive, which is good. But it's fragile. Swinging at it at 130 miles an hour with a metal face is not a good idea unless you've figured out how to protect the chip. And protecting the chip gets in the way of designing a good ball with perfect flight, distance, and spin."

"I have to take your word for it," Lena admitted. "I'm not really familiar with chip technology – or golf ball construction, for that matter."

"So, let me just say that I think I have a pretty good solution now."

"So why are you telling me this?" Lena asked.

"Well, back then at Puetz, I was thinking that maybe you could come and help me run the business. But then you took the job at The Perfect Tee, and I never got a chance to ask you."

"Oh, I see. So why now?"

"Well, you've been running your online store for a while, and I was thinking maybe you're ready for a new challenge."

"Oh." Lena smiled and sat back against the cool wooden slats on the back of the chair. She took the last couple of sips of her drink, and thought about what George was suggesting. He reached over and took her glass.

"How about I refill these, and we'll continue?" he offered.

"Great. Cranberry vodka tall."

Yes, The Perfect Tee was up and running, and except for the battle between her two technology chiefs, it was humming along nicely. Every month or so, they would add some new code to the software that helped women find golf clothes that fit them even more perfectly – to a tee. Perfect fitting was their competitive advantage, and while they had a head start on other online clothing companies – golf or otherwise – she knew they had to keep improving the technology and the shopping experience, or they'd be leapfrogged by a competitor in the middle of the night.

Still, the release of each new software version – one after another – had lost its thrill. She hadn't thought much about it until now. The company needed her leadership, particularly until the division in her tech staffs was resolved, and so far, she hadn't focused on trying to find someone she could groom as a successor. It seemed too early to consider moving on. But George seemed on the verge of suggesting just that.

"Here," he said, returning to the table with their drinks. "I didn't know if you wanted lime or not, so I said no. Don't want to OD on citrus."

Lena smiled. She liked his sense of humor.

"I thought about what I just said, and I wanted to clarify," he started up where he left off. "I don't want to hire you, and I don't want to suggest you should quit your job. I'd really like to consider a joint venture."

Lena was intrigued.

"What do you think I could contribute?"

"Marketing expertise, your website as a sales outlet perhaps, your venture-capital connections. I need capital to move ahead."

"That's reasonable," she said slowly, thinking over the implications for her small staff and her VCs. The staff might be up for a new challenge, too. Or at least some of them. It wouldn't require much of her software developers' time — just her marketing staff's attention and maybe her CFO's.

And while the VCs might not go for it, they'd probably like to have the chance to see the project first and get the first right of refusal to any deal. But before she brought it to them, she'd have to figure out why the last company that tried to build such a golf ball failed.

In any case, this project might be just the kind of adventure she needed to spice up her work life again.

Lena smiled at George. She felt lucky. She could have gone to a different tent this afternoon and missed George. She might have struck up a conversation with someone else when she entered the tent, or George might not have seen her.

That reminded her: she needed to find a Cutter & Buck executive to thank for the hospitality. It was important to take care of relationships.

Lena raised her glass toward George and nodded.

"I'd better do some schmoozing," she said. "But here's to possibilities. Let me think about this for a couple of days, talk to a couple of people in the company. Can we meet toward the end of next week or is that too late?"

Kim

As she drove home from Snoqualmie Ridge and her impromptu meeting with George, Lena wondered how success at this new RFID project might help build her reputation as a business executive, and if it did, would she really deserve it? Would she just be lucky — in the right place at the right time — or did she have any management or strategic talents to bring to bear?

More importantly, she realized, did she need it? Did she need more success? Lena had no reason to believe she was special — no one had ever told her she was — but she'd grown up wanting to escape normal, boring and forgettable Nebraska where she'd spent her childhood. She hated being normal — one of the masses, a forgotten minion among the earth's billions of forgotten minions. She wasn't someone special, but she wanted to be.

Now that she was the CEO of a respectably successful and growing company, the stakes seemed to have been raised: was this not just the new normal? She knew reporters at the Denver Post who had gone onto jobs at the Wall Street Journal and the New York Times, and came back to visit. In late-night bar commiserations, Lena gleaned that they still didn't think they'd "made it." They still needed to prove themselves. What would it take? A Pulitzer? Then would it be two Pulitzers?

Securing the job at The Perfect Tee helped Lena feel a little less normal. Having "CEO" as her title elevated her professional status to one of authority, not just one taking orders. It was better than being a middle-management lackey at TrueWeb, the most mediocre company in America.

Now when she was introduced to business partners as CEO, she got a different reaction. Outsiders and insiders alike were more attentive. Some of the engineers who worked for her, like Ken, still dissed her behind her back for her lack of an engineering background, but most of them put some effort into faking deference.

But there were times that even the patina of success signaled by the three-letter designation of CEO felt like simply that: a patina, a façade, a cover-up. She had been lucky: she knew Sarah from TrueWeb, and she was available when Sarah was looking for someone to take over the day-to-day management of The Perfect Tee two years before. Otherwise, Lena would be working at another mediocre company, writing press releases, conference call scripts, and talking points for executives.

Of course, having won the USGA Women's Senior Tournament two years before — especially having won it as a rookie in the competition — gave her some cachet. It was nice to have done something — even if it was just play a game — better than anyone else, if only that one time. But after failing to repeat her victory at a regional golf tournament a month later, she'd given up on serious competition.

The regional tournament in Walla Walla had brought

her notoriety anyway — not the good kind, and not because she didn't win. After Lena ended up in the middle of the pack instead of on the leaderboard, Kurt, her ex-husband attacked her in her hotel room.

Lena's marriage to Kurt ten years earlier had been the worst mistake of her life. Getting married was more of an accommodation to tradition than a fulfillment of desire. Kurt seemed erudite and interesting enough for a guy with little education and a decidedly dead-end blue-collar job, but they married before she knew him very well.

Kurt's nice façade faded soon after the wedding. He hated her well-heeled and well-connected friends, and he mocked her success, while, at the same time, took the lifestyle her work afforded them for granted. He drank, watched TV, and sulked.

Less than two years into their marriage, Kurt was convicted as an accomplice to the murder of a young nurse in the apartment complex where he had been a maintenance worker. Lena had divorced him while he was in the federal penitentiary in Colorado, but prison overcrowding had triggered his early release. Immediately, he drove to Walla Walla to avenge Lena's decision to leave him.

Coming so quickly after her win on the USGA stage, the incident became national sports news. It wasn't the kind of thing that Lena wanted to taint her recently won notoriety, and the only way she knew to make the story die a quick death was to refuse to talk with reporters about it. But, still, plenty of people in the golf world remembered it, and she was thankful that George had not brought it up.

Being famous for the wrong things, being famous for the right things; what difference did it make which it was?

How it made you feel about yourself was more important than how it made others see you. Pursuing George's initiative was likely to be very hard and time consuming, but it might bring Lena a little more self-respect. Instead of taking someone else's company — Sarah's — and making it successful, she could be involved with a new idea from the start. She could make something new happen. It might help whittle down the chip she carried on her shoulder about her low-class upbringing, or get over the embarrassment of her marriage to Kurt.

Lena wished that she could have talked to Kim about her mental perturbations, but he had no experience with existential angst. He wasn't introspective, let alone tormented with questions of his worthiness or insecure about his place on earth. He was a software engineer, and designing software was all he wanted to do since he started playing with code back in 1978 in the lab in the basement of his high school in Seattle. He never worried about what writing code said about him, what it proved about him, what others would think about his success or failure. He just wanted a job at Microsoft, which he got twenty years ago, and since then, he'd been content. He'd also made a bundle in stock options. Being Kim was easy.

Easy, except for losing his wife Stacy, to Parkinson's. That had been excruciating for him, and Lena believed he must have missed her unflappable, calm personality — especially when he compared it with Lena's own mercurial and unpredictable moods.

Whatever problems Lena and Kim had, they were her fault. Three years after Stacy's death, he was ready for more of a commitment to Lena; she was not.

"I don't know if this is the best time," he broached the subject one evening not long ago, "but I would like to talk about merging our households sometime in the near future."

Lena had laughed, not meaning it as an answer, but amused at the way he had phrased his proposal.

"You mean you'd like to live together," she restated his suggestion behind a wry smile.

"Yeah."

"Why didn't you say so then? 'Merging households' doesn't sound very romantic!"

"Okay," he nodded. "I am an engineer."

Then he rose up and leaned forward over the restaurant table they were sharing and kissed her — more of a peck on the lips than a kiss.

"Do you want to live with me?" He tried again.

Lena had only made it worse for herself, turning his question from one of household economics into a question of romance. Now she had to find a way to reject his proposed arrangement without rejecting him.

"Kim," she started slowly, sitting back in her chair as if increasing the physical distance between them might make her message clearer. She couldn't think of the right words.

I'm not ready seemed too trite and silly. They'd been seeing each other exclusively for two years, and she was well into her fifties already. If not now, then when? I'm not feeling it — while true — was not only harsh but raised the obvious question of why she had continued to sleep with him for so long. The truth was she had been hoping for something more in her second marriage — something that would make up for the horrendous first one and prove that she was capable of real commitment. But she knew her relationship with Kim was unsatisfying – for both of them – and would only get worse if they lived together. He wasn't proposing marriage, but the distinction was insignificant.

"Kim, I don't know," she answered quietly. "Maybe a time will come when I can appreciate you fully and commit myself to us as a couple. But I can't promise that. Definitely not now."

She finally looked up to meet his eyes, and he nodded solemnly. "I expected as much. That is why I didn't ask if you loved me. I asked if we could share some kitchen space."

"Love is not something you can compromise on, Kim," she heard herself pleading. She wanted to sound as calm and rational as he did. It was ironic: he was the one with the emotional attachment and yet she was the one who was coming across as the irrational romantic.

"I know," he answered. He paused and leaned his forehead into his hand. "I'm embarrassed to ask this, because it sounds so petty. Like petty jealousy."

"Ask what?" Lena wasn't sure she wanted to know. She doubted the conversation was going to get any easier.

"Is it Ryne?"

Lena didn't sit up. She stayed slumped in her chair and looked away. "I haven't seen him for months. Why would you think that?"

"Because you used to light up around him like you don't around me. Because back before we started sleeping together, something happened with him that knocked you on your ass emotionally for weeks. And because you won't look in my eyes right now."

Lena smiled at his honesty and met his eyes. He stirred his coffee and gave her time to answer.

"Let's leave it for tonight," she finally suggested instead. "I will think about your question, and I will think about whether I think I can make a commitment, but I am begging off right now. Is that possible?"

The sad thing was that she liked him, and she respected his intelligence. They shared views on economics, religion, and most of the social issues of the day. They had little to argue about. And ever since he helped her recover from Kurt's attack, she'd appreciated how much he cared about her.

But the only commitment she could make was to accept him as the Steady Eddie in her life - temporarily. She turned to him when she needed someone to listen to her whine about work. He was always her best bet for a golf partner on the weekends in Suncadia. And occasional sex with Kim kept her from the horrid fate of some of her co-workers: risky one-night stands to alleviate themselves of unrequited, itchy sex drives.

It couldn't last, though.

After their dinner conversation that night, Kim continued to put up with their tepid affair, and she knew he was hoping she would let down her resistance and let him into her life for good. Waiting. And while she was almost sure it wasn't going to happen, she couldn't totally reject the possibility that someday she would discover that he was just right for her; maybe she'd even fall in love with him.

He was right about Ryne, though. Lena remembered the first time Kim and Ryne met. It was a post-tournament picnic Brandt and Carly hosted one Saturday evening at their weekend home on the second fairway at Suncadia. After golf, Ryne stayed for the party instead of returning to Seattle as usual for his Sunday editing shift at the Seattle Times. Kim usually drove up from Bellevue on Sunday mornings to play with her back then, but that weekend, he came up early so he too could accept Carly's invitation.

"Hey, techie," Ryne had nudged Kim companionably as the evening was just getting started. Lena had known Kim for only a month or so, but she had told Ryne about her new techie friend and his Microsoft job. "How's the code holding up? The Chinese happy with it yet, or are they still on your case?"

Kim didn't welcome the conversation. Of all of the ways Ryne might have approached him, it was the worst. Kim took what he did very seriously. Plus, he considered his work as a security software engineer as highly classified. He didn't readily talk about it with anyone and took offense that Ryne would treat it so lightly. He mumbled an unintelligible answer about confidentiality and retreated to the far corner of the big patio, where he stood most of the rest of the night, sulking.

Lena and Kim had finally become lovers, but Lena was not in love. At least not with Kim.

All of this occupied her mind during the long, tedious drive back into Seattle during rush hour. She pulled into the garage under the building of loft condos where she lived and took the elevator up to the top floor, continuing her solemn reverie.

"Oh, you're here." Lena was startled to walk into Kim as she opened the door to her condo. She'd been thinking of him, and even though they had a standing date for dinner on Wednesday evenings, she had totally forgotten about it.

"Oh, Christ, it's Wednesday!" she exclaimed.

"I love you too," Kim answered sarcastically. He stood at the door with his car keys in his hand, apparently ready to give up on her and leave. He held the door open so she could shuffle in with her briefcase in her hand and her work blazer on a hanger over her arm, and he closed it behind her.

"Oh, honey, I'm sorry!" Lena threw her stuff on the chair inside the condo's front door, and turned to kiss him. He stood still and tall, his face out of reach of her lips.

"Wow! You're really mad, aren't you?" She stepped back. "I'm really sorry, but I have what could be really good news to tell you."

Golf Balls

Walking through the RF Inc. corporate headquarters two months later reminded Lena of her time at TrueWeb.

Although it had been more than three years since she had lost her job as a speechwriter there, the memory of those hallways and conference rooms, the stifling atmosphere of her boss's office, and the burnt coffee and rotting orange-peel stench of the company's coffee stations made her shudder. Getting fired by calling her boss incompetent had turned out to be one of the best life-changing moves she'd ever made.

She tried to keep those visceral feelings at bay as the receptionist led her past scores of light maple doors that lined the long, fluorescent-lighted hallways, paved with strips of patterned gray carpeting. She peeked into conference rooms, their long tables littered with detritus from meetings, and remembered the vertigo she felt when the wheeled chairs around the tables at TrueWeb slid backwards under her as she sat down on them.

The overall effect of the 1990s décor was to lull employees to sleep, and like many high-tech companies in the Northwest, TrueWeb had fought against the somnambulant atmosphere with coffee stations, snack kiosks, and free colas. It didn't work for Lena.

The receptionist let her into the "2 Southwest" conference room, as dull as its nomenclature. The white walls were lined with white boards covered with messy, half-erased engineering scribbles – boxes, arrows and connecting lines, acronyms and question marks. It had been that way at TrueWeb, too.

Lena was happy she no longer spent hours in an office like this. Perhaps it was overreacting, but she thought it felt like prison. Even before her job at True Web was spoiled by a new, incompetent boss, Lena had limited her time in the office as much as possible to avoid the stultifying atmosphere, largely by working hard while she was there, and leaving as early as possible every night.

Setting up the workspace at The Perfect Tee, Lena and Sarah built an environment as different from TrueWeb as they could – without foregoing floors and ceilings or putting it in the middle of Puget Sound. The Perfect Tee offices in Pioneer Square, the historic downtown neighborhood in Seattle, were a little shabby and musty, but at least they weren't antiseptic and homogenized. Further, at the Perfect Tee, leaving empty cola cans and lunch trash behind in the meeting areas wasn't accepted as a sign of a busy person, it was the sign of an inconsiderate slob.

Lena vowed to not let the RF setting affect her attitude. After their serendipitous meeting at the Cutter & Buck tent two months earlier, she had researched the idea of a radio-frequency golf ball, talked with Sarah about getting involved, and then set up the meeting to explore The Perfect Tee's possible role in it. She and George talked about the project a half-dozen times by phone, and, by the time she showed up at the company's bland headquarters, Lena was personally vested in the idea.

"Hey, there's my hero!" George nearly skipped into the conference room at the sight of Lena, his arms full of papers and his laptop computer. He let them spill onto the table and gave her a friendly hug. "Any problems finding the place?"

"Not as long as there are Google maps," she answered cheerfully, surprised at how friendly and energetic George appeared. Her old CEO at TrueWeb shuffled into meetings mumbling to himself and refusing to look anyone in the eye. George was older than TrueWeb's CEO had been when she worked for him, but her new partner carried himself with the bounce of a man twenty years younger.

"Google maps? Old technology!" George kidded her. "No GPS?"

"Only on the golf cart." He laughed at that, and Lena sat down across from him while three men and two women filed into the conference room with cups of coffee and laptops, and took the empty seats at the table.

George introduced his staff to Lena, referring to her as a USGA amateur champion as well as CEO of The Perfect Tee. To her right, a serious and stylish marketing executive named Marlena. Next, a neatly dressed man who worked for Marlena. Around the table: the company's SVP in charge of manufacturing, a woman who headed up distribution, and the company's chief financial officer.

Far more serious and less gregarious than their boss, the team could have been chosen for the way they tempered their CEO's cheerfulness. It was a good sign that

George chose people very different from him, instead of looking for personality clones.

"Let's get started, then," George said, passing out an agenda for the meeting. "Lena, let's skip over a regurgitation of our conversation on the phone, and tell us right up front what concerns you have regarding the product, so we know what we're up against."

Lena was ready.

"Thanks," she said, nodding toward George. "I'm not sure I can tell you anything you don't already know, but let me lay out my thoughts about the challenges we face with this product."

It worried Lena that everyone but George immediately started typing on their laptops. Too serious! She imagined one of them raising their hands and asking, "Is this going to be on the test?" Even in her own office, she wasn't accustomed to people hanging on her every word. She wondered if George's easy-going approach was his "outside voice," and inside his own company, he was a true ogre.

"I don't know if you need to take notes here," she said, tentatively. "I'd prefer we just talk things over today."

Everyone but Brian, the CFO, sat back, apparently pleased to be able to sip coffee and have a conversation, not a lecture. But Brian still sat at attention, as if waiting to take dictation. Maybe it was he who created this stultifying atmosphere. She smiled at the others and continued.

"First, let me tell you what I'm not concerned about," she started. "I'm not concerned about the technology; your reputation is stellar there." She hoped that would put even Brian at ease, but it didn't change his posture one micron. If anything, his face tightened even more.

"I'm not concerned about the golfer's desire for our product. I have very up-close and personal experience with that," she managed to continue, turning slightly to block Brian from the center of her vision. She got a little chuckle from George, and the others joined a half-second later, as if following orders.

"These are the issues I understand that faced the company that tried this before. One, cost. The technology RG embedded in the balls was still relatively expensive at the time, but George thinks you guys have solved that problem. So, good.

"Two: Let's call it golf etiquette. No one wants to play with someone fussing around with radar equipment or looking for balls. Past solutions to finding these radar balls required a special piece of equipment. As George and I have discussed, we now can design an app for that," she said. "We can probably get around the equipment issue if people are already carrying smart phones. But, still, it has to be easy and quick to use, or players are going to get hassled by their partners for taking too long to find a ball — even if it is a Pro V1. Looking for your ball with a radar gun is just kind of dorky."

Lena looked around the table to see if anyone wanted to jump in. She didn't want to conduct a monologue if it was going to test someone's patience. But they were nodding quietly and sipping their coffee while Brian typed.

"Third," Lena continued, "and perhaps most importantly, these balls will not be 'conforming' under current USGA equipment rules. That means, that without a nod from the USGA, the ruling bodies won't allow people to post scores played with these balls on GHIN, the handicap recording system, or play them in competitions – amateur or pro. I think that is our biggest obstacle. But, then, with bifurcation now being discussed, who knows?"

Marlena interrupted. "What's bifurcation?"

George jumped in to answer, which Lena appreciated. It was complicated: bifurcation referred to any instance where the PGA, which governed tour players and instructors, and the USGA, which ruled over amateur golf, accept different rules. The concept had been tested back when the two organizations debated use of the belly putter, but they ended up agreeing to ban it. However, bifurcation had been allowed in determining when players would have to stop using certain kinds of banned equipment, like long putters or square grooves on wedges.

George explained this quickly and then nodded to Lena to continue.

"Maybe people are just going to stop caring what the USGA and PGA think about anchoring and belly putters and radar-equipped golf balls, and play whatever they like," Lena started again. "A very low percentage of golfers post their scores anyway, so for most folks, the rules are irrelevant."

That seemed to resonate with Ray, the SVP of manufacturing.

"Can I jump in here?" he asked, looking oddly at Brian instead of George for permission.

"Sure," George and Lena answered in sync, while Brian sat stoically with his fingers still poised above his laptop keyboard.

"I think our biggest issue is going to be the latter one: overcoming USGA rules, as Lena suggests. But I also think we face a universal problem in the golf equipment industry." Ray looked around for a prompt to continue.

Lena leaned in with interest, and George nodded. "What's that?"

"Golf is such a game of tradition that golfers don't really accept big innovation easily," Ray continued. "Only a couple of truly new ideas get accepted in a decade, and those are usually things that improve golf scores, not peripheral things like radar ball locators. We will need to find a manufacturer who thinks that golfers would to glom onto this in this decade. Otherwise, they'll be loath to make the investment."

"Okay," George said, encouraging Ray to continue.

"The problem is that the established ball brands in the sport, Titleist, Bridgestone, Top-Flite, Srixon, Pinnacle, Maxfli, Nike, Noodle, etc., are looking for break-through technologies that improve performance," Ray said. "Our technology isn't meant to do that. And ball makers may not want technology that increases sales in the short run but would decrease them in the long run because golfers lose fewer balls."

Marlena jumped in. "The keys to solving this, I think, are two-fold," she said. "One is understanding the trade-off between lower replacement sales and higher initial sales price due to the unique radio technology. The other is finding a golf brand that doesn't currently have a best-selling ball. They're probably our best bet."

Marlena seemed to have put a great deal of thought into the idea, indicating she was willing to explore it further. She passed around a nicely formatted spreadsheet that delineated the major golf manufacturers who might fit the bill, their annual revenue, their other products, and their main marketing channels. Lena immediately felt camaraderie with Marlena — another fan of spreadsheets.

"Excellent," George said, reaching for his copy of the spreadsheet. "Lena, would you continue?"

"Yeah, sure," she said. "Given that this ball doesn't necessarily improve performance, I'm uncertain about our options for marketing channels. Again, so many products are introduced each year, it seems that we face a big hurdle in breaking through the clutter. I'll be glad to bring in my marketing VP at some point down the road to help you think about this, Marlena, but she and I have talked about it a bit."

Marlena nodded and Lena continued. "I think you are right: the right approach is to find a manufacturer who needs to generate interest in their entry into the ball market, and in that case, can provide much of the marketing. And, while we have the expertise at The Perfect Tee in online sales, I'm not convinced that will be the way to market this new ball."

Ray jumped in his seat, looking like he couldn't wait to disagree with Lena.

"We should remember that any new ball on the market will be more successful if the key benefit of the product is clear, and to be clear, that has to be one thing, not two," he said.

To Lena's surprise, Marlena didn't appear to be bothered by Ray stepping into her marketing turf and answered him calmly. "I agree," she said. "But I guess the problem then becomes one of credibility. How do you enter a market as focused on performance as golf is, and not market your ball on its performance?"

Lena was impressed with the team's ability to disagree without rancor. A team built on mutual respect was much easier to manage than the team she had in the IT department at The Perfect Tee where someone was always trying to prove he was the smartest person in the room.

"Good questions that we'll need to resolve," George said, cutting their debate short. "But, Lena, as long as you are here today, tell us your thoughts about funding."

"Yes, funding," she said. "We talked about that being one of the things The Perfect Tee can help with. I don't know yet whether my VCs are looking for new investments right now, but there is a lot of uncommitted cash sitting around in corporate coffers these days, so we may decide to investigate more than one source of funding simultaneously."

At that, Brian finally looked up from his screen.

"I think you should probably leave the financial and funding issues to me," he said stiffly. "You are not an accountant, are you? Have you ever done M&A?" He turned to George. "I certainly wouldn't expect to turn this aspect over to her."

Lena raised her eyebrows and sat back, surprised by his sudden pugnaciousness. Maybe she had misread his stiff attentiveness wrong. Maybe more than attentive, it was vigilant. Ready to protect his turf, ready to pounce on any intruder. She'd noticed how Ray had checked to see how Brian reacted to his comment before proceeding. Had he sprung on Ray in the past too?

"No one is going to make any financial decisions without you, Brian," George assured him. Lena could hear George's voice tighten. The two men looked at each other frostily. Was there some unpleasant history between them? Perhaps Brian frequently questioned George's financial credentials as well. Maybe even his leadership.

George and Brian finally broke off their icy stare.

"Okay, great start, Lena," George said, shaking off the exchange with Brian. He stood up and walked to the white board. "I think we should get organized here and decide what projects we need to tackle over the next couple of weeks, and assign ourselves to them."

As the group worked through assigning tasks, Lena sat back and observed. Lena felt good about her progress so far in becoming a corporate leader. She'd managed to keep The Perfect Tee chugging down the tracks without derailment, and the trains were running on time. But she could learn a lot about managing high-level employees from watching an experienced executive like George, and she didn't get many chances to do it. Especially, she wanted to watch how he handled Brian over the next few months.

It wasn't always fun, of course. While she enjoyed walking into the office each day, Lena hated three-hour meetings with the company's engineers, marketers or finance team. But this golf-ball project might be just the change she needed. What The Perfect Tee had done involved some new software, and interactive tricks, but it all added up to building a new kind of marketing channel, not introducing new consumer products. Introducing a new golf ball to the world – not just one with slightly improved spin or distance, but one with a different value proposition – could be just the thing to keep her from slipping into the doldrums.

When the meeting ended, George escorted her to the RF front door.

"Hey, I'm sorry about that little thing with Brian back there," he said. "I seem to have issues with finance guys. Being an engineer, I guess, doesn't carry much cachet with them. I've learned a lot about finance running this business, but those CFOs always seem to need to prove me ignorant. I know I need them, though, however disagreeable they are."

"Ha!" Lena laughed. "And for me, my nemesis is engineers. Not you, of course, but my software guys. They love to throw their code and algorithms in my face and watch me flinch. I guess we all have our demons."

"Yes, and funny how we not only tolerate them, but we pay them a bunch of money to get under our skin!" George leaned forward and gave her a quick hug. "But, before I let you go," he said, "let's set a tee time. I want a commitment from you."

Kim couldn't join George, his wife Tina, and Lena for their golf outing. He was in the middle of budget planning for his department. At least that was his excuse, but he and Lena had not seen much of each other since the new golf ball venture had begun to take up so much of her time. Lena knew she was distracted by the project, but there wasn't much she could – or that she wanted to – do about it.

The threesome teed up the following Friday on No. 1 at Tumble Creek. Lena would have preferred to play Prospector, but the course's soggy bogs and washed out fairways weren't in good shape yet. Lena had given up playing the course until the weather stabilized and she could walk down the fairways without hip boots.

"I hope you're not expecting much," Lena said, putting

her tee in the ground at the white tees on the first hole. "I haven't been out at all the past two weeks."

"Is that called setting expectations or sandbagging?" George teased her.

Lena laughed. "I'm pretty sure it's not sandbagging. I really expect to suck."

"Well, it's been two months for me," George said. "Tina and I went to San Diego in April to get a jump on the season. But, I haven't had a chance to play since then."

The morning was not warm yet, although the sun was shining with the promise of making a difference by mid-day. Lena felt the cold muscles in her back pull tight as she took a couple of practice swings. It was hard to make a full turn with tight muscles, and a back spasm was always just one small miscue away.

Her drive was mediocre. She pushed the ball to the right. Luckily, the distance to the bunkers from the white tees was far enough that her ball ended up short of the sand, but hidden from view in the rough.

"Well, I hope I set expectations appropriately," she said, pulling her tee out of the ground and ceding the tee box to George.

"Breakfast ball?" he asked, offering her a mulligan on the first tee shot of the day.

"Nah. It's not likely to get any better," Lena said. "It will be mid-summer before I get much of my form back. And that's only if you don't make me work too hard."

George's drive was straighter but not much farther, and with the sixty-yard advantage Tina had from the forward tees, they all ended up with a long 200-yard shot to the first green.

"Just so you know," Lena warned George before he lined up for his fairway shot, "that's a false front you see up there. It's another twenty yards to clear the fringe. And it's really uphill. I'd take an extra club."

She was not only trying to help her new partner score better, but she also wanted to see how he accepted advice from another person — especially advice from a woman. It would be good to know as they moved forward on the joint golf-ball venture.

"Thanks. I probably would have under-clubbed," he said. He sounded grateful.

Lena and George hit their shots well enough to have a putt for birdie, although it was hard to tell from the fairway. It took Tina two more shots to get up the hill, which wasn't bad. Lena could remember when it used to take her three shots to get to the green from the forward tees. It wasn't that long ago.

The three players finished their round in less than four hours, not unusual on the private course, especially on a weekday. They turned in their carts and clubs to a club worker, and met in the small restaurant in the clubhouse for a quick sandwich before Tina and George headed back to Seattle.

Tina had turned out to be one of the pleasant surprises of the round for Lena. Not only did she seem totally at ease on the course, she didn't appear to harbor any distrust toward Lena. That came as a relief. A jealous wife was as likely to threaten their good working relationship as anything. And the fact that Tina played well made it more fun to recount their rounds.

"What do you think it would take for me to get to the

point that I was playing bogie golf?" Tina asked Lena after they'd settled their small-change bets on the round. Lena had pocketed two dollars from George for beating him both on their net scores and for putting, and gave Tina a buck for winning their putting contest.

"Well, you're pretty close, so I don't think too much," Lena said. "And, obviously, you putt well. That got me pretty far. How often do you play?"

"Maybe ten times a year."

"Wow. Given how little you're playing, you're doing very well already." Lena laughed. "I used to play sixty rounds a year and didn't score much better than you did today."

"I'd love to see you work on it more," George said, patting his wife on the back and leaning forward to steal a sip of her beer. As the couple's designated driver, he'd ordered a Diet Coke, but he clearly would have preferred an adult beverage. "Maybe Lena would be willing to play with you more often."

"I'd love to," Lena assured Tina. "But, until we determine who our golf ball partner is going to be, I have an idea we won't have many days when we can play hooky and sneak off to the course."

Tina looked rejected.

"But, if you're ever going to be up here on a Sunday, let me know," Lena added quickly. "I have a regular Sunday twosome, and you could join us, with or without George."

"Just Sundays? How about Saturdays?" George wondered. "We're usually more free on Saturdays."

"I have a regular foursome on Saturdays," Lena lied. Actually, it was just a threesome — she and Carly and Brandt.

They had played regularly with her during her year of practice for the amateur tournament, and they had retained their regular Saturday morning tee time for the third year in a row. Sometimes Kim joined them and that wouldn't be possible if Tina took the fourth spot.

"It's George who is usually free on Saturdays," Tina leaned toward Lena and whispered conspiratorially. "He's got his own foursome on Sundays."

"Well, then, you'll just have to come up by yourself," Lena said.

Trouble

L ena's and George's trips to the East Coast and down to California to talk with golf equipment manufacturers started in earnest in July.

Lena turned her duties as key relationship manager with the clothing manufacturers who provided inventory for The Perfect Tee over to Jordan, her marketing vice president, a woman who Lena thought deserved the opportunity to prove herself.

Not having to go through the same negotiations about pricing and inventory with the same manufacturers for the third year in a row was a relief to Lena, but the talks were new and exciting to Jordan. Lena could identify with Jordan's desire to finally be the one to make decisions – not just the one shuttling negotiations back and forth between decision makers. Lena thought Jordan would make a fine CEO someday.

Out on the road, visiting potential ball manufacturing partners, Lena and George turned out to be a pretty good pitch team. They handed the discussion off to each other, back and forth, in a way that communicated a good relationship and a solid strategy. But their audience, usually a couple of guys at least two steps away from the C-suite, were too far down the corporate ladder to be real decision makers. Who knew if their story ever rose far enough in the companies to reach someone who could have pulled a trigger?

On a couple of trips, Lena and George brought their clubs, and played somewhere. But most of the time, Lena flew in for a meeting one day and returned to Seattle the next, getting back to the office mid-morning and in time to get eight or ten hours in before retreating to her condo and collapsing from exhaustion.

Tiring as it was, it was better than the trips she used to take back at TrueWeb, where she served as travel agent, public relations spokesman, handler, and baby-sitter for the executives she traveled with. At least now she only had to take care of herself; George acted as a grown-up and peer, not like some of the helpless executives she'd chaperoned in the past. And she wasn't shunted to the back of the room while the important discussions took place, as she had been before.

Finally, after two months on the road, they broke through. They were visiting a company in La Jolla, outside of San Diego, and as usual, they had made their hour-long presentation, reviewing the technical details of the radio technology and the issues of durability, reliability and performance. Then, they discussed the omnipresent elephant in the room: the question of USGA acceptance.

"If the schism between the PGA and the USGA over the anchored putter is any indication, we might see golfers relax their own approach to the game's rules," agreed Gina, a marketing executive at GTI, a small manufacturer of golf equipment.

That simple sentence was their big break. Up to then, none of the manufacturers was willing to gamble that golfers would thumb their noses at the USGA and play a ball that didn't conform to the organization's regulations.

"I'm glad to hear you say that," George said with obvious excitement. "We, too, believe that the rules hegemony is breaking down. The fact is, most golfers never post a score, let alone establish an official handicap. They play clubs that are non-conforming, carry fifteen sticks in the bag and never hit out of a divot."

"Right," nodded Gina. "In fact, you've come at just the right time with this issue. We're considering establishing ourselves as the everyday golfer's brand. This could be our first entry into the ball market, and it fits with our new image."

And, as seems to be a rule of the universe, once one manufacturer accepted that premise, two others came to the same conclusion. Suddenly, Lena and George had three potential ball makers to work with, and serious negotiations began.

As much fun as it was to get close to realizing their idea come to fruition, the travel and extra work started to wear Lena down. Lena worked hard to not let the joint venture take the place of her No. 1 commitment – to The Perfect Tee. That meant that her hours in the office grew longer and longer as she tried to make up for her time on the road.

But cracks started to develop at The Perfect Tee, and her already tepid relationship with Kim took a serious nosedive.

At work, the bickering between Ken and Taylor, her two IT executives, had become more intense and more disruptive. Apparently, they had both perceived a power vacuum created by her frequent absences, and they each decided they should fill it, to the exclusion of the other.

Lena tried to diffuse the competition, first by encouraging them to improve their relationship outside of work. She invited them, their wives and their children to a late afternoon tour of the Seattle Aquarium, followed by a ride on the Ferris wheel on the waterfront and dinner at Fisherman's Restaurant. While the five toddlers tested her patience, the developers seemed to have a good time and put aside their competition for the evening.

But the tension returned immediately once they were back in the office the next day.

Lena tried a more direct approach. At their regularly scheduled weekly one-on-one meetings, she confronted each of them about it.

With Ken, it was as difficult as she expected.

"Why does it seem that you and Taylor have started to compete with each other instead of working together on the e-commerce platform revision scheduled for the fall?" she asked, making sure she wasn't accusing him of anything, even though he was, she surmised, the perpetrator of the troubles. "Have I failed to recognize your contributions to the project or Taylor's?"

"No," Ken answered. He sat mute. He apparently wasn't going to elaborate or offer an alternative explanation.

"Then what's happening?"

"I don't know what you're talking about," Ken responded. "I'm working on system upgrades in finance. I don't know what Taylor is doing."

"I would think you would know intimately what he's

doing," Lena countered. "You need to work together to make sure this new line is fully integrated in the purchase paths, inventory management, accounts receivable and payable, and financial analysis. It's not just a matter of throwing a bunch of new things up on the website."

Ken looked at her with derision. "I know much better than you do what it takes to build an e-commerce platform," he said, condescendingly.

"Then, have I failed to delineate your different responsibilities?" Lena tried again. "Or are you two disagreeing over the approach to the new product release?"

She got nothing but a blank stare and a bit of a sneer from Ken. The meeting ended with no progress.

With Taylor, she got a bit more defensiveness and less condescension, but it was clear that whatever was causing him to disagree with Ken, he wasn't going to point a finger.

Lena came out of the meetings realizing how much she had lost control over the company's tenor during her absence. She needed to fix things fast if she wanted the momentum they'd built over the past two years to continue.

Lena confided in Jordan, who suggested she reach out to a consultant who worked on cultural and leadership issues for help. Lena demurred. She wasn't ready yet to give up on resolving the personnel issues by herself. And she didn't like the idea of spending hundreds of thousands of dollars on consultants when that money could be used in marketing to build their customer base.

And then, there was Kim. Put off by her constant travel, he stopped feigning interest in either tales of their progress on the ball project or her road warrior complaints.

Over restaurant dinners whenever she had time to spend with him, they sat mostly silent, each checking their smart phones for texts and e-mails more often than they exchanged in-person sentences.

With everything else piling up on her, Lena decided she'd have to worry about Kim later.

ONE WEEKEND, LENA AND GEORGE participated in the amateur tournament at the Indian Wells Golf Resort near Palm Springs, Lena as a minor "celebrity" due to her status as a former USGA champion. She hadn't embarrassed herself, shooting a respectable five-over-par from the white tees. And the three amateur contestants who played with her had gushed over her long drives and precision putting enough to make her feel special.

After their rounds, she and George met over lunch at the Indian Wells clubhouse with a marketing consultant from Boston who had worked with Titleist in the past on various campaigns. He was attending the tournament, prospecting for new clients, so they had to pay him only $15,000 to have lunch with them, a sum that seemed outrageous afterward, given the amount of practical advice they got from the meeting.

At least they agreed with the consultant on something: there was a lot of room for bottom-fishing in the golf industry. While the major brands signed up Tiger, Phil and Rory and other first-tier players to promote their products, most amateurs weren't good enough to play the equipment or the balls the pros hawked for them.

"I think about ten percent of the amateurs who play a Pro V1 can actually take advantage of it," the consultant conjectured. "The rest of them are wasting their money on five-dollar golf balls."

"Right, but how do you get amateurs to accept a brand that isn't endorsed by the pros?" Lena asked. "Can you succeed with a brand that isn't played by Tiger or Phil? It seems that even Wilson Staff – the quintessential amateur brand – has had to give up and sign up some pros."

"Oh, there are even lesser brands than that that are signing on pros," the Boston marketing genius said. "On the other hand, there is Tour Edge. They've never gone for the big marketing deals, and they seem content marketing to the average player. But it is amazing how many people have never heard of them."

"Yes, but even Tour Edge clubs meet USGA standards," cautioned George. "We're looking at breaching that bulk-head."

"It's all perception," admitted the Boston guru. "It's all about reaching out to those amateurs who don't care what the USGA thinks. And there's more of them than you think."

"Who don't give a shit," George completed the thought for the threesome. "But we already knew that. The question is: how to reach them."

They racked up a $500 bill at the restaurant and then another $100 taking a taxi to the Palm Springs Airport, having resolved little for the expense. Lena and George lamented the extravagance at the airport before parting ways. He was heading to New York on RFID business, and Lena was relieved to be heading back to Seattle.

Boarding her flight back to Seattle, Lena was relieved to find an empty seat between herself and the passenger in the window seat of their exit row. It was very rare. Alaska Airlines flights were usually booked solid, and on weekends, when families flew, the flights were not only full, but usually noisy as well.

Settling into her seat, Lena pulled on the seat belt to lengthen it to accommodate her one-hundred-thirty-pound frame. Who the hell sat here before and needed only six inches of seat belt? She suspected the airline cleaning crew went through the plane shortening up the seat belts to make travelers — who could afford flights they could only dream of — feel fat. There was no other explanation for why she always — always — had to lengthen the belt when she sat down. She'd seen more heavy people than tiny ones on these planes.

She hadn't learned as much as she had hoped from the consultant on the trip, but altogether it still had been a pleasant one for Lena. She got to play golf at one of the best courses in the Coachella Valley, and she and George had spent the night before drinking wine and talking about bucket-list golf courses and condo prices late into the night. Rarely did she have a chance to relax and drink for an entire evening.

As she took her aisle seat, Lena glanced over at the man sitting by the window. His bright white shirt — starched, fitted, and accessorized with designer cuff links — caught her eye. He was unexpectedly well-dressed, considering they were boarding in ultra-casual Palm Springs and heading for Seattle, where 'casual Friday' had morphed into 'casual everyday' back in the dot-com era, and most of the city's professionals had never gone back to formal business attire. He sat slumped sideways, snoozing against the plastic shade he'd drawn down over the window.

What a lucky break. Not only was there an empty seat between them, but her closest fellow passenger might sleep all of the way to Seattle. She could read her golf magazines and catch up on e-mails in peace.

Lena had just dozed off over an article in Golf Digest about Tiger's new romance when she was startled by a tap on her shoulder. The man in 14A was awake and wanted to use the restroom. She frowned; the seat-belt sign was still illuminated. But she unbuckled her seatbelt and let him out into the aisle. When he returned, she stuffed the golf magazine in the seatback pocket in front of her and pulled her laptop out of her messenger bag. It was time to clean up her inbox.

But 14A had other ideas.

"Do you play golf?" he asked, leaning toward her over the open seat between them and nodding toward the magazine sticking out of the seat pocket.

"Yes. Do you?" she answered, booting up her computer. As she waited for her browser to fire up, she looked over at her seatmate and was surprised by his good looks. He was at least her age and short, but strikingly handsome. Perhaps it was because of his height that she hadn't noticed anything beyond his starched shirt and cuff links. She was usually drawn to tall men like Kim, Ryne and – regrettably – her ex-husband, Kurt.

"My, you are a very pretty woman," the man said, startling her, returning her silent compliment.

"You are too kind," she answered demurely. "But you didn't say: do you play golf, too?"

"Yes, I love the game," he said. "Are you good? You look like you would be." Lena wondered why he thought that.

Were her shoulders beefy? Was it her high-end golf clothes? Or her tan legs and white feet?

"Probably good compared with most amateurs," she responded, hesitantly. She generally didn't talk about her golf prowess with men. Most male golfers believed that they could out-drive every woman, even those on the LPGA tour. They thought that women's tournaments were too easy, that the forward tees were overrated, blah, blah, blah. The conversation usually turned testy from the very beginning.

But her seatmate didn't look like he wanted an argument. "What's your handicap?" he asked earnestly.

"About five."

"Oh, my," he answered, obviously surprised. "Where do you play? Oh, I'm Larry, by the way. You are … "

"Lena. Nice to meet you."

For the next ten minutes, the conversation flowed easily, all about golf, and Lena let her computer go to sleep without connecting to the internet. They talked about how often they played and where, and about recent PGA tournaments and leaderboards. Eventually Lena told Larry about the Senior Women's Amateur Tournament she had won. He was impressed.

After the flight cleared the bumpy air over the San Jacinto Mountains and turned north up the coast, the flight attendants rolled the beverage cart down the aisle. Lena ordered a free vodka-cranberry, courtesy of her MVP Gold status, and Larry ordered a club soda with lime.

"And what do you do for a living?" Larry asked after the flight attendants moved on.

"I run a small e-commerce site that sells golf clothes

to women."

"Really? Are you the CEO? Is it a company I have heard of?"

"Yes, and I doubt it, unless you are in the market for women's golf clothes." She laughed.

"No, I guess not. But tell me, and I'll look it up when I get home."

Lena described The Perfect Tee's marketing niche, and then Larry told her about his consulting business in grocery distribution based in Sun Valley.

After they had exhausted the subjects of golf and work, Lena and Larry sat in silence for a few minutes, and Lena's thoughts returned to work. She had just reopened her laptop when Larry tried to pick up the conversation again.

"I was just thinking about my son, Brandon," he started. "He's fifteen and I've really been wanting to get him into golf."

"You have a son?" Lena asked, and immediately regretted it. Larry took her apparent interest as license to launch into a long monologue about not just Brandon, but all his seven children. Lena cringed. This was the reason she usually avoided conversations on airplanes. Family stories were nearly always tedious and usually accompanied by a mind-numbing showing of family photos. Without much encouragement from Lena, Larry continued for several long minutes, and then segued to a long complaint about his "third" wife. Lena only half-listened as he detailed his dissatisfaction with his marriage.

Seven children? Who the hell would want seven children? Funny how she could think she had so much in common with a person, and, then, all of the sudden, something so polarizing popped up that she realized they were not alike at all. Now that she thought about it, the evidence against Larry was piling up. He lived in Idaho. He had seven children. He was dressed like the Seventh Day Adventist salesmen who came to her door when she lived in Denver. He drank club soda. He had three wives — now she wondered if that indicated serial monogamy or polygamy. Maybe he wasn't Mormon, but it all added up to the likelihood that he was. And while Lena didn't harbor any ill will toward those who practiced the religion, she didn't want to date one of them.

Without Lena's reciprocation, Larry's monologue soon cooled and then stopped. Lena decided to give up trying to work; opening her laptop just seemed to encourage Larry's chatter. She leaned back, closed her eyes, and let her mind drift back to the tournament she'd just played in Palm Springs. She replayed the round in her head, smiling as she remembered the best shots of the day. Sometimes she worried about how much her memory was worsening with age, but if she could still do the play-by-play after a round of golf, she figured she was okay.

Her thoughts were interrupted by Larry's low voice, almost a whisper.

"You are perfect," he said, and she suspected that all the time she'd been day dreaming, he'd been watching her. "Why didn't I meet you before I met my third wife?"

Lena looked at Larry, irritated. "Oh, I think you'd probably find out pretty quickly that I'm far from perfect," she countered. Actually, I'm probably your worst nightmare.

"Are you married? Have a boyfriend?" he asked, and she realized the topic of her marital status hadn't come up.

"Yes, I have a boyfriend," she answered, protectively.

It was a lie, but a safe one.

"How serious?"

"I don't know how to answer that," she said. "But I think you should know that regardless of my boyfriend, I'm probably not your type."

"What do you mean?"

Lena wondered how direct she had to be to nip Larry's interest in the bud. She decided: very.

"I drink, I swear, I play cards. Sometimes I smoke," she started. "I don't believe in God, and I have slept with more men than I can count. In the past year." She articulated every word clearly but quietly, looking steadily into his eyes. When she was done, she leaned back against her seat again, closing her eyes and folding her hands in her lap. Certainly, he would take a hint.

She was wrong. "All can be forgiven," he answered softly. "I think you're perfect."

"Well, thank you," she said flatly, keeping her eyes closed. She felt trapped. Like many women, she wanted to be admired, desired and coveted, but only from a safe distance. This misguided admiration felt cloying and dangerously close.

Without another word, Lena rose from her seat and headed back to the restroom. She hung out with the flight attendants in the rear galley, making small talk, as long as she could. Lena returned as the plane started its descent for landing, and she noisily busied herself, putting away her laptop, packing up her magazines.

"I have a layover of a couple of hours before I leave for Sun Valley," Larry announced as they waited their turn to slip into the aisle and pull their bags from the overhead compartment. "Could you keep me company for a little while? I think we could really have something special."

"I'm so sorry," Lena feigned disappointment. "My limo is here already, and I can't keep it waiting. Besides, Kim is expecting me home by seven," she said. More lies. More safe lies.

Still, Larry walked next to Lena down the concourse and reached out for a hug as they neared the security exit. Lena quickly turned down the corridor, slipping past his reach, feeling his eyes on her back as she fled.

Leaving

The attention from Larry occupied Lena's thoughts for the next few days. It had been creepy, but it was also erotic and serendipitous in a way. It reminded her of Isadora Wing's "zipless fuck" in Fear of Flying. What if Larry really was the man of her dreams? What if he wasn't Mormon? What if the club soda was just an antidote to a night of heavy drinking the evening before? What if he could have supported her in a fashion that would have given her the freedom to pursue her love of golf and her desire to travel the world?

While she tried to dismiss it as an interesting but unimportant incident in a traveling person's life, Lena found herself comparing Larry – as an incomplete, unknown package – with Kim, and Kim wasn't coming out far ahead. Ahead. But not far.

It didn't help their relationship, as if anything could have. While she had no intention of following up on Larry's offer to contact him once she had time to think – in fact, she had tossed his business card in a trash barrel before she left the airport – the conclusion was unavoidable: she clearly would have opportunities to find alternative relationships if she chose to look. And had the time.

Yes, Kim was as good looking as Larry. But he was more likely to show up for a flight in sweats and a tee shirt than a buttoned-down, starched shirt with cuff links. Yes, Kim had money, but he was not prone to spending it on nice vacations or surprise gifts, like she suspected Larry would be. Yes, Kim had seen her at her worst, but she wasn't sure that was a good thing for romance. Probably Larry would be less attractive, too, once she got over the thrill of someone new. But she didn't know.

All she knew was that she and Kim were not going to work out.

Still, he had his good points. What Lena appreciated most about Kim was that he hated domestic drama and confrontation as much as she did. When she was a child, growing up in an isolated farmhouse on the Nebraska plains, her parents' late-night arguments frightened her. She had no escape. She lay in her narrow bed upstairs and listened to their fights escalate, waiting, hoping for the end, hoping that it would come with the sound of her father's car scattering of gravel as he sped out of the driveway toward a more hospitable reception at the bar down at the intersection of the county roads.

When Kim finally packed up and left, it was far less dramatic. There was no scattering of gravel, just the quiet announcement that he had decided he needed a break from his job and the confession that he needed to put some distance between himself and Lena so he could think.

"What are you going to do? Where are you going?" she asked, curious more than concerned.

"I'm going to caddie for Lionel." His friend had won his PGA tour card on the Web.com tour the year before, and was looking for a new man on his bag. "My experience caddying for you at the Women's Senior Amateur last year seemed enough to convince him I'd be good at it."

The two men had known each other since kindergarten, and Lionel could bet that Kim would be able to show up, keep up, and shut up for rounds on end.

"I'm taking a leave of absence from Microsoft," Kim added. And with neither of them shedding a tear, he walked out her door with the one bag he kept at her condo. She went to the window and watched his Lexus hybrid pull out into traffic and disappear around a corner.

She was glad that he had left Cali with her and Bounty. She would be good company for them both.

Soon, though, Lena regretted they hadn't talked more before he left. Not knowing how soon he might return or how their stalemate might be resolved, she felt in limbo. For the past four weeks, they were not sleeping together or discussing why they weren't sleeping together; they weren't discussing the continued disintegration of their relationship; and they'd never again discussed whether they might have a future with each other. They were both avoiding confrontation, which meant avoiding understanding as well.

LENA DROVE UP TO SUNCADIA the Friday evening after Kim left. She met Terry at the Swiftwater Winery after her friend closed her wine bar, and Lena quickly unloaded the sadness, the ambivalence, and the relief she felt at Kim's departure.

"It seems like it was for the best," was Terry's summation. But when Lena didn't immediately agree, Terry slipped off her bar stool and gave her friend a hug.

"I'm sorry. I just want you to have what you want," she said.

"Oh, crap, I don't know what I want," Lena said, slowly shaking her head back and forth. "I didn't even want to talk with Kim until he left. And now, I wonder if he's really the love of my life and I never gave him a chance."

"You gave him a chance," Terry countered, climbing back on her stool. "I think you gave him a number of chances. Face it, chica. He just didn't turn you on."

"Oh, come on. It wasn't just about sex."

"I'm not saying it was." Terry grabbed the bottle of red a waiter had delivered to their table. She filled two glasses and handed one to Lena. "When I say he didn't turn you on, I'm not just talking about sex. I'm talking about everything. He just wasn't intellectually or emotionally right."

"How do you know?"

Terry gave her friend a look that Lena interpreted as "do you think I don't know you?"

"Okay," Lena finally conceded. "But, you don't have to be so crass about it."

"Okay, what would you call it?"

Lena thought about that, seriously, letting the first sip of wine sit on her tongue for a minute. What was it? If she had sat down at eighteen and listed the qualities she wanted in a prospective boyfriend or husband, Kim would have scored well. He was wealthy and successful. He was loyal and monogamous. He was tall and good looking, athletic and trim. He was intelligent, nice, polite, cultured and well-read. He was a feminist and a liberal.

And he wasn't many bad things. He wasn't a control

freak, he wasn't creepy, he wasn't abusive. He wasn't a kleptomaniac, an insomniac, a necrophiliac. His hands didn't sweat, his breath didn't stink, he didn't have acne. He didn't even snore and, really, when she thought about it this way, the only way his departure made sense was just what Terry said.

He just didn't excite her.

"So, it boils down to something people call chemistry," Lena mused and chuckled at the cliché. "All those other things that I once thought were important, that our mothers would have told us were important, really don't matter?"

"Pretty much," Terry agreed. "Maybe they mattered back when women had to worry about whether they would find a man to support them and their children. Whether he would beat her, whether he would stay out of trouble and out of jail. Whether he'd die young and leave her alone and poor for the last twenty years of her life."

Lena raised an eyebrow. Terry usually wasn't so loquacious, but she had obviously warmed to her subject.

"Yeah, not my concerns," Lena finally answered. She was independent financially. She was reasonably successful and had plenty of work to keep occupied and friends to keep her company. She didn't need a man any more than a fish needed a bicycle, except that fish didn't have sex with bicycles, and fish, as far as she knew, weren't picky about what other fish shared their bicycle.

All she wanted was someone to have good sex with and who would be fun to travel with through the rest of her life. Was that asking so much?

And while Kim had great qualities and so few nasty

ones, what he lacked was a spark that made him fun. She wanted to laugh until her stomach hurt, just once in a while, right in the middle of chewing a mouthful of food, right in the middle of parallel parking, right in the middle of pulling the laundry out of the dryer, just because of something he did or said that she wasn't expecting. She wanted to be surprised by a wild theory; wanted to be surprised by plans he had made for the weekend. She wanted to be surprised and thrilled at a three-dollar present he found for her birthday. She wanted to look at him in a quiet moment and want nothing more than to get him naked, in bed, and underneath her.

But it wasn't Kim she thought of when she imagined these things. It was Ryne. And she hadn't seen Ryne in nearly three years.

What surprised Lena about all of this, as she rode the train of thought in her head, was that the older she got, the sillier her choice of men got. Why, when she was eighteen, was she so sensible about men, and now that she was post-menopausal and over fifty, she acted like a hyper-hormone-poisoned teenager?

Lena shook her head, pulling herself out of her self-absorption and changed the subject. Terry had been patiently waiting for her to finish her reverie.

"What's happening with you and Tom?" Lena asked her friend. "Are things getting better or worse?"

"Definitely worse," Terry muttered, letting her head droop so far forward that her nose nearly disappeared into her wine glass. "I really think it's over."

"Why?"

"Tom moved out last Friday."

"Oh, Terry, why didn't you tell me?" Lena leaned over to put her arm around her best friend's shoulders. "No wonder you've been so philosophical tonight. I would have expected you to be more of an emotional basket case."

"I just don't have anything new to say about it." Tears were gathering on Terry's lower eye lashes.

"But you guys have so much going for you!" Lena argued. "I've never known anyone I thought was better for you."

"I just can't do it," Terry said. "I am thinking of filing."

"Filing? For a divorce?" Lena sat back on her stool, shocked. "You sure?"

"No," Terry said, impatiently. "I said I'm thinking about it. I'm not sure."

"What is it that doesn't work? Same old, same old? Control issues?"

"Pretty much," Terry said. "I can't get used to his need to tell me what to do."

"Maybe he's just trying to give advice, not orders," offered Lena. "Maybe you're just too used to living alone; you don't know how married folks talk to each other. They don't always say 'please.'"

"Oh, we don't talk as much as yell," Terry sniffed. "But it's more than that. He watches TV all the time. He doesn't want to go and do things. He won't hike, he won't play golf. He watches TV and gets impossible when his team loses. His temper is scary. He's never really directed it at me, but it is intimidating."

Lena nodded. She remembered shrinking away from her ex-husband Kurt when he lost his temper. No matter how self-assured she was intellectually, Kurt's physical superiority often gave him the upper hand in their arguments.

"Well," Lena added, wistfully, "commitment to marriage isn't easy."

"Oh, you're the expert?"Terry looked askance at Lena.

Lena held her friend's eyes for a long moment. "Yeah, I guess not."

"And since when have you become such a proponent of commitment? Weren't we just talking about your issues with Kim? Weren't we just talking about your lack of commitment?"

"Uh, I thought we were talking about the fact that he doesn't turn me on."

"Same difference,"Terry said.

Not really. But Terry had a point. It was Lena, not Terry, who hadn't been in a committed relationship for, what, the past ten years? Granted, her first (and last) marriage ended in a disaster, which may give her some excuse for avoidance, but not a life-long exception.

Still, it seemed that she wanted Terry's marriage to work out worse than she wanted to get married herself. Could commitment be practiced vicariously?

Sinking into her thoughts over her warming glass of Cabernet Sauvignon, Lena wondered where her inability to commit came from. Nothing in her life had ever lasted more than a few years, including her life with her parents, who died young. Her first dog Stripe disappeared after only five years. Her jobs, her one marriage, her relationships since then – all short. Maybe she just didn't have any experience in sustained interest. If she'd had some special talent or passion – the violin? ballet? tennis? math? – as a child or young adult, maybe she would have learned something about perseverance. Maybe she would know what it meant to stick with something through its ups and downs.

But wait! Give yourself a break! She sat up straighter. Didn't she just win the Women's Senior Amateur Tournament two years ago after committing to eighteen months of practice and focus? Didn't that prove something? But eighteen months? She slumped again. What was that compared with a lifetime with a marriage partner? Nothing. She was just the kind of person who jumps from one thing to another. Journalism to speech-writing to golf to running a business.

Terry broke into her sour thoughts, bumping her elbow. "Don't look now, but guess who just walked in."

Lena turned to look.

It was as if she'd conjured him up. Ryne was standing at the wine-tasting bar, flirting with the female bartender and looking over the wine list. He leaned his tall frame forward so he could rest one elbow on the bar, and gestured enthusiastically with his free hand as he joked with the tiny woman taking his order. His gregariousness was effortless. A thick lock of black hair fell down on his forehead, and the waitress tried to reach far enough to brush it away for him. And she probably just met him!

"That's what I mean," Lena said out loud.

"What you mean about what?" Terry asked, confused by her friend's non-sequitur.

"Oh, I was thinking a bit ago about how much fun Kim wasn't and how much fun Ryne was. Do you see that?" she nodded toward Ryne. To Lena, Ryne's charisma was obvious. How could anyone miss it?

"Yeah, but I also see trouble," Terry cautioned, turning her head to appreciate her friend's view. "I don't know if this is good."Terry was the one person who knew the power that Ryne had held over Lena that summer three years ago and the effect his sudden departure had on her, and Lena could hear both jealousy and legitimate concern in her voice.

"But you're the one who said it," Lena laughed. "You're the one who put your finger on it. 'Kim just doesn't turn you on,' you said. I don't know what it is about this guy, but he definitely does."

The two women didn't even pretend to look elsewhere. They watched Ryne lean farther over the bar and say something that made the young woman look surprised and then giggle. She poured him a glass of wine from a bottle behind the bar, briefly covered his hand with one of hers, and took his credit card. As she walked away to run his tab, Ryne turned sideways, his eyes starting a slow sweep of the tables around the room. Lena felt her pulse quicken.

Where had he been these past three years? His gaze slowly made its way around the bar toward her corner. She hadn't seen him anywhere — not on the golf course, not at the lodge, not at the winery, not at the Brick in town. If he was working on the book he had started writing three years ago, where was he doing it? Suncadia seemed like the perfect place to get away from distractions and to allow creative juices to flow, but he obviously had gone somewhere else to do it.

Ryne's sweeping gaze passed over her, and then returned to her face with a snap. He smiled and lifted his glass toward her. He nodded at the bartender, signed for his drink, straightened up, and slipped through the crowded bar toward Lena's table.

"Lena, dear!" he exclaimed, leaning forward to brush both of her cheeks with his lips. "And Terry. Good to see you," he turned to her friend and gave her a quick side-saddle hug.

"Lena, Lena, Lena! What have you been doing with yourself?" Ryne leaned forward and rested his elbows on the table, cradling his wine glass in both hands. His dark blue eyes held hers. Lena felt her ears grow hot and her palms sweat. He had always had this effect on her. She blinked and looked down at her chest. Could he see her heart pound through her slim tee-shirt?

Lena didn't know how to start answering his question. She wanted to tell him everything. The tournament, the job, Kim, Bounty, the golf ball. Everything. And nothing. She also wanted to wrestle him to the ground, jump on top of him, and tear her clothes off.

Well, not really. But nearly.

She gestured toward the empty stool next to her.

"Do you have time to join us?" she asked. "Maybe then I can tell you."

Lena was surprised, even given her earlier thoughts, how excited she was to see him. Wherever he'd been, he didn't look much different than he did that morning three years before when she asked him to leave her condo. His hair was still a bit shaggy, with only a little more gray, and he hadn't lost his tan. He hadn't lost any weight either, and to Lena, that was a good thing. He was robust, not skinny like Kim. A nice body to hang onto.

They'd spent just that one night together three years ago, and she had rated the experience a ten out of ten — until breakfast, when he told her he wasn't ready to give up

Kimberly, his waif of a girlfriend. He left, and she hadn't seen him since then.

Ryne had blamed his ambivalence on the fact that he and Kimberly worked at the same newspaper. He said she had him over a barrel; he couldn't break up with her or she'd rat on him. It was not kosher for an editor to sleep with a reporter from the newsroom, even if she didn't report directly to him. And it didn't make things any easier that she was just barely more than half his age.

If her one night with Ryne had been the most important thing in her life at the time, Lena might have been crushed by his indecision. But, she was preparing for the amateur golf tournament, and, in a way, she had been glad that he wasn't going to be around to distract her.

In a way.

Shortly after that, she'd won the golf tournament in Georgia. Then there was the Walla Walla attack, and after that, the new job, settling back into her condo in Seattle, and making a relationship of sorts with Kim. It seemed like a short story, but it felt like it had been a long, long time since she'd looked into Ryne's eyes. She had missed him.

IT SEEMED INEVITABLE FROM THE moment that Ryne walked over to her in the winery: they would end up in Ryne's duplex for the rest of the night and well into the next morning. Terry graciously abandoned them around ten o'clock, allowing the two former lovers a chance to catch up without a chaperone. As soon as Terry was out of sight, Ryne and Lena left the winery. They drove quickly to Ryne's place and, after a hot reprise of their first night together, they sat up in bed, catching up on the past thirty-six months, smoking cigarettes, and drinking an expensive Côtes du Rhone that he brought back from France.

He had taken a leave of absence to work on his book, but as much as Lena tried to get it out of him, he refused to tell her what it was about. He'd spent two years in a friend's apartment in Aix en Provence, writing, drinking wine, and hiking. The hiking looked good on his legs, and the drinking had improved his wine savoir. And perhaps due to good editorial judgment, his stories lacked any mention of women he'd found interesting or spent time with. He stuck to geographical details, vintages, and travelogue.

"Did you win the lottery or something?" Lena chided him. "Two years? No income? Expensive wine?"

"The lodging was free except for propane and electricity," Ryne reminded her, "so it wasn't that expensive to stay."

"Still."

"Okay, this is it," he grudgingly continued. "My mom's oldest brother died and I'm the last of the clan. Mom's gone, her sister died three years ago, and I have no siblings. It wasn't much, but the old guy was good to me. Other than a few thousand he left to some charity in Spokane, I was the only heir."

"Nice!" Lena exhaled a cloud of smoke. "I mean I'm sorry he died. Did you know him well? When I said 'nice,' I just meant 'nice to get a chunk of change out of the blue.'"

"Nah, don't worry. I hadn't seen him in years. He was holed up in a nursing home in Spokane, the one run by the charity that inherited some money from him. He stopped recognizing me about three years ago when his last sister died. I think the grief wiped out his memory. He was alone, but I quit stopping to see him when the doctor said it wasn't helping. Anyway, he was ninety-five at least. Maybe older."

"You know, not to bring up a sorry subject, but I really wonder what it's like to be that old," Lena mused, stubbing out her cigarette and leaning over to dribble some more wine into her glass from the bottle on the nightstand. "I mean, I remember when I was twenty-five and I thought I'd never want to be fifty! And now I'm past that mark, and I see old folks and I think, 'I never want to be that old.' But I wonder. Maybe however old you get, it just doesn't feel old."

"Well, if you stay in the kind of shape you're in, it probably isn't as hard growing old as it is for some people. I think it's the aches and pains that get to people eventually," Ryne said, sounding a bit like he was speaking from experience. "And you do look great. How is it you're still in such good shape? Are you still playing golf every day?"

"Thanks for the compliment," Lena smiled and gave him a kiss on the forehead. "But, no, I've been a working woman for the past two years. It's not so much about exercise. Sometimes I just don't have time to eat."

Almost apologetically, she told him about The Perfect Tee. Her story about the business she'd taken over and how she managed her bevy of engineers and quartet of venture capitalists seemed mundane compared with his tales of Southern France. But either out of satisfaction with their sexual reunion, or out of intellectual curiosity, Ryne stayed engaged with her story.

"I'm so proud of you," he said quietly after she had spent herself telling him about her successes.

"What do you mean?" she said. "What do you have to be proud of? You weren't here."

Ryne looked surprised. He turned to her and leaned back slightly, as if he expected to get slugged for insolence.

Lena laughed. "Just kidding," she said. And she meant it. But then she added, "Still, I never really understood that expression. To be proud of something, you should have to be part of it."

"And I wasn't."

"No, I'm not talking about you and here and now," Lena tried to allay his concern. "I'm talking in general. When people say, 'I'm so proud of you,' aren't they talking about their own pride? And if you have something to be proud about, shouldn't you have had something to do with it?"

"I suppose …" Ryne sounded a bit intimidated by her sudden passion for the subject.

"I mean this," she said, trying to explain. "When I was a kid, my uncle would come over, and my mom would show him my grades, and he would say, 'I'm so proud of you.'"

"Like I just did," Ryne said, frowning.

"Yeah, but don't take this personally. I'm not just talking about you."

"Oh." Ryne didn't sound convinced.

"I mean, what did my uncle do to help me get good grades? Nothing. Absolutely nothing."

"I see what you're saying," Ryne said, seemingly warming to her topic.

"That's why I don't really get fanaticism about sports teams," Lena continued. "I mean, other than buying an occasional ticket and tee-shirt, exactly what have I done to make the Mariners a better team?"

"Obviously nothing," Ryne joked.

She laughed. He was right; the team needed a lot more

than her contributions to ever become more than an al-so-ran in the American League.

"Well," he concluded after they let that thought sit and ruminate. "I think that's one thing I like about you."

"What's that? That I've done nothing for the Mariners?"

"No, your integrity. Like your golf game. That tourna-ment. You won that out of sheer effort. No one gave it to you. Your parents didn't put a club in your hands when you were three."

"Yup," she said. "I guess that's part of it. But let's not forget. I wasn't born on the streets of Calcutta, either. I had advantages."

"You are one complicated chick," Ryne laughed. "I will take nothing for granted with you."

"Oh, let me show you something else you never ex-pected," Lena said, grinning. She turned over and threw her leg over his hips.

THE NEXT MORNING, as they lay in bed, slow-ly waking up and talking, he pissed her off by scoffing at the idea of a radio-frequency-enhanced golf ball. He only raised the same issues she had — would it improve anyone's game, would it be accepted by the USGA, would any man-ufacturer want to produce it — but it seemed so inappro-priate, given the setting, for him to blatantly shoot down the concept.

Lena felt her heart pounding in her chest the way if felt when she encountered an asshole on the highway. Sudden-ly, she was hot and angry. She flipped the covers back and turned to get out of bed.

But Ryne slipped his arm around her waist and held

her. He didn't try to pull her back into bed. He just held her. She could have easily broken free of his gentle hold, but she didn't. With his other hand, he smoothed her hair away from the back of her neck and kissed her between the shoulder blades.

She turned and slipped her legs back onto the bed.

Ken v Taylor

Back in the office Monday morning, Lena held her regular weekly meeting with her direct reports. Jordan reported significant success in securing some new lines for the styles The Perfect Tee would offer in a year or so, and Lena tried to lead a group applause when she finished her presentation. But, the response was lukewarm, and Lena realized her morale problems were getting worse.

Ken and Taylor were not talking to each other. Sitting on opposite sides of the conference table, they pouted in sullen silence during each other's weekly reports. And, worse, it seemed that their two-way dispute had somehow spread to a three-way quarrel that now included Kevin, the e-commerce chief and internal customer of Ken's and Taylor's programs.

"I have a list of priority issues a mile long, and I can't seem to get anything going on them," Kevin complained. He looked back and forth from Ken to Taylor, but they didn't look up from their laptops.

"What are the most urgent issues?" Lena asked.

"Most have to do with customer service and order paths," Kevin said.

"What's the deal, guys?" Lena asked. Ken and Taylor

pretended like they didn't hear. Lena raised her voice. "Ken? Taylor? What's the problem?"

"Manpower," Ken mumbled, eyes glued to his laptop screen.

"Yeah," Taylor contributed.

Lena guessed the real problem was the amount of time the two programmers were spending getting in each other's way and building warring coalitions. Forcing a confrontation in the meeting wouldn't be productive.

"Kevin, give me a list of your top ten priority issues, and I'll sit down with these two and get things moving," she said. "Why don't you and I meet this afternoon."

It was clear to Lena that she was going to have to spend more time understanding the software tiff. The quarrel between Ken and Taylor had gotten out of hand before she realized it, and that made her wonder how many other things she had been ignoring.

Further, the crux of the disagreement between her two developers was not as silly as the way they were acting. It involved a disagreement over a serious matter. Ken was in charge of the e-commerce platform and database management; Taylor built the software brains that helped customers input their measurements and build their avatars. He also led the team that built the software that digested the manufacturers' specs that made it possible for the company to provide the perfect fit – the company's most significant competitive differentiation.

Taylor was pushing for a broadening of the company strategy to build on the golf clothing expertise, bringing in tennis wear first, then ski wear and other sportswear. To do that, he needed a pool of developers to design a more universal and flexible code that would more easily digest manufacturer specs for the new industries.

On the other side, Ken wanted to acquire and integrate more sophisticated financial management software to improve the company's ability to forecast its earnings. The financial planning and analysis folks were struggling to get relevant numbers from the e-commerce platform early enough in the quarter to predict costs on the warehouse and distribution side. Without that information, it was hard to give guidance to the company's investors about financial results. It even hindered their ability to forecast pricing and sales levels.

It was a serious debate about resource allocation and the company's capital structure that was Lena's job to parse. At the least, she should have been leading the debate and providing a process for making a decision. By having the CFO lead the budgeting process that summer, she'd neglected the up-front strategic issues that should have laid the foundation for the company's budget, and the CFO didn't have the authority to make those decisions for the company. So, no one had done it. And now Lena had to admit, the two developers were operating — however childishly — in a leadership vacuum that was no one's fault but her own.

The day after the staff meeting, she took a rare break from the office and drove out to Sarah's quiet neighborhood in Issaquah. It was a warm, sunny afternoon, and the two old friends walked out of Sarah's back door and down a path through an obsessively manicured greenbelt that bordered on her backyard.

"You know, I've always appreciated the way you and

the VCs pretty much leave me to manage the company without micro-managing," Lena told Sarah as they wended their way behind the huge brick and cedar-shake mansions. "But I need to settle this disagreement between my IT guys soon, before it rips the company in two. To do that, we need to talk big picture."

"Big picture what?" Sarah asked. They pushed through a gate that led out of Sarah's section of the secure greenbelt and across the street, where Sarah punched in a code to enter another gate.

"We need to decide if we're going to extend our clothing lines into other sports, or are we going to focus our efforts improving our financial systems," Lena started. "If you and the VCs are looking to do an Initial Public Offering at this point, we would need to beef up our accounting and audit systems. But I'd like to continue to build the breadth of the business before we do an IPO, and that entails different kinds of IT work."

"You don't usually come to me with these kinds of questions, Lena," Sarah said. "Don't you and the VCs usually discuss these issues?"

"I thought I'd talk with you first for a reality check."

"I have very little stake left in the business," Sarah said, "and no interest in directing strategy at this point. Keeping those brats of mine out of trouble is a full-time job these days, and I haven't even been reading the notes of the board meetings your man sends me."

"Yeah, I know," Lena said.

"So, is it really something else you wanted to talk about?" Sarah knew her so well, and Lena had been betting on that. It was why she had taken a couple of precious hours to drive out to the suburbs to see her.

"Of course." Lena chuckled. "It's always something else, isn't it? I think our problem in management is this damn female introspection hang-up. Why can't we just go to battle like the guys and not worry about what it means about us or our management abilities all the time."

"Oh, Christ, I have no idea," Sarah laughed. "I'm not introspective enough to answer that! And so, what's on your mind?"

"Engineers," Lena summed up her problem in a word. "I don't know if I can manage these guys. All they have to do to flummox me is start doing their engineer talk and tell me that I 'wouldn't understand.' They have a way of getting under my skin that they never seemed to pull with you."

"Well," Sarah answered, "that's not true. They always drove me nuts too. The difference is that I was so excited about creating this thing, that I didn't care how much personal abuse I had to endure to get it done. Maybe the problem is that the excitement is gone already, and now you're dealing with the unpleasant shit."

"Oh, it's not all unpleasant," Lena countered. "I enjoy going into work every day, and I get along with everyone else. It's just those IT guys."

The women passed through another set of gates and wandered off the path, down a steep bank, and sat on a bench overlooking a small lake. The water was perfectly clear, and the developer had covered the shallow bottom with beautiful granite stones. Lena wondered how he kept the lake so algae-free, and then she noticed a faint chlorine odor and noticed there were no water birds hanging around.

"I probably don't want to know what kind of volatile organic compounds I'm breathing right now, do I?" she asked Sarah.

"Probably not," her friend answered. "Sometimes it really smells like bleach down here. It's just a tiny whiff today. I have no idea what they dump in to keep it pretty like this."

"Well, anyway," Lena brought the subject back to The Perfect Tee, "when I talk with Ken, in particular, I get attitude constantly, and I guess part of the problem is that I thought this CEO title would immediately make everyone heel."

"You mean like a dog heels?"

"Yeah. I know it sounds naïve, but I can't believe that being the boss – even in these days of the so-called flat organization – doesn't mean anything."

"It really doesn't," Sarah said. "I don't have to tell you: CEOs get dumped every day. By boards, by palace coups, by their own misdeeds."

"Then why do we do it?" Lena leaned forward and rested her elbows on her knees.

"Power."

"But obviously, there isn't any."

"Yeah, hence the conundrum, huh?"

Lena looked back over her shoulder and saw Sarah grinning.

"Lena, I don't have any answers," she said. "But then you know that. I think you just needed a day out of the office in the sunshine and a friendly shoulder to cry on. You are welcome to come and do that anytime, you know."

"Thanks," Lena said, straightening back up and leaning against the bench's back rest. "You are right. I just needed to get out and clear my head for an hour. Now, I guess I'd better get back and call the VCs about this strategy thing."

LENA STARTED CALLING THE VCS to set up a meeting when she got back to the office. She hadn't tapped their expertise or business savvy very often, not wanting to be the high-maintenance CEO in their portfolio. But this strategy question was one thing she should have involved them in, and she was disappointed that they hadn't tackled it together before now.

What was stranger, though, was the reaction she got from Blake. He was the VC who had always been the most difficult to get along with and seemed closer to Ken than to her. He was the least enthusiastic about the RF golf ball project and most critical of Jordan, for reasons that escaped Lena. It didn't surprise Lena that he reacted badly to her request for a strategy meeting. He nearly always argued that he was too busy to go to her meetings.

What surprised her, though, and bothered her even more, was that he'd already talked with Ken about building new financial analysis and reporting tools. So, had it been Blake who was pushing Ken to expand the budget for financial systems?

"Why?" she asked.

"I think we should get prepared for an IPO," he said. "The sooner we prepare, the better our numbers will be and the smoother the process will go."

"Why didn't you talk with me so we could work this into our strategy and budget?" Lena asked, trying to sound logical and not hurt by the sleight.

"You've been out so much, it's hard to reach you."

"That's bullshit," Lena responded, getting angry despite her effort to approach Blake calmly and as businesslike as possible. "I have my cellphone with me twenty-four hours a day, and I've never been in a place where I didn't get reception. I get e-mail on it. I get texts. I can answer phone calls. You could have — "

"I have to take another call," Blake interrupted. The conversation ended abruptly.

After she talked with all four of the VCs, she gave up on the idea of a strategy session. They were all too busy to squeeze in a two-hour meeting at that point, so she'd be on her own for a couple of months more.

Meanwhile, she had to decide whether to confront Ken about keeping his conversations with Blake a secret, or just let it go. He may have been instructed by Blake to keep quiet about it, or he may have seen this as an opportunity to set himself up as the obvious heir to the CEO throne, once the VCs tired of Lena or Lena tired of The Perfect Tee.

Lena also wondered what an IPO would mean for her future. Taking the company public by issuing stock and listing on an exchange was always one of the most obvious exit strategies for the VCs. But back when she first came on board, Blake and the other VCs had indicated that they were going to be patient and wait until the company's revenues were large enough to attract the kind of institutional investors who would stick around a while, not the fast-money types who bet on penny stocks.

Rather than waste any more brain cells worrying about it, Lena decided a better use of her energy would be to concentrate on helping Kevin get his priorities met. She pulled up his list of priorities and tried to focus.

It was deadly dull stuff, and her reunion with Ryne over the weekend wasn't helping her concentrate. Her mind kept wandering back to it. Infatuation and sexual obsession were two things that could give falling in love a bad name. They were distracting enough, but then she kept remembering she had another problem: "the other guy."

Although it was clear that her relationship with Kim had deteriorated, they'd never officially broken up. Now that Ryne was back in her life, Lena had occasional panic attacks, realizing that neither Kim nor Ryne was aware of her relationship with the other, and this love triangle wasn't likely to be resolved easily. Someone was going to get very angry, and probably, that was going to be two someones.

Most of the time, though, she felt lightheaded remembering the weekend with Ryne. She hated that feeling. It reminded her of the short affair with Greg. She'd met him at the Mount Si Golf Course outside of Seattle before she decided to compete in the senior amateur and after losing her job at TrueWeb. After a head-spinning four-day affair, which pushed every other thought out of her head, Greg simply disappeared and ghosted her. She'd felt sheepish, not so much because he'd turned out to be a flake, but because she had devoted so much energy and time to the silliness.

Now she seemed to be blindly diving into a risky romance with Ryne. Unlike Greg, Ryne was a known entity. She knew where he worked. She knew where he lived and who his former girlfriend was. She had been around him long enough to know something about his temperament and something about his personal issues. That helped ease some of her doubts.

But it wasn't without its own caution flags. She didn't

know for sure that he was ready to fully turn his back on his relationship with Kimberly, his former girlfriend.

Over the next couple of weeks, she was sure that he didn't have time to see the other woman, at least at night or on weekends. He was at Lena's condo nearly every evening after work in Seattle, and they were either at Lena's or Ryne's home in Suncadia every Friday and Saturday night. Now Lena was concerned about how their relationship had evolved so quickly. Was this real or was she being fooled?

The sex was great. Not just good and fun, but great. It was addictive in a way that her brief fling with Greg had suggested it could be; but with Ryne, it was more than a suggestion. It lasted unabated through the first month after Kim had gone on the tour, and a short time after that, Ryne began to leave clothes and toiletries behind in her condo in Seattle to make it easier to get up and go straight to work in the mornings after he spent the night there. He really seemed to be as infatuated with her as she was with him, but not in the cloying way that it felt with Kim.

Soon, she needed to get up the nerve to tell Brandt and Carly about it. Carly had been skeptical about Ryne's ability to detach himself from his young, adoring employee back three years ago. She'd rolled her eyes when Lena told her about the one-night stand, when Lena tried to deny that it was the cause of a two-month golf slump. Now, Carly was likely to think that Ryne was going to be no better for her and for her work at The Perfect Tee than he was for her preparation for the USGA tournament.

After all the consternation, it turned out that she didn't need to worry. Brandt and Ryne had been friends long before Lena had met either of them. Getting back together for a round of golf the next Saturday pleased everyone, even Carly.

Lena and Carly had a quick, whispered conversation in their shared cart once their drives ended up on the opposite side of the fairway from the men, and Lena was surprised that Carly didn't seem worried about Ryne. He had a special kind of charisma, Lena realized, that softened hearts and made people accept him for the imperfect person he was happy to be.

Having Kim — the calmest, most grown-up of all her friends — out of the picture and out of town had simplified things, oddly.

"I like Kim. I like him a lot," Carly assured Lena. "But he's not terribly charming. So, what are you going to tell him?" Carly asked as they waited in their cart for the men to hit their fairway shots.

"I haven't figured it out," Lena grimaced. "He's such a nice guy you just hate to hurt him."

"But you'd better tell him soon or you might end up with a mess on your hands. Imagine: Kim comes home unexpectedly and finds you and Ryne in bed together."

"Yuck. The most cliché of romance clichés, huh?"

"Yeah, but could happen," Carly warned. "He doesn't tell you about every movement he makes on tour, does he?"

"No, but I would expect he won't come back until Lionel takes a break before the FedEx Cup Playoffs."

"Is Lionel playing in the Playoffs?" Carly looked surprised.

"I doubt it, but I'm sure he and Kim will go and watch. Soak up the atmosphere. And if Lionel gets a win or a few top tens in the next few tournaments, who knows? Maybe he will get a chance to go."

Over beers at the Inn at the end of the round, the foursome settled into a comfortable silence, punctuated only by an occasional "wow" or "ouch" as they watched tour players amaze and disappoint golf fans on the TVs above the bar. Lena had relaxed into a TV trance – the kind that only golf on TV can cause – until she jumped at a hand placed on her shoulder. She turned to see Jim Treacher.

"How'd you play today?" he asked her, glancing over at Ryne whose own TV trance was holding firm.

"Good, not great," Lena answered, declining to reciprocate and ask about his round. "Good to see you," she smiled and turned back toward the TV. She had little hope that her indifference was going to end the conversation that quickly, but she tried.

"Aren't you going to introduce us?" Jim persisted, nodding toward Ryne. Ryne turned to see Jim standing behind them. In a blatant power move, Ryne stood up to tower over Jim, and stuck out his big hand for a shake. Lena imagined that Ryne was probably gripping the ex-banker's hand tightly.

"Ryne Morris," her boyfriend introduced himself.

"You mean like Ryan Moore, the pro?" Jim shrank slightly, seeming to lose some of his composure, whether due to Ryne's height advantage or because he thought he was talking to a tour player.

"No, Ryne, not Ryan," Ryne answered with a hint of exasperation from having heard the question a million times. "Morris, not Moore. I'm a good six inches taller than he is. And older. A lot older. And you are?"

"Jim Treacher," the older man regained his posture, answering confidently. "One of Lena's golfing buddies."

"Oh, really?" Ryne feigned a deep interest in the man's relationship with Lena. "How long have you known each other?"

"A couple of years, right, Lena?" Jim looked to Lena for support under Ryne's intense stare.

"We did play together a couple of times a few years ago," Lena responded, shifting her position behind Jim so she could roll her eyes. If he wanted to remind Lena of that awkward pass he made three years ago, this didn't seem the time. Ryne smiled and clapped Jim on the back a little hard.

"Well, perhaps you can play together again sometime, when she's not too busy." Ryne winked, turned back to the TV, and sat down, clearly showing he was through with the conversation.

Jim raised his eyebrows and looked back at Lena. "Pretty confident of himself, isn't he?" he whispered conspiratorially.

"He should be," Lena said simply, reaching over and placing her hand possessively on Ryne's back.

"Oh." Jim shifted in his golf shoes. He moved sideways and wedged his body between them, turning his back to Ryne. "I've been wanting to talk to you about that new business project of yours."

"What business idea?" Lena asked, puzzled.

"Word gets around," Jim said. "Your golf ball."

"What about it? And how did you hear about it?" She couldn't remember talking with Jim about the RFID golf ball project.

Jim ignored her second question. "I would like to discuss a possible investment. I think the idea has some potential, but you will probably need some financing and some real business leadership, and you know those are my things."

"Well," Lena blinked and frowned. How arrogant. The man worked at a frickin' bank, not a manufacturing business. She took a second to shake off her disdain and calm her voice. "This isn't the place to discuss this. And, I wouldn't want to have any conversations with you until my partner and our VCs are in the room."

"Absolutely," Jim responded quickly. "I thought we might set that up."

We? Who is this "we"? Once again she was amazed at his arrogance in placing himself in a relationship with her that he had no right to assume.

"I'll think about it," she said flatly.

"You know it's going to be hard to get a ball on the market that doesn't meet USGA standards," Jim continued.

"I believe we are quite aware of our challenges, but thanks for the advice," Lena said even more coolly.

"Maybe you can call me next week after you talk with George about it," Jim suggested. Obviously he had done enough research to know who her partner was.

"I said I'll think about it," Lena spat.

"Great. I'll await your call." Jim placed his hand on her back. She wasn't sure if it was meant to be a friendly gesture, a possessive gesture or a pass, but its effect was to make her shiver uncomfortably.

He nodded toward Ryne. "Say goodbye for me."

THE NEXT WEEK, JIM CALLED. His tone, absent Ryne's

presence, was more confident and businesslike, and his interest in the golf ball venture had morphed from an interest in investing in the project to buying it outright.

Lena had considered not talking to him when her assistant asked if she should forward his call. But, *he's not going away, I might as well get this over with.*

"Well, that's quite a different proposition from what you laid out last Saturday," she responded. "I thought you were interested in investing, not controlling."

"True," Jim said. "But I wanted to see if you have set up that meeting with George so we can discuss this, businessman to businessman."

Lena's heart raced, and her face turned hot. *Was he really suggesting that this was an issue between himself and George, and didn't involve her?*

"Are you trying to cut me out of the conversation?" she asked, hearing her voice rise a couple of tones. "This venture is fifty-fifty between George's company and mine."

"I wasn't suggesting -- "

"You just said 'businessman to businessman,'" she cut him off. "That's clearly trying to push me aside."

"I meant 'businessman' in the gender-neutral sense," he tried to recover.

"Well, I'm not too impressed with your ability to clearly articulate your intent," she fired back. "It's never been a strength of yours, I realize."

There was a pause on Jim's end of the line.

"Ouch!" he finally reacted. "I thought we could talk as friends."

"Jim. We're not friends. You tried to make a pass at me once and now you appear to be trying to cut into my – "

"That wasn't a pass," he cut her off. "That was a serious job offer."

"Really? 'I would get to see more of you,' you said. That's not a pass?"

"I would say that to a young man I liked to be around, too."

Lena held her breath. She had not wanted to go down this conversational path with him, and she was disappointed in herself for doing so. She slowly let the air out of her lungs, blowing a windy hiss into the receiver.

"Lena this is about business, not about relationships," Jim continued, pedantically. "Don't get the two mixed up."

"I think we have discussed this enough," Lena snapped back, trying to end the call. "Why don't you write a letter to George and me and clearly express your interest, and then I'll see if George wants to meet with you."

"You don't, do you?"

"Don't what?"

"Don't want to meet with me about this."

"No. But I'm willing to read a letter and assess your honest intent. I wouldn't want to turn down an offer that might add to our chances of success."

Jim took a moment to respond. "Okay, if you want to proceed that way, I'll think about it," he said. "One way or another, you'll be hearing from me again."

Ryne

Two days later, George called her in the middle of a meeting with John, her CFO.

"Who is this Jim Treacher fellow?" George asked.

"He called you?" Lena felt her heart rate quicken.

"Late yesterday. He said he had approached you with an interest to invest in our golf ball venture, and you refused to talk with him."

"Oh, my god," Lena said. She was embarrassed to utter such a cliché, but nothing else seemed to fit the current circumstance. "I can't believe this. He said that?"

"Yeah, so who is he?"

"Christ, George, this is really complicated, and I need to finish my meeting with John. Can I call you back in an hour or so?" Lena wanted time to calm her nerves and think about how much she should tell George.

When she called him back later that afternoon, she had decided to tell him everything. She started with how they met, innocently, on the golf course, and how they had eventually parted ways after what she interpreted as an inappropriate pass by a married man whose wife was out of town. She told him what she knew about Jim's banking days and the conversations they'd had about the golf ball venture.

"Got it," George said. "I figured there was more to this."

"That doesn't mean that we shouldn't talk to him," Lena quickly conceded. "Perhaps he could be of some help. But, first, I don't want to cut my VCs out of the picture by pursuing some sort of financing that precludes sticking with our known investors."

"I agree. What do you think we should do?"

Lena was relieved. George was clearly seeing her as an equal in a way that she didn't expect Jim ever would.

"I think it might be time to talk with the VCs and gauge their interest," she suggested. "I need to get together with them for some business at The Perfect Tee anyway. Then we can see if there's a reason to follow up with Jim. But in any case, I wouldn't expect him to back off until we've met with him together."

"Right. Do you want to set something up with your financiers? Maybe next week?"

"Okay, let me work on it."

"Oh, and by the way, you should know that Jim mentioned something about an ex-husband. I didn't want to talk with him about something personal, so I cut him off. I know about what happened in Walla Walla, and I don't need to hear it from him. But it's clear that he has some pretty strong feelings about wanting to insinuate himself in this deal, even if it means leveraging nasty personal stuff."

Lena felt her head swimming. How many times had Jim made her lose her composure in the last week? Would he have pursued this in such a manner if she were a man?

"I don't know what to say, George. It's pretty damn hard to believe he would bring up my past in this way."

"Look, Lena. I don't want anyone to go into your past

and dig up something that has nothing to do with our business venture," George said calmly. "But perhaps you and I should talk about how to handle this sometime so that we aren't sideswiped by the issue when it really matters."

"My troubles with my ex-husband are easily Googled," she responded. "Why don't people just do a search and read all about it?"

"I don't mean — "

"I am not worried about it, George," she cut him off. "I know you don't want to focus on something like that. But I agree. At some point, we should probably get on the same page about how to handle things like this."

"Sure, Lena." He paused. "Hey, don't let this jerk get under your skin. We'll deal with him in whatever way is appropriate after we talk with the VCs."

Lena left work early, exhausted by her developers' spat and the conversation with George.

She pulled out the keys to open her condo door but, to her surprise, she found it unlocked. She certainly didn't leave it that way. Yes, she was a bit discombobulated, worried about work and about what Jim was going to do to their golf-ball venture, but she always locked the door.

The confusion ended when she closed the door behind her and turned around. "Oh!" she exclaimed. Kim's bags were strewn in the front hallway. He'd come home. Bounty and Cali bounded over the pile of duffel bags to give Lena her big, wet welcome-home kisses. They were more excited than usual, undoubtedly due to Kim's arrival.

Now, suddenly, her worries over Jim and her developers disappeared. What was she going to do about the fact that Ryne's clothes were in her closets and dresser? His toothbrush was in her bathroom. How the hell was she going to explain this to Kim?

Lena glanced quickly around the small condo. Kim's stuff was there in the hallway, but he wasn't. She breathed a sigh of relief; maybe she would have some time to put Ryne's stuff out of sight, but if she did that, then what would she do when Ryne came in later that evening? There was no easy way out of this.

Maybe the best thing to do was just to pack up a bag, head up to Suncadia and let the two of them work it out without her. Yeah, it was the solution of a coward, but right then, it seemed like the only escape from what promised to be a nasty, disturbing ruckus.

She was halfway up the stairs on her way to pack for Suncadia when she heard the door open behind her and Cali and Bounty jumped up to greet Kim as if they hadn't seen him for months. Kim's sun-tanned face was turned up at her while he absent-mindedly petted the dogs' heads. He smiled broadly and spread his tanned arms, expecting her to run down into them.

Instead, she sat down on the stairs, speechless and shaking. At least she wasn't in bed with Ryne when Kim had come in, as Carly had predicted.

"Hey, aren't you glad to see me?" Kim asked, visibly confused. He reached for the grocery bag he'd just placed on the kitchen counter and pulled out a six-pack of Budweiser. He pulled a can loose and popped the top. "You want one?"

"No," she said sheepishly. "I just got back from a meeting at work. I'm thinking of going up to Suncadia for a couple of days, so I was just heading up to pack."

"Really? Couldn't you tell I was home?" Kim gestured to his bags in the hallway. "You're going to leave me here alone when I just got back?"

"Uh … ," Lena couldn't think of what else to say. "What're you doing back?" she changed the subject. "Don't you guys have a tournament this week in Portland?"

"Things just got a little ugly out there all of the sudden, so we decided to take a break," Kim said, sitting down at the kitchen counter bar and taking a big swig of his beer.

"What do you mean?" Lena walked back down the stairs and put the five remaining beer cans in the refrigerator. "What happened?"

Kim told the story backwards: he and Lionel returned to Seattle for a two-week break. That was because Golf-Week was chasing them down for a story about Lionel's political opinions. That was because some of the tour players had been bad-mouthing him to the golf media about his nasty attitude.

"Nasty? I've always thought Lionel was a real sweetheart," Lena said. She sat down on the bar stool across from Kim. "How could anyone think he was nasty?"

Lionel, Kim explained, had given an interview to the Seattle Weekly. Hadn't Lena seen it? It was titled "A Liberal on Tour," and was about how Lionel's liberal politics made it hard for him to make friends on the tour. He disagreed with their privileged and adamant anti-tax stance, and he shunned their prayer groups. He'd even gone so far as to ask one of the more vociferously religious players to quit leaving religious pamphlets in the locker room in deference to the possibility that some players may not share his religious views. He'd called them "the Christian Mafia" in the interview with the Weekly, and since then, he'd gotten the cold shoulder from the other tour players, and enough stink-eye to ruin his game. Kim and Lionel decided to take a break from the tour and let things cool down.

"Yikes," said Lena, summing up her reaction. "I get a little freaked-out by all that on the Golf Channel, too," she said in solidarity. "The way they thank God for helping them win, like God chose them over all the other players."

"Yeah, Lionel called them arrogant. I guess if you believe in a god who stands around worrying about you all the time, it's a small leap to think he's rooting for you in every tournament. I just could never figure out how come they don't win every week, then. Is God just being fair by spreading the wealth?"

Kim made her laugh. She remembered how his calm rationality always helped her moderate her own mercurial temperament, especially when it involved politics or religion.

"I don't blame you guys for wanting to get away," she said. "But is Lionel going to be able to keep his card if he skips a bunch of tournaments?"

"I don't think he was going to be able to keep it anyway," Kim said. "He's played okay, but he's probably going to have to go back to the farm tour next year. He's not even in the top hundred right now."

Kim shook his head and got up to help himself to another beer. Just as he closed the refrigerator door and sat back on his stool, Ryne opened the condo door and walked in.

Lena stood and froze. Then, turning on her heels, she

left the two men alone, escaping to the condo balcony, closing the door after her. She leaned her arms on the railing with her back to the windows and the scene inside. God, I want a cigarette.

IT WAS EXTREMELY UNCOMFORTABLE, BUT in the end Lena was surprised how civilly the two men treated each other. It was as if they had known what was going on, or at least suspected it, and she had been the naïve one, thinking she was keeping secrets.

After some awkward shuffling and surreal small talk, Kim and Ryne shook hands, Kim gathered up his bags, called for Cali and left. Once the door closed, Lena came back into the condo and stood looking at Ryne, waiting for his reaction. He said nothing, and they sat on the kitchen bar stools for a long time in silence, sipping beer. Finally, Ryne stood up. He crushed his beer can on the side of the sink and threw it in the recycle bin.

"Let's take Bounty for a walk and then go down to Cactus for dinner," he said, suggesting the Mexican restaurant down on the corner, across from the lake. "It would be good to get out of the condo for a little while."

For a few days, the uncomfortable encounter left Lena embarrassed, in part for the fact that it happened, and then for the fact that she had abandoned the guys and left them to work it out on their own. While that may have been for the best, the chagrin chilled her sex drive, and she spent the next weekend alone in Suncadia, sharing her embarrassing tale with Terry over wine at Terry's wine bar, while Ryne flew back to New York to talk with his publisher. But, her libido came crashing back by the middle of the next week, when she spotted Ryne in the distance, entering her condo as she walked home from work in the rain. She picked up her step. "He really is gorgeous," she said out loud to herself, earning a puzzled look from an Amazon employee passing her on the sidewalk.

Kim didn't call or e-mail or text. She heard that he left town a couple of weeks later as Lionel returned to the Tour, and her biggest concern became Cali. She didn't know who was taking care of the mutt, and she and Bounty missed her.

After things returned to normal between Lena and Ryne, it seemed that resolving the Kim issue was a catalyst of sorts. She found it easier to focus at work and began to believe that she and her developers were going to be able to resolve the budgeting issue, in spite of interference from Blake. On the weekends, she listened while Terry struggled with deciding whether to file for divorce. Her friend finally decided to give the relationship another try.

And Lena and Ryne took advantage of the beautiful Northwest summer weather and long days of sunlight, playing nine holes of golf when they got up to Suncadia on Friday nights, and sleeping late and enjoying a lazy breakfast and a long walk with Bounty on Saturdays. She played with Carly and Brandt on Sunday when Ryne went back to work at the newspaper. Her golf was solid, and it became for her what most weekend golfers want it to be: a relaxing and rewarding game that occasionally disappointed her, but generally delivered enough great shots and unlikely one-putts to induce a smile as she shook hands with her playing partners on the eighteenth hole.

The Party

In August, Terry held the birthday party for Lena she had promised to host at her wine bar.

Ryne, Carly, and Brandt came, as Terry had predicted back in June, but Kim didn't. Neither did Terry's husband, Tom. George and Tina drove up for the party and rented a unit for the weekend at the lodge. Lena had invited Kate and Elysse from Tumble Creek. Kate came with her husband, but on finding out that Jim Treacher wasn't invited, Elysse responded with regrets; she had another commitment for the evening.

A few other golf club members and her golf instructor from Suncadia came as well as some wine-bar regulars from Roslyn, the police chief, the fire chief, and the mayor, which indicated the extent to which Terry — more than Lena — had cultivated some gravitas in the community. Some of Lena's neighbors from the lodge showed up. Lena knew everyone who came, even if they didn't really constitute the kind of tight-knit group Terry had proposed bringing together as their new "community."

The wine bar looked great that night. Terry had placed dozens of colorful votives around, giving the shop an aura of romance and sophistication, although Lena worried that they might send the century-old building up in flames. The ambiance, wine, candles, and music made Lena yearn to retreat to her condo in the lodge with Ryne. But she couldn't walk out of her own birthday party.

Lena whispered to Ryne that he should wander around and mingle so she could keep her mind off the later, private activities they planned for the evening. He winked at her and obliged, and Lena did her best to keep Terry's mind off Tom. Bounty wandered underfoot, evaluating every human at the party, and stopping next to the most likely food sources.

For an hour, Lena fielded dozens of questions about her now-years-old senior women's championship, but not surprisingly, no one asked her about The Perfect Tee. Either the folks in Roslyn had no idea that she was running the golf-clothing website company, or they simply had no interest. In either case, the evening reminded Lena how good it was to have a "rounded" persona — not just businessperson, but also sports figure. That way, she always had something to talk about with nearly everyone.

Except for the county official who had come with the mayor. He wasn't a golfer, had no interest in the sport, and seemed confused about why Terry had invited him to her party. At one point in the evening, he sidled up to Lena, figuring out that she was the guest of honor, and pummeled her with questions.

"Where are the celebrities?" he asked Lena. "I thought there would be some Suncadia executives or someone at this party that I needed to meet. Why else was I invited?"

Lena had no idea why the politician thought there would be any headliners at her party. And, if a Suncadia executive met his definition of "celebrity," Lena could only feel sorry for him. Apparently, he had become accustomed to getting petty favors and goodies because of his low-level public office, and when confronted with an evening out that yielded no payoffs, he was not only disappointed, but terribly confused about what to do with conversation.

Slipping away under the guise of needing to "powder her nose," Lean motioned for Ryne to follow her. They let Bounty into the generous bathroom with them, and kissed sloppily. Lena pulled away to check her lipstick in the mirror. Most of it had ended up on Ryne's face, and she handed him a paper towel to wipe it off.

A knock on the door surprised them, and Ryne responded in a deep, radio voice: "Who's there?"

"Brandt and Carly."

Ryne unlocked and opened the door.

"What are you guys doing in here?" Brandt asked rhetorically, pulling Carly into the restroom behind him and relocking the door. "Carly and I need some smooching, too!" He reached for his wife and pantomimed a noisy smack on her lips.

"Hey, don't you guys have a room?" asked Ryne. "We already have dibs on this one."

"Nice birthday party," Brandt said to Lena. "The local officials even showed up. You must be some kind of draw," he teased Lena.

"They're Terry's friends," Lena said. "I barely know them, but they help fill out the room. If we were just depending on my friends to show up, we could have just had this party in this bathroom."

"Like we are now," Carly said, lighting a cigarette. It

was probably against the fire and health codes, but none of the other three cared. She took a deep draw and passed it to Lena.

"We'd better go back out," Lena said, exhaling smoke. "I don't want anyone to wonder what's going on in here. The way gossip spreads around this town, who knows…"

Another knock on the door interrupted her.

"Who is it?" all four bathroom inhabitants answered at once, which triggered a rash of giggling. Carly tossed the barely-smoke cigarette into the toilet and flushed it. They tried to silence their giggles and snorts by covering their mouths. It was fruitless, and none of them made a move for the door. It took another knock and a plea through the door from Terry to get them to calm down and unlock the door again.

"What are you guys doing in there?" she asked as Lena opened the door. Terry seemed more amused than angry. The foursome smiled conspiratorially and followed Bounty out of the restroom like clowns exiting a Volkswagen.

As Lena came out, Terry grabbed her arm and pulled her aside. "Someone is here looking for you, and I didn't know how to get rid of him," she whispered.

"Who?"

"Elysse is here with that guy, Jim — you know the one that tried to proposition you that time?"

"Oh Christ! I thought Elysse said she had other plans."

"Well, apparently her plans involved Jim, and now they're here. And they brought some other guy."

"Maybe I can escape out the back." Lena looked around the room for Ryne, but he had already moved into the small crowd.

"You can't do that! This is your birthday party," Terry pleaded.

"Oh, no. You're right," Lena assured her. "Not after all you went through to put this together. Maybe I should just get this over with and go talk to him. Where is he?"

"He's over there, talking to the stranger who came with them." Terry pointed to a far corner near the shelves that held imported wines for sale.

Lena moved forward, keeping plenty of people between herself and Jim, trying to see who else he had brought, uninvited, to her party. At first, she didn't recognize the short, dark-haired man who was talking to Jim with his back toward her. But he turned briefly to throw his blazer over a chair, and Lena caught her breath. She recognized the starched shirt and the cuff links.

"How could he have ended up here?" she whispered to Terry.

"Who is he?

"It's some strange guy I met on a plane once. He was a little creepy. And Mormon, I think. Larry. Larry is his name," Lena stared, shocked and confused, unable to believe her eyes. "How the hell does he know Jim?"

Terry shook her head, and stared along with her.

"Oh, shit!" Lena grabbed Terry's arm. "I think they're coming this way."

Lena turned and ducked back into the bathroom, locked the door, lowered the toilet seat and sat down. She buried her face in her hands and shook her head back and forth.

This was just about the worst nightmare she could imagine. Larry had occupied her thoughts – unsettlingly –

for a couple of days after they had met on that flight back from Palm Springs two months before. But since Ryne had walked back into her life, she hadn't thought about him once. Now, apparently, he had hooked up with Jim, and who knew what problems the two of them would cause her. Two jilted potential lovers with money and some shared mission; Lena could only guess what that was.

Were the two conspiring to get their hands on her golf-ball business? she wondered. If so, that posed a serious threat to her effort to be taken seriously as a woman executive. Love triangles? Jilted lovers? Combine those with The Perfect Tee's morale problems and internecine battles, and she'd lose all credibility with her VCs and just about everyone else in the industry in Seattle. This was the last thing her reputation needed.

ON A MONDAY MORNING EARLY in September, Lena was surprised by an e-mail from GTI, one of the manufacturers in southern California they had solicited for the golf ball venture. The missive — it copied both Lena and George — requested a return visit from the two partners, reprising their scouting visit earlier that summer. But, better yet, it also said the company might allocate significant dollars to research and building a prototype based on the RFID ball in the next year's fiscal budget. All they needed to do was work out the details.

Lena was ecstatic. She called George first, and got his voice mail.

"Call me! Did you see the e-mail from GTI? Great news!" she recorded.

Then she called Ryne. He was out, too, so she left a

voice mail and then skipped into the big bullpen that represented most of The Perfect Tee's workspace, looking for a live person to share the good news with. Unfortunately, it was early and the only person she could find was Ken. He accepted the news with a stoicism befitting a Buddhist. He and his VC-partner-in-crime were probably the only two people involved in The Perfect Tee who wouldn't be excited about the news.

Lena didn't let Ken's negative attitude spoil her mood. She swept back to her desk, pulled her cell phone off the pile of clothing catalogs and called Terry, who squealed at the news, as if on cue. Lena had told Terry about the golf-ball project the night of her birthday party at Terry's wine bar. It had been Terry who had finally talked her into coming out of the restroom and facing Jim and Larry. With Ryne standing next to her as a kind of bodyguard, she managed to stay composed while listening to their proposition.

Larry and Jim, it turned out, had known each other for a couple of decades. As a banker, Jim had financed Larry's grocery distribution business, and the two had remained friends. Small fucking world. How unlikely was it that two men — who had each independently sought a personal relationship with Lena — were now hitting her up for a business relationship together.

In neither case was she interested in what they were proposing, but to humor them enough to get the uncomfortable situation over with, Lena stood and listened. Having Ryne next to her helped minimize the uncomfortable undertones that had characterized the confrontations she'd had with the two men in the past. Still, Lena couldn't wait for their pitch to end. To hurry it up, she said little other than "uh-huh" from time to time. In the end, she took their business cards and said she'd keep them in her Rolodex in case she changed her mind about needing their help.

Thanks to the fact he had Elysse in tow, Jim was easier to shake off that night than he had been in the past, and Larry left with them.

"That guy can't take a hint, can he," Ryne said, watching the two men pick up their coats and escort Elysse out the door. "And that guy, Larry? He seemed a little too slick. How many times do you think he's been married?"

"Three," Lena answered without hesitating. "Three times."

"How do you know that?" Ryne was obviously taken aback. "Have you met him before?"

"Oh, yes. On a plane coming back from Palm Springs once. I had no idea that he knew Jim. Sometimes this world is just a little too small."

GEORGE RETURNED LENA'S CALL ABOUT the GTI e-mail around mid-morning.

"Yoo-hoo!" he shouted into her ear when she picked up the line. "Thanks for your call this morning! I try to avoid my inbox on Monday morning. I would have missed it."

The best thing about going to Southern California in early September was the great golf weather. The first line of business GTI had arranged for them when they arrived the next Monday was a round of golf with the CEO and CFO at The Grand, a beautiful, perfectly manicured course just east of La Jolla and GTI's headquarters.

Lena had missed her regular round with Carly and Brandt to return to Seattle on Sunday night and catch the

5:50 Alaska Airlines flight direct to San Diego that morning. That helped her tamp down the guilt she felt playing on the dewy grass Monday morning while her employees were sitting down to their regular, mundane tasks of running a retail business back home. She rationalized that the business owed her a make-up round for her long workdays over the summer.

They decided on match play, George against the GTI CFO, Bruce; and Lena against Dan, the GTI CEO. According to their official handicaps, Lena had to give Dan six strokes, which was probably generous, as it quickly became apparent he was as much of a sandbagger as most weekend players. His handicap had to be in the single-digits, Lena figured after watching him play the first few holes, not the eleven he maintained he carried. But she played well enough to overcome both his home-course advantage and his inflated handicap, and they came to the last hole tied.

By the time they reached the eighteenth green, the sun had burned through the morning gloom and had started to dry the greens, quickening their pace. As they walked up to the putting surface, George caught up to her.

"Great round," he said softly. "It's a nice way to start negotiations, isn't it?"

"How are you doing in your match?" she asked, realizing she had not paid any attention.

"Oh, Bruce waxed me," he said. "Our match was over back on the fourteenth hole."

"Another manhandling by a CFO, huh?" she teased him.

Lena was glad that George and Bruce had continued to play the last four holes anyway. Who wouldn't on such a beautiful morning?

"You don't think I should let Dan win, do you?" Lena whispered to George. "I mean, is it to our advantage that I win or that we let him win?"

"Lena, this is golf, not a negotiating table," George chided her cheerfully. "Play to win. You always should. I'd be disappointed if you did anything else."

"But you…"

"I lost because I'm rusty. And he's a better match-play golfer," George cut her off. "Don't read anything into that."

With each of their balls lying on the green in regulation – two shots on a par-four – Dan and Lena both had putts for birdie. But as a member of the club and regular player, Dan knew the roll of the green. He had played his ball short and right, less than eight feet from the cup. Lena had misread the green, and her ball hit the surface and flew thirty feet past the hole. Clearly, the advantage was Dan's.

Whether he did it on purpose or not, George had also flown his ball past the flag, and it lay just off the green, ten feet farther but on the same line as hers. With a good read from his putt off the fringe, she might be able to tie the hole, at least. Otherwise, she was likely to lose to Dan, the sandbagger, on the last hole.

It's funny how competitive I still am, she thought. Here she was, playing a friendly match with a guy who could quite possibly make their golf-ball dream a reality, and all she wanted to do was beat him. And she was thinking of him right now only as a sandbagger, not as the CEO-who-can-make-all-of-this-effort-worthwhile. For most of her life, she didn't think she had that kind of cut-throat instinct, but maybe it had been there all along. It was kind of thrilling to feel herself rise to the occasion.

Bruce, uncharacteristically, had missed the green, and his chip from ten yards in front wasn't going to help any of them read their putts. His ball landed a couple of feet in front of the hole, and he putted in. Bruce feigned a little bow and retreated to help Dan read his putt.

Lena marked her lie, picked up her ball, and stepped aside to watch George's putt. It was a tricky double break, but his ball slid just past the hole on the high side, giving Lena exactly the read that she needed. George was better at team play than he acknowledged.

"Settle down," she mumbled to herself as she replaced her ball and crouched down behind it to recreate George's putt in her mind's eye. "This isn't the US Open."

She stood up and waggled her putter, triggering the muscle memory she'd built up over the past few years. "I can't believe how nervous I am," she admitted aloud to the three men on the green with her. "You'd think I'd be over that by now."

"I don't think even Tiger gets over it," laughed Dan. "But don't worry; I won't use it against you at the table this afternoon."

"Use what? Making it or missing it?" Lena asked, moving into position. Dan didn't answer. She made a couple of short, smooth practice strokes, and lined up.

"Confidence," she said to herself, took the putter back and smoothly rolled the ball through a slight break to the left, a slight break to the right and into the hole.

"Your turn," she said, standing up straight, smiling at Dan, and picking her ball out of the hole. She couldn't have wiped the smile off her face if she tried, even after Dan stroked his short putt in for a matching birdie.

"I'm afraid we're going to have to play another match or two sometime to determine a winner," Dan said, shaking her hand happily. He seemed relieved, and Lena didn't know if it was because he hadn't lost or because she hadn't.

"Did you fly the green on purpose?" Lena whispered to George as they waited by the carts for the club employees to cursorily wipe off their clubs, collect their five dollars each, and carry the bags to the bag drop.

"I'll never tell," George smiled at her and winked. Then, his face got serious. "Do you really think I'm that good?"

The New Job

Lena suggested that she should change out of her golf duds before going to the GTI office for their meeting, but Dan insisted they all were dressed just fine for the GTI culture. And, indeed, when they pulled into the surface lot that surrounded the nondescript two-story office building that housed most of GTI's executive and research staff, she saw that he was right.

The bevy of Priuses and Jettas lined up, nose to glass, in front of the building bespoke an informal and practical lifestyle — not a BMW or Lexus in sight. The reception area was sparsely decorated in Scandinavian teak, the only clutter being a disheveled pile of dog-eared golf magazines on the coffee tables. Everyone — man or woman — they passed in the lobby and the hallway on their way to the conference room wore khaki shorts or trousers and some version of a golf shirt, complete with resort or club logo, even though some of them sported the pasty-white skin of Seattleites in the winter.

"Thanks for making the trip down," Dan started the meeting, as the other three morning golfers dove into the trove of sandwiches and chips waiting for them in the middle of the conference table.

"I'll bring in some of the staff I expect will join us, but first, I think it would be good to reach a basic understanding of what each of our companies will contribute to the project," the GTI CEO continued.

Bruce, George and Lena all nodded, their mouths busy chewing. Funny how hungry you could get playing golf in the morning!

"To keep the meeting informal and short, I appreciate your willingness to have the first meeting without lawyers," Dan continued. He looked down at his sandwich.

"Do you mind if we put off the rest of the meeting until we finish eating?" he asked, his voice nearly pleading. The others simply nodded, unwilling to stop eating long enough to talk.

Once they'd devoured the lunch, the group settled in to determine what their partnership might look like. When they were nearly done, the org chart was still missing someone to stitch the process together — a key liaison between George's company and Dan's who could mediate issues, watch for things that were falling through the cracks, and make sure that deadlines would be met, if not beat.

Dan stood on his toes to draw an empty square at the top of the org chart they'd scribbled on the white board and turned to Lena and jabbed at the box with his colored marker.

"I think this is Lena's job here," he said, sweeping his glance from her face around the table, expecting and getting the unanimous agreement it appeared that he had expected.

"That's a big job," Lena said. She hoped she didn't sound unsure of herself. She wanted to retain the respect she had apparently garnered from both George and Dan, but she had blurted words out before she could censor them.

"Yes, it is," Dan agreed. "That's why we want you do it."

Lena paused. Filling the box at the top was a big responsibility, but to admit any reservations about doing it was absolutely the wrong way to build the kind of authority she'd need to keep the team together and functioning.

"I can do it," Lena said, breaking the expectant silence. "That'd be terrific. I'd love the opportunity. Thanks." She almost followed "thanks" with "for letting me do this," but quickly edited it out. She was getting better at this authority thing already.

"Excellent," Dan and George said in unison, and Lena could tell that the men had discussed having her lead the joint venture before the meeting. She didn't really care.

Now she needed to find the time. Something in her life had to give. But what?

On the plane back to Seattle, Lena and George luxuriated in first class; the upgrade a treat that George sprung for out of his own pocket. Clicking their first glasses of wine, they toasted the progress they'd made in just a few months.

"Did you and Dan talk about having me lead this venture before we got to San Diego?" Lena asked, leaning back against the window with one leg tucked up under the other in the roomy leather seat.

George smiled and swirled his wine, holding the glass up to inspect its color as if it were a fine Bordeaux instead of the cheap California red blend Alaska Airlines had chosen for its wine offering of the month.

"Yes, we did," he finally admitted, looking her in the eye. "I wanted to be sure we had his support so that you would be able to take over without anyone questioning your fitness for the job. It's not going to be easy, Lena, if it does happen — who knows, maybe the lawyers will fuck this up and we'll never get a definitive agreement. But if it does, holding two engineering teams together isn't always easy. A lot of egos get involved."

Don't I know it! Lena thought.

"Is this what you had in mind when you first talked to me about your idea back at the golf tournament?" she pursued. "I always wondered what you thought I could bring to the table."

"No, when we first talked, I was thinking we'd skip the brick-and-mortar stores and sell directly online," George said. "But with GTI, it doesn't look like we'll go that way. They already have the sales relationships and reps, and so things are turning out differently. But I like the way you handle yourself in meetings and on the golf course. Great putt today! I like how you've built solid teams at The Perfect Tee."

Oh, boy. If only he knew about the tough battles that she was fighting trying to keep her team functioning. She'd talked with him briefly about the battle between the two developers before, but she'd always made it sound a little less threatening than it was.

"Oh, well, maybe it will all fall apart before we reach agreement," she muttered to herself, not expecting George to hear.

"What? Don't start jinxing us with that negativity." George laughed. "I have a good feeling about this."

Lena was glad someone did. She turned and stared out the window at the fading light on the ground below. When she got back, she'd have to call a meeting of her executive staff and bring them up to speed on today's developments. While they weren't going to be involved in the golf-ball venture much in the next few months, she would, and she needed to let them know what she was doing.

Lena hated to call too many special meetings with her top management team; she remembered the feeling of being left out as a mid-level executive at TrueWeb. The top execs frequently huddled in special meetings to discuss some pending venture or secret project — each with its own secret code name — leaving the rest of the company to wallow in rumormongering as they tried to figure out what was going on. It wasn't likely that many in her small company would pay much attention to the RF venture if they weren't working on it, although there might be some grumbling about how much time she'd be spending away from The Perfect Tee to focus on it.

She had some serious work to do over the next few months, getting her own shop in order and taking over the golf-ball team, and she was starting to accept the fact that she wouldn't have time to play golf for a while. Good thing the season was ending at Suncadia. She hoped she would still have time for Ryne, though. The thought of him — her first in hours — brought a smile to her face and flash of heat through her body. She couldn't wait to get home.

WHEN GEORGE AND LENA MET at the Edgewater Hotel's small dining room that looked out onto Puget Sound the next Monday, they had more than the GTI venture to talk about. A business development consultant had contacted them, revealing he was representing "a leading golf-ball label" that was interested in their RFID technology.

They had visited a number of golf-ball companies over the past few months, and George and Lena had no idea which one of them had hired the consultant. George leaned on his bankers to see if they could figure it out. So far, no results.

"Where does this put us with GTI?" Lena asked.

"We continue to work on the agreement," George said matter-of-factly. "We don't know whether this is a serious inquiry or just an attempt to get some intelligence on the project."

"It seems like it's a different kind of deal, anyway," Lena surmised. "It's possible that an established ball maker might just be interested in your technology, not in a real partnership."

"That's what I would guess. We should talk to the guy, but if that's the case, I'm not really interested in collecting royalty payments. I really wanted to see this thing through to the end. But, money is money, Lena. Enough money and I guess we could be talked into anything." He was sounding more like a CFO all of the time, Lena chuckled to herself.

George picked up the short lunch menu and quickly set it back down, apparently having made up his mind.

"So how are things going here at home?" he asked.

Lena put down her menu and blushed. Freshly back in Seattle after a rainy weekend that Ryne and Lena had filled with golf on TV and a doubling of their usual sexual activity, Lena first thought that George was asking about her personal life. She took a drink of water and a deep breath to slow down the sudden acceleration of her heart rate, and then realized he was asking about The Perfect Tee. He didn't know anything about her love life, and he had no reason to know anything about Ryne Morris.

"Oh!" she exclaimed, "it's going fine. I met with my team this morning to bring them up to speed on the GTI meeting. And I think – I hope anyway – that I'm making some progress on the Ken and Taylor situation. I just had to reestablish some control over the budgeting process and find a way to fund both of their pet initiatives. At least some of each of them."

"Well, good. Those kinds of things can really devour your energy." George nodded with apparent empathy.

"That reminds me," Lena said, "I meant to ask you what happened to your CFO in that last meeting in LaJolla. Wasn't he supposed to come down to join us?"

George paused and took a deep breath. "Brian's gone," he said, laying his hands out flat on the table as if trying to calm his nerves. "It got to the point that we weren't working together so much as working against each other. It was a terrible thing to go through."

He shook his head, and Lena imagined the messy details that the dismissal of a top executive like Brian entailed. She still faced the possibility with Ken, and the prospect kept her awake some nights.

"You know," George commiserated. "I encourage a lot of dissension and discussion. I think it's healthy. But outright insolence and insubordination tears your team apart, whoever it's directed against."

Lena considered sharing her issues with Ken more honestly, now that she knew about Brian. Maybe she would, if things continued to deteriorate. But for now, she didn't want to look like she was struggling to manage her team. It was easier, she considered, for a male executive to admit an isolated incident of weakness or failure. As a woman, any chinks in her armor could be interpreted as overall ineptitude.

After they ordered, they settled down to plot their strategy with GTI.

"Do you think we need to hire an investment banker to help us with this?" Lena asked.

"God, no. It's not that big of a deal, and our profits don't need to be eaten up by Wall Street types yet. I'm sure they'll find a way to make money on us at some point, but let's keep the wolves at bay for now. I think we can handle this with our own lawyers," he assured her. "And I plan to have a new CFO on board within a month. I've got candidates going through interviews now."

"Good. But at what point to do you want to test my VC's interest in funding our half of the project?"

"Let's wait until we determine what this other new party wants, we may have enough outside attention to pique their interest in the project."

"I have to tell you, I think Blake will not like it," she said. "He seems to be really itching for an exit strategy — that is an IPO of The Perfect Tee."

"I am surprised," George shook his head. "What are your revenues?"

"It's looking like we'll reach $200 million this year. I don't think that's critical mass for a public company, but apparently Blake does."

"It costs at least $3 million a year to be public," George

agreed, "and that's a bare minimum. It would eat up most of your profits."

"Another way for Wall Street to get their hands on all of the wealth generated in America." Lena laughed, and they clinked their water glasses in solidarity.

IPO?

When Lena called her VCs to set up a meeting, she told them the agenda would start with an update on The Perfect Tee and their plans for Christmas sales. Then she would introduce George Tatlinger from RF Inc. to discuss the golf-ball joint venture they had been working on. She wasn't looking for a commitment from them, but she wanted to ask for their advice on a couple of issues and listen for any indication that they might be interested in backing the project in the future.

She didn't reach Blake directly, but left him a voice mail. He responded by e-mail. Lena expected him to object to any new projects that might delay a public offering or take the company's eyes off the ball and lose some potential growth as a result. And he did.

"I don't support this venture. I have told you that from the beginning," Blake said in his e-mail to Lena. He copied the other VCs. "The Perfect Tee is too young to have this kind of distraction on the part of its CEO. If the company is going to reach its potential in the women's golf clothing market, it needs laser focus" (Lena cringed at the cliché) "and continual improvement to be sure that other start-ups don't have the opportunity to steal market share."

Blake didn't mention his interest in a near-term IPO, which Lena thought was disingenuous. He ought to put his cards on the table so the other VCs would understand the real reason he disliked the new venture. He wanted to keep The Perfect Tee story simple. Investors liked their IPOs to reflect uncomplicated, focused business strategies that were easy to analyze and compare with obvious competitors.

Lena expected all of that, but Blake surprised her in his e-mail by declining to come to the meeting at all. He was going to be on the East Coast at a board meeting of one of the companies he'd recently helped go public.

He concluded the e-mail by relenting that he would reconsider his position on the golf-ball project if they came to him with a signed agreement with a manufacturer and a joint-venture structure that would guarantee that Lena would not be distracted from The Perfect Tee business by the project. Since Lena had just agreed to sit atop that joint venture, she doubted that she could say anything that would change his mind. She wasn't sure she had convinced herself that it wasn't too much of a distraction, either.

On her way to the VC meeting, she remembered how Blake used to beg her to play golf with him. When the four VCs interviewed her together for her job as CEO, they all took great interest in her tournament win. But it was Blake who kept needling her to play golf with him.

She had looked him up on the golf handicap network where serious golfers post their scores and receive their handicaps. He played to about an eleven – about eleven strokes over par on average – which made him better than 95 percent of American golfers, but also probably made him think he could easily beat a "girl," she imagined. Guys could be like that.

Oh, let them dream. And let Blake stew. She couldn't think of a single reason to play golf with him. If he beat her, she would never hear the end of it, and she'd wish she'd never taken the job at The Perfect Tee. But if she beat him, he would be embarrassed, and she'd never get another agreement past him as long as she was CEO of The Perfect Tee.

Without Blake, the meeting went well. The VCs seemed pleased with the Christmas marketing plan that Jordan had put together.

When George joined the meeting to discuss the golf-ball venture, the VCs grew silent, and Lena worried that Blake had managed to turn them all against the idea. But after they finished presenting the technology the men softened a bit. Lena wanted to believe it was because of their excellent preparation, but she started to wonder if the shortening fall days weren't wearing on everyone's energies. Maybe they just wanted to get out to their suburban enclaves before it got dark and the traffic picked up.

With few words, the VCs stood up, gathered their North Face rain parkas and wished Lena and George well. The meeting was over. The three had barely filed out of the rented hotel conference room before they were on their cellphones, telling their wives how soon they would be home.

THE GOLF SEASON WAS DRAWING to its usual chilly, rainy, and windy end early in October, and Lena found it depressing. She'd played about one-fifth as much that fall as she had before she took the job at The Perfect Tee. Two years ago, golf had been her job, not an escape, and at times, she'd tired of practicing and even playing. But now that it had become recreational again, golf was relaxing and took her mind off her work worries. And she didn't get to do it enough.

Finally, on the third weekend of the month, Indian summer flooded the course with warm, soft air and sunshine, and the pleasant weather spread all the way to Puget Sound, stilling the winds that usually pushed over the Cascade divide.

George's wife, Tina, and Lena had picked that weekend for a Sunday round at Suncadia before everyone packed up their clubs for the season. Ryne usually worked on Sunday, but he had taken the day off to play with them. Lena decided that Tina should ride in the cart with her for two reasons: it would cut down on Ryne's and Lena's tendency to publicly display their affection, which Lena didn't want her partner's wife to witness; and it would help Tina navigate a course that was new to her.

Although it wasn't her favorite of the three courses at Suncadia, they decided to play Rope Rider since Tina had never played it. The course opened five years after Prospector, and the year it opened, it was one of only a handful of new golf courses opening across the country. With a minimum of competition, it was named the best new public course of the year by Golf Digest.

Rope Rider was much easier than Prospector, Lena's usual haunt, and Lena shot under par for her round from the men's tees. She credited the great weather, but Ryne and Tina wouldn't accept it. At Swiftwater Cellars, the winery that doubled as the Rope Rider clubhouse, they took turns plastering her with compliments. She hadn't heard so much admiration for her golf game in a long time, certainly not since her victory at the USGA tournament. Their admiration seemed to morph into a kind of attraction – clearly it had a long time ago for Ryne, and now, Lena suspected it had made a similar kind of leap for Tina. She wasn't sure of it, but when they slipped into a table at the Village Pizza in Roslyn later that night, Lena made sure to sit across from Tina and next to Ryne.

Once separated from Tina by the table, Lena felt more comfortable, and with a pile of Trivial Pursuit cards to entertain them before and after eating their pizza, the three new friends played until they were kicked out of the restaurant at closing time. Ryne and Lena dropped Tina off at the lodge.

"Let's play again soon!" Tina exclaimed as she stumbled, a little drunk, out of the back seat of Ryne's old BMW sedan.

"Sure – but it'll probably be next summer before we get this kind of weather again," Lena said, rolling down her window but staying in the car.

"Then, maybe we'll have to play in the rain," Tina said cheerfully, waving goodbye and accepting the open door the bellman had waiting for her at the lodge entrance.

"Whew, I'm glad that's over!" Lena turned to Ryne as they pulled away for his duplex. Lena had left Bounty at Ryne's place when they got up that morning. Although she hadn't done it for that reason, by staying at Ryne's for the weekend, Lena avoided walking into the lodge with Tina and chancing an embarrassing good-night parting.

"Did she seem awfully fond of you tonight, or was it my imagination?" Ryne looked at Lena a bit possessively. "I've never seen anyone that touchy-feely with you."

"Except for you," Lena said. "But yes. It was a bit unnerving. Do you think she's got a thing for me?"

"Yeah, I do. But I'm bigger than she is. I'll beat her up," Ryne joked, faking a laugh.

"Well, I'm glad it's funny for you. You know I have to work with her husband."

"Oh, she'll probably be over it once she sobers up," Ryne assured her. "She's married, after all."

"Yeah, but people have been known to change their minds after very long marriages," she said. "I just want to make sure I'm not sending the wrong messages."

"Well, just keep busy sending them to me, and you'll be alright."

"Why do you think I made sure I sat next to you at the restaurant?"

"I thought it was because you like me. But I'll take it either way. And speaking of how much you like me, I can't wait to see you wake up tomorrow with a smile on your face." Ryne looked at Lena, raising and dropping his eyebrows conspiratorially.

Lena grimaced. "My god, you need some new material!"

But he did just as well as he promised.

THE BUDGET WAS READY FOR review by the VCs at the end of October, on time, but not by much. The stickler was getting Taylor and Ken to agree on IT priorities and to stop their intra-company battle long enough to do so.

Early in the month, Taylor burst into her office to complain that Ken was leaching his good developers, followed closely by Ken knocking on her door to bitch that Taylor was sabotaging his efforts to upgrade the financial accounting system. Ken said Taylor was exaggerating what he needed in his budget to build out a new platform that would accommodate new lines of sportswear. Taylor asserted that Ken was inflating his accounting system developer staff so that he could leach developers over to other, unapproved projects.

At times, it was like managing an office of twelve-year-old boys who scuffle in the schoolyard and then blame each other for throwing the first punch. She didn't want to lose either of them right before Christmas, when IT issues could cost millions in lost sales, but she didn't want to simply split the difference and give them both some portion of the increase in the budget they maintained they needed.

Instead, she called a meeting with Ken, Taylor, Jordan, and the CFO John to go over their budget requests. As head of marketing and supplier relations, Jordan argued that the company really needed to get started on the sportswear platform in January in order to meet their goal of adding new merchandise by mid-year, so she sided with Taylor. As CFO, John said he was inclined to back Ken because any new accounting software would make his life easier, even if there was no IPO.

"No IPO?" Lena feigned ignorance. "What IPO?"

John sank back in his seat and tried to look small. Lena felt a little sorry for him. He didn't know she was pretending to know nothing about Ken's push for an IPO.

Ken tried to recover for John. "We've been looking

ahead to making sure our systems are ready, even if it is a ways off," he asserted.

"How far off do you think it is?" Lena asked.

"No idea," Ken said, which was true — there were no such plans, yet. "But we should not put ourselves behind the eight ball."

Lena felt her face burning, and tried to tamp down the anger. "Other than your hypothetical IPO, what part of this additional budget request can you justify?"

"I can send you a break-down," Ken said.

"On my desk by this afternoon, please."

"Yes, sir." Ken was obviously steamed. But Lena surmised that he was probably more worried about Blake losing faith in his ability to make things happen than he was about Lena's disapproval.

KEN'S NUMBERS CAME IN THAT afternoon, and they still looked padded. With John's help, she tried to separate fact from fiction, and by the time she left for the day, long after the city had gone dark, she felt like she had the situation under control.

It was never easy presenting a budget to VCs, Lena knew, but when she and John showed up in the investors' Bellevue office at the end of the month, she felt prepared.

When the VCs came into the conference room, Lena was surprised: Blake was absent again — no big loss — but so was Doyle.

"Blake's having some issues with two of his investments on the East Coast," explained the older VC, Nick. "Both companies reported earnings last week, and both missed analysts' estimates. The stocks have dropped 30 percent each, and he's scrambling to figure out what went wrong."

Lena thought it was odd that Nick would be so willing to share Blake's problems. But from the look on Nick's face, he wasn't feeling very sorry for his fellow VC. He looked at Lena, rolled his eyes and shook his head. "I think they were a little aggressive in their timing," he answered her puzzled look. "I'm not surprised. But that's neither here nor there. Let's get started."

"Where's Doyle?"

"His baby is due today. Second one, a boy," said the fourth VC, Kyle. "We let him off the hook."

The budget review went quickly. Neither of the investors brought up the issue of an imminent IPO. Obviously, they were not agitating for as quick an exit as Blake was, and they seemed pleased with the profit projections for the next year – humble though they were.

As they closed the files for the budget review, Nick asked John to step out of the room so the group could go into "executive session." John quickly gathered his files and ducked out. Lena was surprised. An executive session wasn't on the agenda.

"Lena, we are a little concerned about you," Nick started.

"Why?" she looked from Nick to Kyle, confused. The meeting had gone well so far, but she sensed that it was headed downhill quickly.

"We want to keep an open mind about this golf-ball venture, but we don't understand how we can get the necessary focus from you on The Perfect Tee when you're also running that project."

"I'm not spending that much time on it," Lena quickly

insisted, annoyed to hear her voice rise as her throat tightened. "I mean, I'm giving The Perfect Tee 100 percent — fifty or sixty hours a week. I'm handling the golf-ball venture at night and on the weekends."

"Well, burning the candle at both ends is expected for start-ups," Nick said in his I'm calm, even if you aren't voice. She'd heard that tone a year before when a copy-cat golf-clothing website threatened their business, and he stepped in to help her legal team bat it away. "But you can't do that and serve both masters. It's enough to keep a start-up going without taking on other projects."

Lena looked down at her hands. She had clasped them tightly on top of her budget files; her knuckles had turned white. She pulled her hands under the table and tried to relax her muscles from the shoulders down.

"Have I slipped up? Have I failed to move our company forward?" she asked slowly, carefully incorporating her own I'm calm, even if you don't expect me to be voice. Two could play this game. "I don't understand where this concern of yours is coming from."

"Lena," Nick shook his head and lowered his voice another notch. "We don't think things have gone badly so far, but we've heard from some of your staff that you've been irritable in meetings and that you've been out of town a great deal. Apparently, there are also some problems in your IT team."

Lena hadn't heard such a paternalistic tone since her former CEO had explained to her why he thought she wasn't cut out for management. That was five years ago. Now, with two years as CEO of The Perfect Tee behind her, she thought she was putting doubts about her capabilities behind her. The VCs had appeared confident in her leadership, but now, out of the blue, her ability to handle the job was being called into question. She felt the small hairs on the back of her neck rise.

Fucking Ken! Lena turned her head to the side so the VCs couldn't see her grimace. Damn him! Was he conspiring with Nick, too? She should have just fired the asshole two months ago when he started pulling this IPO stunt with Blake. She shook her head, relieved that the VCs couldn't hear her thoughts. She didn't want them to know she could even think in such profane language.

"We've also heard from an ex-banker who said you rebuffed his efforts to help you and George," Nick continued. "We started to wonder what is going on over there. And who is this guy?"

Instantly, Lena knew whom Nick was talking about. "Jim," she said flatly. Her head was spinning. How could Jim do this? When was he going to get out of her life and leave her alone?

"You know him," Nick said. It wasn't a question.

"Jim Treacher," Lena said. "A couple of years ago, before I came to The Perfect Tee, he propositioned me. He wanted an affair. I turned him down, of course. He was married at the time."

"Are you serious?" Kyle, the younger VC, leaned forward. "Are you sure it's the same guy? Is it, Nick?"

"Oh, yes," Lena answered for him. "He's been after George and me to give him a piece of the action in our golf ball in exchange for his 'advice,'" she said, adding a bit of snarkiness to the last word. "He's even brought in a business consultant to help him weasel into our deal."

"But did you hear him out?" Nick asked. "Maybe he has something to offer."

"I told him we needed to talk to our investors first," Lena paused and swept her hand to indicate whom she was talking about, "and that would be you guys."

"He told me that he wasn't even given a chance to discuss it with you," Nick countered.

"I don't see why we should have," she retorted, keeping her voice low as possible. "Should we entertain any yahoo who calls wanting a piece of the action? Divulge our plans and technology to someone we don't trust? Who can steal our IP? Who has contributed nothing but interference?"

"He's not a yahoo." Nick was getting as heated as Lena was. He clenched his fists and sat up straighter in his chair. "He's a banker, and he knows quite a bit about the project you're working on."

"Any information he has about our project is information he stole," she countered. "No one had permission to share details or even a broad outline of the project with him except for me and George. And we have given him nothing."

"Maybe he can help, though," Nick persisted.

"The only thing Jim knows about a golf-ball venture is how much money might be made from guys like him who lose twenty balls a day in the woods at Tumble Creek. And," she paused, waiting to be sure she really wanted to say it, "he's only pursuing it because I jilted him."

"Well, that's your word against his, I suppose," Nick said, lowering his voice as if he were embarrassed to say it.

"When it comes to sexual harassment, it usually is."

"Well, do you think he goes after the business of every

woman he's ever propositioned?" Nick raised his eyebrows.

"I have no bloody idea. I don't know how many women he has propositioned. But what is surprising me now is that you would listen to a man you don't know, a man who hasn't been in business for years, who has never been in the golf business and whose only connection with this project is a passing acquaintance with me. You're going to take his word over mine?" Lena could no longer hide her anger. Her voice rose and she hovered over her seat, her weight on her hands on the table.

"No …" Nick pushed back in his chair in reaction to her body language.

"You know," Lena was practically shouting now, "you have a fairly significant amount of money invested in a company that you've trusted me to run, that I've been running competently, and I simply can't figure out how this man has managed to impress you to the point that you would even raise this issue with me, let alone question my judgment."

That, Lena admitted to herself, sitting back down, was what infuriated her. It was her old CEO at TrueWeb all over again – doubting her ability to develop strategy, manage a business, lead a team.

"Okay, you've made your point," Kyle broke in. "Let's just all calm down here." He waved his hands over the table as if to clear the air. They sat in uncomfortable silence for a few moments.

"Back to your IT teams' problem, Lena," Nick returned to the topic. "What is the issue there? Do you need help with anything?"

"I don't think so, but I'll let you know," Lena sat back in her chair and tried to relax her shoulders. "It appears that Ken believes we should do an IPO sooner rather than later, and that's made for some interesting conversations around the budget. That's all." It was a lie. There was much more to the IT problems than that: back-biting, stealing other teams' personnel, refusing to cooperate. Lots of unnecessary disruption.

"Why would he think that?" Kyle feigned surprise.

Lena considered divulging the discussions Ken and Blake had held behind her back, but decided against it, since Nick already knew that Blake was behind the push for an IPO.

"I don't know, but we have already worked through it, and as you saw today, there is no money in the budget to prepare for an IPO," Lena said. "On the legal side or the finance side."

"Good. Well, I will take your word for it that you have your personnel issues under control," Nick said, throwing her a small nod of confidence before he stood up to end the meeting.

Hackers

The meeting was a disaster, despite the approval she got for her budget. Nick was clearly questioning her judgment, her commitment to The Perfect Tee, and anything else she did. All she could hope for, she thought as she drove back to the office, was that Christmas sales went well, they would be pleased with the results, and Nick would get off her case.

But he had scared her, and she reacted by working longer hours over the next month so that she could devote a full sixty hours a week to The Perfect Tee and spend her nights and weekends catching up on the golf-ball project. She told George about the meeting with Nick and Kyle, and he seemed sympathetic. He was fine with her conducting most of their joint business in the evening or on weekends. His wife, Tina, must have been a very tolerant or independent woman. Or both.

With her work at The Perfect Tee and on the joint venture, Lena had less time for her friends or for Bounty. She got up extra early — after extra late nights — made a cup of coffee in her Keurig and took Bounty for a walk around the Amazon campus near her condo, just to get a little time with her.

Lena didn't see Brandt and Carly for weeks. They rarely came to Suncadia anymore since the cold, rain, and wind made golf no fun — actually, nearly unbearable. She saw Terry when she got up to Roslyn, but mostly, she stayed in Seattle over the weekend to catch up on her golf-ball responsibilities. She lifted the "no work on weekends" rule for her team at the company, now that summer was over. If it weren't for Saturday night pizza with Ryne and his dwindling sleepovers, she would have been entirely without non-canine companionship.

But it helped that they were making good progress on the golf ball. The agreement between GTI, RF Inc., and The Perfect Tee was signed at the end of November, and they avoided talking with the other "established golf label."

Ryne was busy, too, working his regular Seattle Times editing job, negotiating with his agent, rewriting sections of his book, and suffering through its brutal edit. But he found time to help with Bounty, taking her for walks in the waning light of the fall afternoons and taking her home with him a couple of nights a week so she wasn't alone, waiting in the lonely condo for Lena. Lena couldn't think of anything he could do that would mean more to her. Of course, it only made her miss them both more.

While progress on the golf-ball was heartening, the atmosphere in the two development camps at The Perfect Tee had gone from tolerable to worse again with back-biting and what she suspected was deliberate sabotage of each other's platforms. That scared her. Christmas sales had started to pick up, and she needed to be sure things ran smoothly so they could meet the budget forecasts she'd just laid out for the VCs.

Finally, she decided the only way to get the two developers out of each other's hair was to suggest they take a month off in December. The work that needed done on platform maintenance could continue– if not improve – in their absence, and she didn't have the energy to intervene in their petty battles. And the nastiness was starting to cost them in another way – they were losing good talent from their pool of developers. There were plenty of jobs for good developers all over Seattle – even across the street – and no software engineer in town had to tolerate a bad culture to make a good living.

She ejected them both at the end of the week after Thanksgiving. Taylor was thrilled to have a chance to spend a month with his family on a beach in Mexico and was out of the door two hours after she talked with him, stopping only for a quick meeting with his direct reports. But Ken seemed suspicious. "Is something going down that you don't want me around for?" he asked her without even pausing a second to think about what he might do with a month off.

"Like and IPO? Not that I know of," Lena smiled. "Do you? Just take a break. It's been stressful for all of us around here," she said. "I'm going to take two weeks off myself. If this place can't do without us for that long, then we're not doing a very good job of building our teams, are we?"

By mid-December, after weeks of an exhausting work schedule, Lena had made her own plans for the holidays. With Taylor and Ken off on their mandatory sabbaticals and Christmas sales humming along, she felt comfortable letting John and Jordan take over while she took a vacation – her first since she started at The Perfect Tee. She was nearly blind from reading legal documents and staring at tiny numbers on Excel spreadsheets on her computer for fourteen to sixteen hours at a time. And she'd done all she could with the RF project for now. GTI was heading into its annual two-week Christmas vacation for all employees, and even the executives were totally out of reach.

Lena reserved a seat on the Alaska Airlines non-stop to Palm Springs at 5:30 Friday evening before Christmas. She'd have five days to herself to relax, read an easy novel, get in a round of golf with whatever strangers she'd get paired up with before Ryne came down. Two weeks over Christmas in the condo where she'd stayed in the past was pricey. Very pricey. But she wanted to feel at home when she got there, and she didn't want to spend a lot of time looking for something new. And money wasn't her biggest worry anymore, thanks to nearly three years of a good salary and fairly frugal living.

By Wednesday night, she was feeling ahead of the game. She'd tied up the loose ends with the RF project and had a final meeting with the financial planning staff, who assured her the company was exceeding its budgeted revenue for the fourth quarter. Ryne had agreed to take Bounty up to Roslyn to stay with Terry over the holidays, right before he came down to meet her in the desert on Christmas Eve.

Lena had cleaned the produce out of her refrigerator, which relegated her to restaurant meals for the next two days — a small price to pay for a sweet-smelling kitchen when she returned. She had stopped her newspapers and mail, and gave an extra key to her condo to her next-door neighbor in case of emergencies.

She was sitting back in her chair with her boots on the desk, chatting with George on the phone, when Barry, one of Taylor's employees knocked on the glass of her office door. She waved him in and held up her index figure to indicate she was just about done.

"Merry Christmas, Happy Hanukkah, and Happy Kwanza to you, too," she tied up the conversation with George. "And I'll see you in January."

"Hey, Barry!" she said, feeling her imminent escape to the sunshine and the Christmas spirit already lifting her mood. "Wazzup?"

"It's not good." Barry's frown instantly burst her happy bubble. "We got an e-mail I think you should know about."

"What about?"

Barry took a seat at her small conference table and adopted the pedantic tone that engineers tended to use when talking to non-engineers, whatever their rank.

"I'll make this simple as I can," he said.

Lena shook her head to indicate that oversimplification wasn't necessary. He was probably not even aware of the condescension in his voice.

"Just tell me what it is," she said. "Don't treat me like an idiot."

As Barry explained it, the e-mail he received was from a self-described "watchdog" who said his purpose was to protect consumers from identity theft. This "watchdog" looked for vulnerabilities in online retail websites and IT systems that might expose consumer's credit cards to discovery by identity thieves.

In reality, Barry explained, these people were blackmailers. Once they discovered — or could fake discovery of — a vulnerability in the company's operating code that hackers could exploit, they "kindly" let the company know about it and offered to provide details and a solution to the problem in return for payment.

"They actually call it a service." Barry sneered. "It's nothing but blackmail."

The blackmailers contacted the company, offering to withhold their warnings to consumers if The Perfect Tee paid them to describe and fix the vulnerability. If the company didn't hire their technicians, then they would have "no choice" but to warn the public. They would do this through the complicity of hundreds of bloggers who loved these games and, to a large part, distrusted corporate America — even little start-ups like The Perfect Tee. Any company in business to make a profit was fair game, in their book.

Lena didn't know much about the world of hackers and cybersecurity. She only knew that they needed to upgrade their credit-card processing system to become something called PCI compliant — a system of checks and balances, and standards of protocol that the credit card companies believed would protect their customers from identity theft. They had begun laying out the budget and plans to meet those requirements, which besides protecting customers would also lower their credit-card processing fees. But meeting PCI compliance was at least a year away.

"How long do these things usually take to develop?" Lena asked. She sat down in a chair at the conference table across from Barry.

"Depends," he said, shaking his head. "If they think you're going to cave, they'll give you some time. If they think they're being rejected, they'll flood the blogosphere with the news of the 'threat' to our database pretty quickly." He made air quotes with his fingers.

"How do we make them think we're going to cave?" she asked. "You know, to buy us some time?"

"Is that what you want to do, or is that what you want them to think?"

"I don't know yet. And how much does caving cost?"

"It depends on who they are. If it's offshore, not too much. But if it is American, probably a lot. Probably a quarter-million dollars."

"Yikes. The legitimate press doesn't really run these stories about these alleged vulnerabilities do they?"

"Not the mainstream press, such as it is, although Target's big Christmas hack last year probably increases their appetite for these stories every year. And the hacker blogs love these stories."

Lena leaned back and covered her eyes with her hands. She needed to concentrate for a minute. She tried to focus on her options, but her mind only wanted to think about how this mess was going to ruin her Christmas break.

Barry waited, cleared his throat and waited some more. Finally, he added, "another risk here is that a group of hackers can get together to launch a denial of service attack if they think you're stonewalling."

"You mean flood our servers with phony requests?"

"Pretty much. They can shut down service at a company with the capacity of Amazon. Blocking our servers is pretty much child's play."

Lena wondered how they would make a payoff to these kinds of blackmailers. Would it be legal? Would it be a capital item or an expense they'd take this quarter? Could they amortize it over some period of time?

She smiled at herself, wryly. Was this what she thought

of when facing a cyber-attack? How she'd handle the costs on the income statement? Something horrible had happened to her in the past two years as she'd managed the company. She shook her head at her own bizarre transformation. The accounting treatment of ransom should hardly be the first conundrum to come to mind.

In any case, Lena had to admit that she was clearly out of her league, legally, financially, and technically. She was going to need help. And she probably didn't have much time. Did she have to let her VCs know? she wondered. That would be really inconvenient, especially if she was going to leave for Palm Springs on Friday.

"Do you think we need to call Taylor?" she asked.

"Yeah, and probably Ken, too."

Lena blanched at the idea of calling her two development heads when she'd ordered them out on sabbatical for a month. She had told them not to worry, not to check e-mails or texts more than once a day. It might take a day — maybe more – to get them both on the phone.

"But, first let's talk to PR and legal. Amanda!" she called out the door for her administrative assistant.

As usual, Amanda seemed to appear at her door before Lena had uttered the last syllable of her name. "Get Jerry and Jordan and tell them we need to meet right now."

She turned back to Barry. "Is there any chance this is a bluff? That they don't have anything, really?"

VERY LATE THAT NIGHT, AS she returned to her condo, she pulled a taped note off the door. "Dinner?" Ryne had scribbled. Oh shit! She and Ryne were going to have a good-bye dinner tonight before she left for the desert. Had he called her? She checked her phone. There were five texts from Ryne between seven o'clock when she was supposed to meet him at the Dahlia Lounge and eleven, when he'd apparently stopped trying to reach her. The last one said he was picking up Bounty and going back to his apartment. He hoped she was okay, and could she let him know?

Letting herself in the condo, she closed the door with her foot while she speed-dialed his cellphone.

"What happened? Where were you?"

"Shit hit the fan," she said, thinking how she was going to make a short story out of the afternoon's developments. "A hacker. Legal got involved. I think we've got a plan, but I have to tell you, I was more worried about how this was going to affect our vacation than anything."

"Really?"

"No, not really. What I was really worried about was how we would account for a ransom payment on our income statement."

Lena had meant it as a joke, or at least, kind of a joke. But either way, Ryne hadn't found it funny. There was silence on the line.

"Sorry, that was out of context," she admitted. "But I couldn't help but filter all the advice I got this afternoon through how it would mess our trip up. It's a disaster anyway. I've got to be back in there tomorrow morning by five to talk to our lawyers and PR counsel in New York. What a shitty way to start a vacation!"

"Well, it hasn't started yet. Maybe everything will get settled quickly." Ryne sounded more positive than she felt. "Get some sleep. I've got Bounty. I'll check in with you mañana."

"Thanks, Ryne. What would I do without you?"

"Oh, I don't know. You did without me for a very long time, my dear. Now, of course, you'd die of heartbreak."

She laughed with him and hung up. Then she frowned. He was probably right.

Over the next day and half, Lena and her team, with help from their PR agency and law firm in New York, decided that the problem wasn't as urgent as she had first thought. Given that Christmas was the next week, they had until after the holidays to respond. Even atheist hackers celebrated at least one of the winter-solstice holidays, they figured. And by then, the PR firm promised to have a strategy outlined that would respond to any blogs that might "reveal" the supposed "vulnerability." And the lawyers would come up with a list of options.

Even as she boarded the plane at SeaTac, though, she wondered if she should have called her VCs. Once she cleared the security lines, boarded the plane with something like a hundred hyperactive children, and stuffed her bags in the overhead bin, she was too exhausted to think about it anymore. Why bother them over the holidays, she finally concluded. She turned off her phone and leaned back to catch a catnap on the plane. It would just have to wait.

Christmas

Christmas was the holiday most likely to disappoint Lena, not only because it was the one that came with the greatest expectations, but also because it delivered some of the strongest memories — good and bad. And thanks to the mind's ability to forget pain, most of the memories that kept popping up were good ones: singing Christmas carols in her old Denver neighborhood on a frigid night, eating cream puffs that her mom only made for the holidays, and adorning Stripe, her first mutt, with Christmas bows.

Being alone right before the holidays gave her time to remember them all — good and bad. There was the time her father decided that giving gifts at Christmas was a pagan ritual, which given his leanings as an atheist should have made it more fun for him. But as a church-going atheist who attended Sunday services in one his few concessions to "fitting in" in their small Nebraska town, he could be frustratingly unpredictable. There were no gifts that year. Luckily, his rejection of Christmas as pagan only lasted for a year, and, by the next Christmas, he had forgotten it.

Lena's plane landed in Palm Springs late at night. She was glad the liquor store between the airport and the condo was still open; she stopped for vodka, Kahlua, Patron tequila and some Cointreau – black Russians for the evenings and margaritas for the afternoons. At the condo she had rented, she tossed her suitcase on the floor of the bedroom and threw some water on her face. Then, she made herself a black Russian, and turned on the gas fireplace to ward off the desert chill.

Settling down in the soft leather chair in front of the fire, she concentrated on Christmases past, trying to order her memories chronologically. She thought that, by focusing on the holiday, she could distance herself from work and accelerate the arrival of a vacation frame of mind. But the hacker threat at The Perfect Tee kept intruding, no matter how much she tried to discipline her thoughts. It hung around the edge of her consciousness, like a tactile fringe hanging on the physical blob of her brain.

Her relationship with her VCs was already on tenuous terms, thanks to the golf-ball distraction. Not telling them about the hacking incident wasn't going to help. And, besides that, she was out of her element – cybersecurity and cyber threats were things that she barely understood.

Despite her management skills, Lena had found herself in over her head in plenty of situations. It seemed like she'd lived a fair percentage of her life that way. One year when she was in high school, Lena was working at the Dairy Queen, making twists, dilly bars and malts, and handing them to customers through the narrow drive-in window in exchange for small change and a rare tip. Her parents had died in a car accident, and Lena moved into town to live with Betsy and her single mother. Lena had to find a job, as an allowance from Betsy's mom wasn't in the cards.

As a Christmas treat for her staff of teenage malt-makers, the drive-in owner, Janice, reserved a table at a nice steakhouse in Lincoln. The girls closed the Dairy Queen early on a Tuesday night before Christmas, dressed up, applied their cheap drug-store make-up, and rode with Janice into the city in the drive-in's van. Lena was excited. The last steak she had eaten was the one her mother had cooked on the kettle barbeque at home the night before the fatal accident.

The restaurant was nice in an early 1980s, Midwestern way: potted plants hung from the ceiling and wood dividers separated diners from each other for privacy. Menus were already waiting for them when they arrived at their table for six, and the girls flirted with the young waiter, asking for alcoholic beverages they weren't old enough to order, and then giggling at their audacity. Janice smiled at their jokes and let them carry on without censure, all the while exuding a motherly gravity that kept the girls' antics grounded.

Shy and visibly uncomfortable around her own classmates, Lena had always received more than her share of Janice's attention. It had been only six months since Lena had moved into town, and she still felt naïve in social settings. Listening to other girls as she walked home from school or as she sat at the lunch table, she was learning about popular tastes and interests: musical groups, fashion, and cool brands. The bubbly popular girls weren't cruel to her, but it was clear that she didn't fit in.

That night Janice sat next to Lena, and they talked quietly while the other girls gossiped. The cacophony at the table kept Lena from having to contribute much. Opening the menu, she skimmed the selections. Where was the steak? she wondered. There was a list of entrees: a rib-eye, a top sirloin, a New York strip, a prime rib, a ham slice, a pork chop and fried chicken. But nothing called "steak."

As the girls gave the waiter their orders, Lena listened. It didn't help. She still didn't know what they were ordering, and the "how would you like that done?" question baffled her. So, when it came her turn to order, she chose the pork chop. It seemed like a safe bet. And the waiter didn't ask her how she'd "like that done."

"I thought you loved steak," Janice said in barely more than a whisper as the waiter gathered their menus. "Why did you order a pork chop?"

"Oh, I had steak last night," Lena lied. In truth, chicken strips, hot dogs, and hamburgers stretched Betsy's mom's culinary talents and financial resources to the maximum.

Watching the other girls cut into their juicy steaks depressed Lena, but at least she got through the meal without displaying her ignorance. Someday I'll figure these things out, and then I won't feel so left out, she told herself.

FORTY YEARS LATER, LENA STILL frequently felt ignorant, although now it was about entirely different sorts of things. Cybersecurity, for example. But after the first night in Palm Springs, Lena pledged to not let hackers and her insecurities ruin her Christmas vacation. She was good at compartmentalizing. The ability to block out what worried her was what made it possible to sleep, work, play golf and, in general, enjoy life. She just had to get busy.

Lena spent her first full day in the desert shopping. At Ralph's she bought plenty of food for their two weeks. She pulled into Walgreens for shampoo, soap, and deodorant.

She bought new sheets at Bed, Bath & Beyond and put them on the bed. The condo came furnished, but she never liked sleeping on someone else's sheets if she didn't have to.

The second day, she cleaned her golf clubs in the bathtub and then took them out to the driving range to see if she could find her swing after weeks of golf abstinence. After that, she had two days to play, slowly regaining her confidence with other snowbirds whose games were even rustier than hers.

Ryne's plane landed late on Christmas Eve, and she picked him up at the curb outside of baggage claim. He threw his golf clubs and carry-on into the trunk of her rental car, and they hurried back to the condo. Lena didn't wait for him to unpack before falling into bed. She was exhausted from an early morning tee-time and was asleep before he pulled back the covers and slipped in beside her.

Lena awoke Christmas morning on one edge of the bed, clutching her pillow and blankets against the cool desert air seeping into the bedroom. Cool enough! She got up to close the window. Crawling back into bed, she wiggled across the mattress and put her arms around Ryne.

"Hey, I was sleeping!"

"Merry Christmas, Ryne."

"Hmmm," he moaned contentedly, sliding an arm under her waist and pulling her closer. She laid her head on his shoulder.

She lay quietly for a few minutes, letting Ryne shake off his morning dreams. Through the window, Lena watched the palm trees sway in the light morning breeze, their height dwarfed by the dramatic rise of the San Jacinto Mountains only a few hundred yards to the west. The slate gray rocks that lined the east flank of the mountains were taking on a pink morning hue as the sun rose.

"You know what I was dreaming about when you so rudely awakened me?" Ryne broke the stillness.

"No, but I really don't want to know. Keep your dreams to yourself. It's one of the few things people never have to share." Lena really believed that. She never told her dreams to anyone.

"Hmmm. I never thought about it that way," Ryne mumbled. "You are one smart cookie."

"Cookie?"

"Cookie. But I mean that in a good way."

"How is that? 'Cause I'm so sweet?"

"Uh, hardly."

"How then? How do you compare me, a living, breathing human being, with a baked piece of sugary dough?"

Ryne snorted. "You know what? It's seven o'clock on Christmas morning, and you're already cross-examining me. Do you know how intimidating that can be?"

Lena wasn't sure if he was kidding. She craned her neck to get a look in his eyes. He was smiling. He didn't look intimidated.

"How could I intimidate you?" she asked. "I'm five-three and you're six-five. You outweigh me by about eighty pounds."

"You think the only thing people are intimidated by is people who are bigger than they are?"

"Well, no," she laid her head back on his shoulder. "But I've always been a little afraid of bigger people."

"Is that all that intimidates you?"

"No, I'm intimidated by lots of things. People who

grew up in the city, people whose parents were corporate types." Lena was a little dismayed that their conversation was going on so long. She had really expected to be well into the process of making love by this time.

"Cities?" Ryne asked.

"Yeah. While I was out there jumping over logs with my dog on the farm, you city-folk were going to art films and reading the New Yorker. Like two camps" She was kidding. Kind of.

"And corporate types?"

"Yeah, you'd all sit around the dining room table at night getting lessons from your parents on mergers and acquisitions, and how to behave in board meetings."

"You are funny girl."

"I know. Some things you just can't shake, no matter how much you think you've outgrown them."

Lena settled back into the comfort of Ryne's shoulder and lay quietly for a while, listening to Ryne breathe and to a couple of raucous crows outside the window. It suddenly struck her how bland the condo's interior was compared with the starkly beautiful landscape of Palm Springs. She waited for him to make the first move toward having sex. No reason to rush, she realized. They had ten days together in the desert.

"So, do you also see the world as two camps, men and women?" Ryne broke the silence, and it took Lena a minute to figure out his segue.

"Not so much. Just big people and small people."

They lay still a couple minutes longer.

"I also divide the world into two camps: those who make love like you and those who don't," she whispered.

"And how many are in my camp?"

"Just one," she said, peeling the covers down. She rose onto her knees and pulled her night shirt over her head, dropping it onto the floor.

"Do you think we'll ever outgrow this?" she asked, leaning down to kiss Ryne, feeling his mouth soften with her invitation.

"God, I hope not," he mumbled through their lips.

LENA SCRAMBLED SOME EGGS WITH shredded cheddar and buttered the toast while Ryne unpacked his suitcase and pulled his clubs out of his travel bag. They took their breakfast and coffee out to the patio and ate slowly, soaking in the warming desert sun. Lena took their empty plates into the kitchen and poured two fresh cups of coffee, and when she returned, Ryne had retrieved a package from the bedroom and placed it in front of her. The box was wrapped in the colorful comic section of the Sunday Seattle Times, which didn't surprise her. That was what her friends at the newspaper had always used for wrapping paper. The shared cultural artifact made her smile.

"What's this?"

"Silly. Your Christmas present."

"You know I didn't get you anything."

"And you didn't need to. This is not something I bought for you. Open it."

Lena pulled the newsprint off the box and broke the Scotch tape holding it closed. She reached in and pulled out a thick sheath of paper. The top sheet simply read "THE TOUR by Ryne Morris."

"It's your book!"

"Yes, and you have the first copy. Well, the first copy of the first draft."

"Oh, my god! Finally, I'm going to find out what it's about!"

"Only if you read it."

Lena thumbed the edge of the thick manuscript, the neatly typed lines blurring into solid gray stripes as the pages fluttered past.

"Wow, this looks like a lot of work."

"Probably the hardest thing I've ever done," Ryne nodded. "But you should know, there's a lot of you on those pages."

"Me? It's about me?"

"No, but you were my muse."

"Can I start it now?"

"No, we're going to play golf, remember? We need to get some rounds in before the hordes descend."

Ryne was right. The desert courses were usually uncrowded on Christmas Day, and sometimes the day after, but once families had finished opening presents and sharing big dinners with the grandparents, the togetherness would start to wear thin. After that, the golfers among them would escape to the links to enjoy the respite from the snow and cold they'd left up north. The kids would be dropped off at the country club pools to be supervised by underpaid but well-toned college students.

Lena's golf game was still a bit rusty — especially her short game, which required a sensitive touch that was easy to lose without practice. But she played much better than Ryne, who hadn't had the three days before Christmas to get his swing back like she did.

They played an easy, familiar course close to the condo, and rounded out the morning with sandwiches on the restaurant patio. Then, eager to get started reading his novel, Lena drove them back to the condo.

Ryne retired to the bedroom for a nap, and Lena made a strong margarita. Then she dove into the clean white pages of Ryne's manuscript, quickly devouring the first two chapters. It was at least partly inspired by her run for the Senior Women's Amateur title, but the heroine was hankering for a spot on the real tour – the LPGA. And unlike Lena, the woman was willowy, tall and blond. Perhaps that was to protect her identity as the muse, Lena hoped. But the heroine seemed suspiciously like Kimberly, the young woman Ryne was dating three years ago when Lena had first met him.

When she looked up from Ryne's novel about five o'clock, it was dark outside. Every time she visited Palm Springs in the winter, she was surprised by the short days. Growing up in Nebraska, she'd been programmed to believe that when it was warm, the days were long. But now it was dark by early evening, and yet, it was still warm enough to grill and eat outside by the light of a few candles.

"How do you like the book?" Ryne asked after they'd finished eating, put the dishes in the dishwasher, and returned to the patio to finish the bottle of wine they'd started with dinner.

"It's beautifully written," Lena started and then stopped. She thought about bringing up the fact that the protagonist looked like his old girlfriend. But she saw no reason to ruin a great day with her insecurities. "I'm surprised how well you've gotten into your woman's head."

"Two sisters and now you," Ryne answered her implicit question. "I've been surrounded by women my whole life."

"That's a good thing," she smiled and tipped her wine glass toward him in a toast.

"But there's some news I haven't told you yet," he said. "My agent called yesterday morning, and we have a deal with Knopf."

"Wow! Really?" Lena was surprised and very happy for him. First-novel deals with premier publishers were getting more and more unlikely these days. "That is really great! When will it be published?"

"Pretty quickly. Maybe by next summer."

"How did you keep that secret from me all day? I would have been blabbing about it the second I got off the plane."

"I wanted to end today on a high note, and my golf game wasn't going to be it." He laughed. "But, if you don't mind a reprise of this morning's exercise in bed, I think that would be an even better way to end the day."

Desert Rain

The next three days, it rained, and the temperature never rose above fifty degrees. Lena was used to playing golf on days like that in Suncadia, where weeks and weeks could pass with no alternative. But it seemed not only unnecessary in the desert; it seemed like an insult. With so little time to enjoy the warmth and the sun, it wasn't fair that three days of their Christmas break should be ruined by rain.

She finished Ryne's novel and started another one that Terry had given her for Christmas. She baked a pumpkin pie and made comfort food in the Crockpot. Twice a day, she checked e-mails, and once a day, she and Ryne left the house to venture into the valley's restaurants, braving the Christmas break crowds. But after spending most of three straight days in the tiny condo – not even being able to sneak in a dry cigarette for the rain – Lena was claustrophobic.

And, as usual, the few days after Christmas left Lena feeling let down. The anticipation of Christmas Eve and Christmas Day – of its presents and food and drink and music – was as real to her at fifty-five as it had been at five. But now, the reality was so much less exciting. She missed the noise, the messy house, and the loud conversations of family holidays with her uncles and cousins. Even after her parents died and she lived for a couple of years with Betsy in town, Christmases were chaotic and noisy.

One Christmas when she was in college, she spent Christmas in Wisconsin with a friend she'd met in her English literature class. They weren't close friends, but Amy felt sorry for Lena when she found out that Lena was staying on campus alone for the holidays. And Lena was too happy to have somewhere to go to refuse the half-hearted offer.

Amy may not have really wanted Lena to come home with her, but Amy's mother made Lena feel like it never would have been Christmas without her. She prodded Lena for information about her classes, family, and boyfriends, as if she'd had no one to talk to for the entire year. She waltzed around the kitchen in stocking feet and an old-fashioned rick-rack-trimmed apron, thrusting food at whatever body happened to pass by.

The house was warm and humid, and smelled like sage and cinnamon. It was comforting and homey, but Amy was impatient with her mother as soon as they arrived, and two or three times a day, she begged Lena to join her for walks in the pine woods that surrounded the split-level house. At night, after Amy's parents went to bed, Lena and Amy played gin rummy with Amy's grandmother. The old woman was nearly deaf, so the holiday din didn't tire her in the least.

Thirty hours into Lena's rain-imposed seclusion with Ryne in Palm Springs, Lena longed for the din and chaos of Amy's Wisconsin home. Yes, it had been claustrophobic in a way, but it was also full of character and laughter. It certainly wasn't boring.

In Palm Springs, the rain made the condo smell moldy, in spite of the pot roast and short ribs cooking in the Crockpot. Ryne apparently didn't mind either the moldy odor or the quiet, and Lena found herself getting agitated by his lazy, relaxed mood. He sat for hours in front of the TV, watching whatever sporting event the networks threw up for him. He surfed the Internet, jumping from one page, one subject to another, happy in its meander and purposelessness. Lena paced behind his back, hoping he'd catch some of her nervous energy and agree to do anything — even go hit golf balls in the rain. But, instead, she left the condo alone, walking down the streets in the rain, fuming at herself for not being able to relax and enjoy the downtime. Isn't that what she had been looking forward to, back in the frenetic early days of December?

Finally, the weather cleared up, but Ryne and Lena still couldn't play much golf. Without thinking ahead, they'd let the tee times at their favorite courses fill up with snowbirds. They found only one late-day opening, which didn't allow time for a full eighteen holes before the sun set behind the steep rise of the San Jacinto Mountains.

Ryne eventually agreed to get up and out, and they visited the air museum by the airport, a trip that fascinated Ryne but bored Lena to tears. Do all guys love war planes and tales of World War II air battles? Lena remembered how often she had returned home in Denver to find Kurt mesmerized by a History Channel documentary about heroic airmen deftly dodging enemy bullets over London or France in the war. Only an empty beer could stir him from the screen, and then only long enough to grab another can, pop the top, and plop back down on the couch.

Excusing herself in the midst of the air museum tour, Lena stepped outside and sat in the sun, watching planes land at the tiny Palm Springs airport, their huge fuselages miniaturized by the backdrop of the massive mountains behind them. A tight trio of women, each about her age, slid by on the sidewalk in an energetic power walk. They chattered incessantly as they approached her, passed, and then disappeared around the bend and down the street.

Lena was jealous. She didn't have many friends like that – probably only Terry and Carly – and none in Palm Springs. And she saw Terry and Carly so rarely these days. Would they even have enough to say to each other to carry on a conversation for more than a couple of blocks? Once this golf ball project was over, once she'd freed the Perfect Tee from this hacking menace, Lena was going spend some time building female relationships.

Lena checked her e-mail that evening. She came out of the bedroom, where she kept her laptop and headed straight for the wine refrigerator. Opening a bottle of Sauvignon Blanc, she waved her wine glass in frustration.

"I wish I had a better grasp of these Internet security issues!" she exclaimed. "I wonder if Kim could help."

"Well, maybe you should have stayed with Kim," Ryne said, not looking up from the newspaper he was reading at the kitchen counter.

Lena was shocked. She turned to face him. "What?" she asked, her voice rising. "What did you just say?"

"Well," Ryne met her eyes, trying to look calm, but his irritation was transparent. "Wouldn't he be able to help you? He's Mr. Internet Security, isn't he?"

"Where is this coming from?" Lena asked. She stopped pouring the wine in mid-glass.

"Look, I am not blind," he answered. He turned away and looked back down at the newspaper. "I know this week didn't go so well, and I'm just thinking maybe you are regretting that you spent Christmas with me instead of him."

"The reason it hasn't gone so well has nothing to do with Kim," she retorted. "It has to do only with you and me. And rain. Don't try to blame this on something else."

Ryne tipped his head sideways and continued to stare at the newspaper. He turned a page and smoothed out the newsprint in front of him.

"Could you look at me?" Lena asked.

Ryne looked up and blinked.

"Well?" he asked.

"Why would you want to bring up Kim?"

"Because it appears you need him right now more than you need me."

Lena had no way to counter that. She wondered if it was true.

The next morning, after a night of no sex, Ryne mumbled that she was getting a little hard to get along with.

"I'm just not good at sitting around and doing nothing," she snapped. "Christ! Aren't you bored?" She meant it as a criticism of his inactivity, but he didn't read it that way.

"You need to learn to chill," he retorted. "This is supposed to be vacation."

"Maybe you could learn to not turn your brain off when you walk through my door," she countered. "You're no fun when you're dull."

"I'm not your one-man circus. I don't perform on cue."

"There's a big difference between being a wet blanket and being a one-man circus," Lena said, and slammed out the door to walk to Starbucks. She wasn't even making sense anymore.

Their last conversation wasn't even a real dialogue. It was more like a couple of overlapping monologues spoken in low, I-don't-care-if-you-can-hear-me tones. By the time she dropped Ryne off at the airport the next day, Lena was happy to get him out of her hair, and he was happy to go. Their goodbye kiss, as he jumped out of the front seat of her rental car at the airport curb, was quick and platonic. She didn't wait to see him disappear through the terminal door before stepping on the gas and steering back onto the street.

Her last afternoon in Palm Springs, Lena sat in the backyard of the condo, overlooking the quiet pool, and pouted. She finished the two half-bottles of wine leftover from their final, tense meals, and used up the last of the Cointreau and Patron. She threw out the unused food they'd accumulated over the week. She went online to see if she could plan a couple of days with Terry in Suncadia over the coming weekend, but was distracted first by an e-mail from Carly sitting in her inbox.

"Want to extend your Xmas break and come to Hawaii with us for a quick trip?" Carly's e-mail message read. She attached a copy of their reservation in Maui.

At first, Lena shook her head, rejecting the idea out of hand. But, before she replied to Carly's e-mail, she got up to refill her wine glass with the last of the cabernet. In the time it took to walk to the kitchen and back to her laptop in the bedroom, she'd reconsidered.

Work had resumed back in Seattle two days before, and from what she could see by her e-mails, the office pace was slowly picking up in the way that the post-holiday work weeks usually unfolded, as if from a slumber. Everything sounded copacetic. Christmas sales had been good, even better than they had expected. Lena missed Bounty, but Terry seemed to be doing well with her. They had been snowshoeing and hanging out in front of the fireplace in Terry's cozy cabin.

She didn't really have to rush home. The next meeting with GTI to discuss the golf ball project was still three weeks off. She could schedule a teleconference with her management team in two days to take the place of the regular staff meeting already on the calendar. The disappointing way she and Ryne had spent their winter break left her feeling like she needed something more – something fun – to distract her before she sat back down in her CEO chair and figured out how to deal with the hackers.

And, finally, the three long days of rain she and Ryne had endured in the desert made it hard to face going back to Seattle's incessant rains so soon.

Instead of hitting reply to answer Carly and Brandt, she picked up the phone and called them. Before she retired to the bedroom to pack and sleep, she'd reserved a seat on a plane to Hawaii and booked a room at the same hotel as her good friends. They'd play some golf and take in the pro tour's Tournament of Champions before she had to return to The Perfect Tee's hacker, grouchy Ryne, and the rest of the long, dark winter in Seattle.

LENA WAS HAPPY TO SEE the leis on the necks of the flight attendants and hear their cheery "alohas" as she was to postpone her return to The Perfect Tee for a few more days. It had been years since she'd flown to the island paradise and renewed her fantasy of a permanent island life. But the ten-hour trip to Maui sapped her enthusiasm.

She kept her planned flight from Palm Springs to San Francisco on Alaska, then transferred to the plane headed to Hawaii instead of the one headed on to Seattle. A trip like this used to be exhilarating and energizing, back when she made cross-oceanic trips to Hawaii in her thirties. But she was forced to acknowledge that her stamina was lagging. As she rose from her seat in Kahalui, she fantasized that Brandt's and Carly's flight would be delayed and she could catch a quick nap at the hotel before they arrived.

Still, an hour later, she smiled at the sight of her two friends blasting through the door at the Makena Resort on time, maybe even a little ahead of schedule. She had had just enough time to check in, put her bag in her room, and go back to the lobby to buy a bottle of overpriced water before she recognized Carly's happy laughter. As usual, Brandt followed two paces behind his wife, struggling to keep up with her long-legged stride, cackling at a joke they shared at the bell captain's expense.

Carly threw her long arms around Lena's shoulders and magically transferred some of her energy to Lena's tired bones.

"God, it's great to see you!" Carly exclaimed, stepping aside so Brandt could give Lena a hug as well. "How was your trip?"

Brandt and Carly took their luggage to the lobby elevator and up to their room, and Lena sat sipping her bottle of water on the rattan and cotton couches between the registration desk and the concierge desk to wait for them. Occasionally, smiling couples floated through the wide, open air entry from the port-cochere, and turned sharply left to confront the hotel registration staff and get their vacation started — disheveled from the long flight from the mainland, but hopeful with the possibility that this vacation, after so many others that had disappointed, would be the one that finally justified all of the waiting, the expense, and the planning they put into one week in paradise.

Lena was almost embarrassed for their wide-open hopefulness, but, still, she recognized a little of herself in the middle-aged women. They dressed in bright, flowered knits that signaled their refusal to accept the mundane deterioration of their own appearance — sagging jowls, blossoming cellulite, flapping upper arms, proliferating brown spots, and thinning hair. Billowing blouses in pink, peach, lime green, and an occasional yellow bespoke their age as clearly as the muted khakis, navy stripes, and taut blue jeans signaled the youth of the spoiled teenagers wealthy enough to go to Hawaii the first week of January with their parents.

Lena would have felt sorry for the husbands of those middle-aged women — sorry for the frustration and exhaustion of a string of petty arguments about where to go first, who should do what, when they should eat, where they should park, et cetera, et cetera — but their too-short shorts and white crew socks pulled up above leather Tevas killed her sympathy. No wonder their wives insisted on calling all the shots throughout the day. If a guy couldn't dress himself better than that, he couldn't be trusted to make any other decision, no matter how trivial.

"Where are your clubs?" Brandt appeared suddenly in front of her, pulling Lena out of her depressing reverie. "Let's go hit some balls!"

Out on the driving range next to the hotel, Lena felt her body and spirits come back to life. Swinging a golf club wasn't only fun and liberating; it used every limb and big muscle. After only a couple of practice swings and a couple of lazy warm-up lob shots, she felt better. The blood that had pooled in the soles of her feet a couple of hours ago found its way back up her legs, into her arms, and up to her cheeks. No wonder people who played this sport were able to eventually shoot their age; not only could the game be played into old age, it also made life worth living a lot longer.

As usual, Lena's long, accurate drives eventually drew a small crowd of appreciative fans of the game – a young pro who was reconstructing the pyramids of golf balls at the driving range stations, an elderly gentleman who had been hitting next to her, and a middle-aged couple who was strolling by the practice area.

The gallery helped Lena focus on the things that produced great swings – a measured tempo; a pretty, balanced finish; and concentrating on a target for each shot. She even surprised herself with how far and straight she was hitting the ball, especially given the exhaustion she had felt earlier.

"How far is that?" she heard the middle-aged woman ask her husband.

"Farther than you can hit," he laughed, unkindly. Lena threw him a disapproving glance, and he added, meekly, "and probably farther than I've ever hit as well."

"Nice! Were you on tour at some point?" the young pro asked, stepping between the couple and Lena. "Lovely tempo you've got."

"Thanks. But no. Never a pro. I won an amateur championship once though," Lena smiled and leaned against her driver to enjoy the rare moment of being admired by a handsome, athletic young man half her age. Down the line in front of her, she saw Brandt turn to Carly and roll his eyes. Her friends pretended to tire of the attention she attracted when she played golf with them, but she knew there were times when they got a bit of a charge out of her semi-celebrity as well.

"How long are you here?" the pro asked. "Maybe we could get in a quick nine holes together."

Ha! Maybe she didn't look as old as she felt. Then, she remembered she was wearing a hat and big sunglasses. Without a close look at her eyes, her forehead, and her thinning hair, there was a good chance the young man had no idea how old she was. In fairness to him, she pushed her glasses up on top of her hat and smiled at him.

"Thanks, but my friends and I are only playing tomorrow and then we're going to watch the tournament for the next couple of days," she said. "I won't have time this week, but maybe on another trip."

She was letting him off easy. Now she hoped he would be kind and not blanch at the wrinkles around her eyes. Without waiting to see his reaction, Lena pulled her sunglasses back down over her eyes, raked another range ball off the pyramid, and lined up her next shot.

Hawaii

The next day, something was off with Brandt, or at least in her relationship with him. Lena and Carly started the round off well, but it was a struggle for Brandt from the first tee, and it got worse. His first drive veered sharply right on a nasty slice, and his ball landed in an "environmental area." That meant he got a free drop, but he'd lost his first ball of the day on the first shot of the day. What little humor he had at the start of the round dissipated quickly.

Lena often rubbed Brandt the wrong way. He seemed like a flirtatious ladies' man, but Lena never seemed to be able to say the right things around him. She felt as if she never met his expectations, whether in her looks, sense of humor, intelligence, or social graces. In the latter category, she had to admit, he was in a whole different league. He loved meeting new people, striking up conversations with brand new acquaintances, securing invitations to parties and golf dates right off the bat with whomever he met. And he was indulgently complimentary of his wife, in a way that paid for his flirtatiousness, but at the same time, always left Lena feeling very inadequate by comparison.

After the first two holes of the day, Lena tried to ease the tension by being effusively positive. Whenever he hit his tee shot, she complimented his "great drive," only to watch in horror with him as the shot sliced off into a pond or duck-hooked into more environmental areas.

"Would you please quit your commentary?" Brandt growled after his third tee shot. "At least until you see where it lands?"

He had a point, and Lena tried. But she couldn't resist the urge to try to cheer him up, and instead of making him feel better, exacerbated his irritation with her cloying optimism. He scowled at every utterance. He muttered and pouted, escalating his bad behavior to the point of throwing clubs. By the fourteenth hole, he was sitting in the cart, refusing to take another shot. Finally, he gave Lena nothing to react to, and she managed to leave him alone.

On the other hand, from the start of the round, Carly ignored Brandt like she might a temperamental teenager, and played as calmly as ever and competently as could be expected after three golf-less months in Seattle. But the mood affected Lena, and she posted one of her worst rounds in many months.

Back at the hotel, Brandt headed straight to the room to take a nap — maybe that's what he needed — and Carly and Lena sat by the hotel pool with a couple of cranberry-vodkas and a bowl of olives.

Lena apologized to Carly surrogate for apparently ruining Brandt's day.

"He'll get over it. He gets that way sometimes. He's a bit like a seven-year-old who doesn't know when he's tired," Carly said. "He'll be over it by dinner."

"I hope so," Lena sighed. "It could be a long three days if he isn't."

Carly chewed the flesh off a large green olive, and since the waiter hadn't thought to bring a pit dish, she put the pit into the ashtray.

"How was the Christmas vacation?" Carly changed the subject. "Did you guys have a good time?"

It suddenly struck Lena odd that they hadn't talked about it yet. The conversation at dinner the night before had touched on the Seahawks, Carly's business woes, and Lena's golf-ball project. Lena had avoided bringing up the problem with the hackers for lack of any good way to justify not returning to the office, even to friends. And she hadn't mentioned the tension of the last few days with Ryne.

"It was great at times, but not all together wonderful," Lena summed up the holiday. "I'd like to blame it on three days of rain, but it seems that we should be better at uninterrupted togetherness than we are, regardless of the weather."

Lena told Carly about the claustrophobia, the boredom, Ryne's inactivity. It came across like a long whine, and Lena felt selfish as soon as she was done complaining.

Carly sipped her rose-colored drink through a straw and gave Lena a little room to reflect on her whine before responding. "Yeah, two people usually have trouble staying exactly on the same wavelength all of the time," Carly said, both accepting and minimizing Lena's problem. "Brandt and I are both pretty high-energy, so it's not so much an issue for us, but I think it is for most married couples."

"A rousing endorsement of the institution!" Lena laughed.

"You're not talking about that though, are you?" Carly sounded surprised.

"Oh, god no. Marriage is the last thing on my mind. Or my wish list," Lena put the subject to bed. "Already made that mistake."

"Long time ago, though."

"Yeah, but not long enough. And Walla Walla wasn't that long ago. Too scary."

Carly nodded. The incident with Kurt in the hotel in Walla Walla, right after he was released from prison, had shocked them all. Carly, Brandt, Kim, and Terry had stayed in Eastern Washington with her the next couple of days through the police investigation. They didn't talk about it much anymore, but it had sealed a kind of survivors' bond among them.

Brandt had recovered his sense of humor and easy sociability by dinnertime, and the evening meal on the patio overlooking the pool and the ocean was relaxing and pleasant. But still, Lena was quick to excuse herself before the temptation of dessert and before pressing her luck with Brandt's tolerance and went straight to bed.

Twenty-four hours later, she recognized that the evening's pleasantness was just the calm before the storm.

IF THERE WAS ONE THING, other than golf, that the three friends had in common, it was their tendency to be inconsistently and unnecessarily pecuniary about the smallest of expenses. Rather than pay the twenty-five-dollar parking fee for a spot in the lot designated for the Tournament of Champion fans, they drove around the neighborhood surrounding Kapalua for forty-five minutes, looking for on-street parking. It would save them a small fraction of the amount they'd spent on their spectator's passes.

Lena could have gotten into the event for free, given the Perfect Tee's relationship with professional golf, but she didn't feel up to making the calls and going through the PGA's PR office at a time when those staffers were busy getting ready for the tournament. Somehow it seemed smarter and easier to pay the sixty dollars for her ticket and get a little of it back by parking a mile and a half from the gate.

The Tournament of Champions was the PGA event that marked the beginning of the calendar year for the tour. It was a chance to see nearly all of the top golfers in the world on one stage, with no amateurs clogging up the fairways. Only those who had won a PGA, Asian Tour or European Tour event the year before were invited. Of course, some of the biggest names – usually Tiger Woods and Phil Mickelson – skipped the event. But there were plenty of fans who were tiring of Tiger and Phil anyway.

The tournament had begun a couple of hours before they arrived. The three friends wandered from hole to hole, moving backwards through the course to catch a glimpse of as many different pros as possible. There was no humidity and only a light trade-wind breeze on the course, and it only took about an hour before Lena realized she'd rather be out playing on such a gorgeous day than watching others – however talented – do it.

Brandt's mood had returned to grouchy, though, and Lena wasn't sure she wanted to risk re-igniting his wrath by making the suggestion. Instead, she found herself trying to cheer him up, and, like she had the day before, she only managed to piss him off trying.

"What a great day," she exclaimed as they rounded a

corner and caught a glimpse of the ocean beyond the sixteenth green.

"You've said that about fifty times," Brandt snapped. He was right, but she couldn't seem to quit saying it over and over in a kind of attack of tourette's syndrome brought on by his mood.

"Sorry."

"Don't say you're sorry. Maybe you don't need to say anything for a change." Brandt had a way of making her realize what it must have been like to have a critical, difficult older brother, and for once she was grateful for having been an only child.

"Brandt, you don't have to be nasty," Carly chided him. But she stopped her scolding there, and Lena wondered if she was afraid of incurring his anger too. The women stopped trying to make conversation, resorting to a kind of sign language to keep from tripping over each other as they followed grouchy Brandt from hole to hole.

Finally, Brandt suggested they grab some lunch and then leave the tournament to play some golf of their own. Lena reacted to the idea a little too enthusiastically, which only brought on more scowling. Deciding it was better just to ignore him than to apologize, she silently led them to the hospitality tent near the eighteenth hole, where they grabbed beers and hot dogs, and sat down at a picnic table in the shade to eat.

"We don't have a tee time anywhere," Carly finally broke their silence as they left the course, walked several blocks, and turned a corner, returning to Lena's rental car parked along the road.

"I don't think that'll be a problem," Brandt assured

her, his mood lightening enough that he didn't snap at her. "With the tournament, most golfers on the island are probably here."

"Where do you want to try?" Lena pulled her phone out of her pocket and turned it on. "Makena?"

"Nah, that's such a sissy course," Brandt snarled. His mood hadn't improved as much as Lena thought, apparently. "Let's try one of the Wailea courses. Or Ka'anapali."

Lena squinted to try to make out the listings on her smart phone, but the sun was too bright. "We'll have to do it when we get to the car," she said, handing her phone to Carly. "The phone numbers for courses are in my contacts. I'll let you try them when we get going."

Lena unlocked their doors with the key fob as they approached the car from the front and slipped behind the wheel. The car seat felt like it might blister the back of her thighs, but eager to get going, she yanked the gear shifter into reverse position, glanced into the rearview mirror, and started to back up. The car hit something behind them, and she heard a nasty scrape under the chassis.

"What? There's nothing back there!" Lena exclaimed. "That's a driveway entrance behind me. What did I hit?"

Lena flipped the car back in park, and Brandt jumped out of the back seat. Afraid the car would move while he was half-in and half-out, Lena shoved the transmission into park and leaned out her window. "What is it?"

Leaving his door open, Brandt walked behind the car and leaned down. "It's a traffic cone. It's stuck under your bumper. The guy who lives here must have been trying to keep cars from parking in front of his driveway," Brandt called out. "Pull forward and I'll yank it loose."

Lena yanked on the shifter, but instead of moving through reverse and neutral to drive, it stuck in reverse, and with a jerk, the car jumped backwards. She stomped on the brake, but it was too late, and Brandt let out a blood-curdling scream.

"Brandt!" Carly yelled, jumping out of the passenger seat next to Lena and rushing behind the car. Lena slammed the sticky gear shift back in park and followed her.

Brandt lay on his back on the pavement holding his knee, his face contorted with pain. He squeezed his eyes closed and clenched his jaw, his head thrown back and his chin pointing at the sky. "Brandt! Are you okay?" Carly dropped to her knees and lifted his head.

"No! No! No, I am not okay! Christ, can't you see that?" he screamed. His eyes popped open and stared straight up at the sky. He hyperventilated in pain. "Shit! Shit! I think you broke my knee cap. My fucking knee cap!"

"I'll call 911," Lena said, scrambling back into the driver's seat and pawing through her backpack for her phone. "Where's my fucking phone?" she screamed, tossing the contents of her purse onto the front seat where Carly had been sitting.

"You gave it to me. It's in the console," Carly shouted back.

"Wait!" Brandt bellowed. "Don't call an ambulance. Just get me to an emergency room. Come on! Help me get up and let's go!"

Lena didn't know if that was the best decision or not, but it didn't seem like a good time to argue with Brandt. She stuffed the mess on the seat back into her backpack, and went back to help Carly get Brandt up on one foot.

With the women supporting him, he hopped around to the back seat behind Lena, yelling "Ow!" with each move. Carly left him leaning against Lena on the driver's side and ran around to the other side to help him lift his injured leg into the car and stretch it out across the back seat.

"Christ that hurts! Jesus!" Brandt settled down into the seat and Lena carefully closed the door behind him and slid in behind the wheel. She didn't even fasten her seatbelt as she backed the car noisily over the cone under the car and then peeled out, leaving the crumpled orange plastic spinning away as she sped down the street.

The Brick

Later, Lena couldn't remember what route they took from the golf course to the emergency room. Carly pulled up directions to the hospital on her iPhone and barked instructions while Brandt continued to scream a stream of profanity from the back seat. Lena just did what Carly said, her head spinning and her heart racing with adrenaline. She saw nothing but the narrow strip of road in front of her and heard nothing but Carly's calm voice giving her directions over Brandt's profanity.

Once they pulled up to the ER's sliding door, she threw the car in park and followed Carly into the lobby. After that, she was little more than a horrified bystander, watching the ER staff lift Brandt out of the back seat and wheel him back into an exam room, while Carly dug through his billfold for his ID and medical insurance card.

Lena pulled her car into the parking lot next to ER and shoved the sticky shifter in park.

"You piece of shit!" she yelled, slamming her fist down on the shifter knob. It hurt badly, and Lena grabbed her wrist with her left hand and closed her eyes. Her ears were ringing. She sat holding her wrist for a long minute, waiting for the adrenaline to subside and the ringing in her ears to stop. When she finally lifted her eyelids, she was shocked at how bright the day was. Somewhere along the way, she had lost her sunglasses.

Brandt stayed back in the bowels of ER for three hours, as a doctor was called in to do what he could to immobilize his knee and stem the swelling. Carly went back and forth from the waiting room to Brandt's gurney in the back, bringing Lena news and trying to make her feel better about what had happened. It was the kind of accident that could happen to anyone. It wasn't her fault. Brandt will be fine. None of the assurances rang very true, and eventually, Carly stayed back with Brandt and Lena sat alone.

Three times Lena got up and went out to the car to have a cigarette – the most she'd smoked in a day in months. Finally, a blue-smocked hospital worker wheeled a sedated Brandt out in a wheelchair, and helped him settle back into the rear seat of the rental car. Two hours later, Lena and Carly helped him into a wheelchair at the departure gates at the Kahalui airport. She hugged Carly goodbye and watched as her friends disappeared through security to catch the next possible flight back to Seattle.

Lena returned to the hotel, called the airline to change her flight to the next morning, and packed her bag. Then she cracked open a beer from the mini-bar and sat on the lanai, watching the sun set over the ocean. It was a sight she'd photographed every time she'd been in Hawaii, but this time, she would be happy to have no photographic evidence of the disaster this spur-of-the-moment vacation had turned into.

The frustration of the day reminded Lena of a nightmare she'd had over and over the past two years, since she left her amateur golf career behind and took the helm at The Perfect Tee. She dreamed she went out to play golf, and for one reason and another and another, she never got to tee up the ball or swing a club. A crowd got in the way, and she couldn't make it to the tee. Or the food that she'd ordered at the clubhouse never came. Each time she had the dream, morning after morning, she woke up petrified that her life was passing before her eyes, unlived and unenjoyed.

In the first year that she started having the dream, Lena thought it was pretty literal: she wasn't getting to play enough golf. But now, it felt more like a metaphor for the frustration of not getting to do what she wanted with her life. What was she missing, though? She was running a company, making decisions, being heeded as the boss. That's exactly what she thought she wanted three years ago when she left TrueWeb. She was getting the chance to prove she could do as well as the condescending CEOs of her past.

So, which was it? Metaphorical or literal? She continued to wonder, waiting for her plane to board at the gate at the humid Kahalui airport the next afternoon. Was it literally the frustration of not playing enough golf? Lena huffed at herself in disgust. Surely, deep down in the unconsciousness that controlled her dreams, lay goals that were larger, more worthy, and less selfish than just playing golf every day. She was living her dream: running a company, sharing her bed with a good man, taking care of an angel of a dog, and maintaining a bevy of friendships that filled out her life.

Of course, now she wasn't sure that Brandt and Carly were going to continue to be her friends; certainly, the accident wasn't going to improve her prickly relationship with Brandt. And since Kim had run into Ryne at her apartment, he probably would never speak with her again. Jim and Larry had turned against her; they now seemed set on interfering with her golf ball venture for no reason other than spite. Even her connection with Ryne seemed difficult. They couldn't sustain a pleasant week together in close quarters; that didn't seem to bode well for a more serious commitment, if it ever came to that.

Compared with her friendship problems, returning to work seemed easy, even if she faced hackers, doubting VCs, and warring tech guys. She boarded the flight and settled into her seat with only one short-term goal: five hours of angst-free, Ambien-assisted sleep.

LENA ARRIVED BACK IN SEATTLE late on Friday, and Ryne and Bounty picked her up at the arrivals curb at SeaTac. Bounty bounced off the interior walls of Ryne's SUV, kissing Lena with big tongue laps, turning around and around in the back of the vehicle, and then leaning into the front seat to start kissing Lena all over again. If only humans were so expressive and transparent!

Ryne drove straight up to Suncadia. The hour-and-a-half drive up and over Snoqualmie Pass offered a chance to talk about what had happened in Palm Springs, but Lena was afraid that Ryne would want to avoid it. She didn't want to start their weekend as if everything was just fine and dandy, and she was relieved when Ryne broached the subject, just twenty miles out of town.

"My flight home from Palm Springs wasn't fun," he said. He let that cryptic sentence hang in the air without further elaboration. It was up to Lena to take the bait or change the subject. Lena picked up his cue, even though she wasn't sure how successful they'd be trying to bridge the wide gulf that had grown between them over the Christmas break.

"I'm sorry," she started. She stopped. That was a good start — accepting some responsibility by offering her apology. But, where to go from there? How could she rein in her proclivity to jump to conclusions and blame him for their discord? It was too easy to blame Ryne without acknowledging her own contribution to the mismatch. But this mattered. She didn't want to win an argument; she really wanted — for once — to find a solution. This was progress in her willingness to make a commitment, she noted to herself.

"I know we didn't do so well in Palm Springs," she said quietly. "I am not really sure why, but I am sorry for whatever part of that was my responsibility."

"What do you think happened?"

Lena focused on the question. Even as she scoured her memory to try to identify exactly what had driven them apart over the week, she considered the significance of Ryne's willingness to get to the bottom of it. He didn't seem to want to smooth over whatever stood between them. Now, she had to swallow her pride and answer him as honestly as she could.

"Okay. I'm not sure. But let me try to be honest about how I felt," she said, dipping her chin in a contrite posture. "I have trouble with quiet and low key. I seem to need some kind of constant activity and distraction. I get bored. I need some …" That was as far as she could get without starting to reach beyond what seemed honest and real.

"Need what?" Ryne asked. Lena appreciated his tone; it wasn't demanding or judgmental. He sounded like he really wanted to know.

"I don't know. I guess I need activity, stimulation, something to fill in the space." Lena paused and tried to make sense of what she was saying. "I'm not comfortable facing the void."

Ryne nodded. He let the silence sit between them for a minute. "I think that's honest. And I know I'm not always the most exciting guy to be around. But I think that's okay. If I tried to be everything for you, I'd fail anyway. I'm okay if you need more than just me to fill your life. I just want you to be okay with that as well."

Lena sighed. She didn't know if that answer was enough. Maybe what she really needed in her life was someone else, someone who was more like Ryne in his public moments and less like Ryne in his private moments. Someone a little crazy, a little manic.

"And I didn't care for that bit about Kim." Ryne said it without looking away from the highway in front of them.

"What?" It took her a few moments to process what he was talking about. She didn't remember the exchange at first, and then it came back to her.

"You know, the bit about how you wished he were there so you could get some good advice."

Lena didn't respond right away. In some ways his jealousy seemed so petty, so unnecessary, given how obviously attracted she was to Ryne compared with Kim. She sat and calmed her temper.

"You know I can't even begin to compare the two of you when it comes to how I feel," Lena said, finally, quietly.

"No, I don't know that," he said, staring straight ahead at the dark highway.

"Well, you should."

"But he's so smart," Ryne countered. "He would 'know what to do.'" He was throwing her words back at her.

"I think you have given me some pretty sound advice, too, over the past few months," she said.

"Yeah, right," Ryne said. The subject of Kim had clearly pissed him off, and she let him stew for a few minutes. It shouldn't be that hard to convince him that her words in Palm Springs meant nothing outside of the context of an Internet security issue, which had nothing to do with him or their relationship. She was surprised, however, that he felt insecure enough about their relationship that one conversation about Kim would have upset him so much.

She didn't like it. That glimpse into his insecurity. She hadn't seen it very often. She liked him strong and unflappable. But that wasn't fair of her. Everyone had their vulnerable moments; she shouldn't expect Ryne to be any different.

And besides, wasn't it nice to know the balance of power in their relationship was perhaps more even than she thought? They both needed reassurance; they both needed to know they were valued. At least, that's how she wanted to feel.

"Ryne," she said. "You are the most important person in my life. Not just right now, but ever. I really mean that, but that doesn't mean that you'll always be the only one in my life. And it doesn't mean you have to be Mr. Excitement all the time, or the best golfer, or the smartest or the fastest or strongest, or leap tall buildings with a single bound. Okay. I just want to be with you. Just who you are."

Ryne said nothing. But she watched his face soften. He was processing what she said. He was taking it seriously.

"Well, that's good enough for me," he said, finally. He didn't look at her, but she could see his eyes had watered a bit. That might have bothered her only a few minutes before, but now she saw it as a good sign.

She let out a long breath and stared out at the highway in front of them. Maybe, she thought, her earlier hypothesis was all wrong. She didn't need someone more manic, more like Ryne at his best all the time. Maybe what she needed was to give him space to be human and vulnerable, and to be willing to talk through their problems when they arose. The fact that they had just done that, alone, seemed to bode well for the future.

RATHER THAN RISK AN EVENING alone so soon after they had argued, Ryne suggested they eat dinner in Roslyn before returning to her condo in Suncadia. He pulled off the interstate at the Suncadia exit and headed straight into town. He turned into a diagonal parking spot in front of the Brick on the corner of the town's main intersection that had been the setting of hundreds of scenes in Northern Exposure.

"Is this okay?" he turned to Lena and asked before turning off the engine. "I don't want to wait for a table at Village Pizza, and I'm guessing you don't either."

"No," Lena said, nodding. "I mean, yes. No, I don't want to wait. Yes, this is a good idea."

Lena swung her legs out of the car door and felt her feet slip on the dirty ice that extended from the curb into the middle of the street. She stood up slowly, seeking a stable stance, and grimaced. The stiffness in her legs and hips was due to six hours on a plane and two in the car more than it was due to age, wasn't it? And the cold! Palm Springs and Hawaii may not have been perfect, but she certainly hadn't missed this weather.

Inside the Brick, the sandy, wet floorboards smelled like winter, and condensation streamed down the insides of the tall, arched windows, cutting squiggly lines into the frost at the bottoms. Lena stomped her feet to shake off the cold, and unwound the knit scarf from her neck.

Roslyn regulars shared the overheated, humid space with a few Suncadia resort guests without really mingling. Every bar stool was taken by locals, and the benches that flanked the trundle tables in the middle of the room were crowded with burly beer drinkers bloated by big unzipped parkas and untied Sorel boots. The resort guests stood in the middle of the floor with their cocktails, having arrived from Seattle too late to secure seats on a Friday night.

Two couples had commandeered the shuffleboard table in the back corner under a wall of lighted beer signs, and competitors and spectators surrounded the bar's two pool tables with beer mugs in their hands.

Lena and Ryne got lucky and snagged a high wooden table by the wall as an older couple slid off its stools. "Good timing." Lena smiled, relieved. "I wasn't in the mood to stand up all night."

"I'd think you'd be tired of sitting," Ryne said. Lena wondered if he'd caught her grimace as she got out of the car. Over the past few months, she'd stopped worrying about the difference between her age and the youth of Ryne's last girlfriend, but on days when she felt closer to sixty than forty, she wondered if he ever regretted trading up in age.

Of course, Ryne was no younger than she was, but the liabilities of age seemed to weigh more on the female side of the ledger, Lena mused as she squinted to read the beer menu posted over the bar. Wine was typically her drink of choice, but beer was not only more socially acceptable at the Brick, but also safer. The wine selection was dismal.

"I'll take the Roslyn Brickhouse lager," she said, slipping Ryne a ten dollar bill for their beers. Ryne accepted the contribution, picked up the dirty mugs left by the departing couple, and stepped over to the bar. Lena surveyed the crowd for familiar faces. She recognized a few Suncadia couples she knew just well enough to acknowledge with a wave. Terry was in Seattle for the weekend, attending a sommelier seminar, so she didn't expect to see her friend's wild hair and open face, but she thought she might see Terry's husband, Tom.

Sure enough, there he was. Lena raised her hand to catch his attention, but then she noticed how close he was standing to a short, tiny blonde who looked barely old enough to drink. Lena quickly pulled her arm back to her side.

"Do you know that woman with Tom?" Lena asked Ryne as he sat two beer mugs and dinner menus down on their tiny table top and slipped back onto his stool.

Ryne searched the room for Terry's husband. Lena nodded in Tom's direction to help him zero in on the tall carpenter, and Ryne frowned at what he saw. "No, I don't think I've ever seen her before. But she looks like a local. Like a local teenager, that is."

The bar crowd was thick enough that Lena and Ryne could watch the couple without drawing attention to themselves. Tom wasn't flirting with the young woman; it appeared that their relationship had progressed beyond the level of tentative, insecure seduction. They stood next to one of the pool tables, hooked together in a side-by-side embrace that telegraphed intimacy, and watched one of Tom's friends sink four solids in quick succession. Tom raised his glass in anticipation of his friend's victory. Cocky, the young man lined up to bank the eight ball into a side pocket, and Tom joined in a collective moan when the ball slid into a corner instead.

"Oh, Christ," Lena muttered, watching the couple, not the pool shot. "This is really, really horrible."

Ryne nodded as the spectators broke up. Tom accepted a relinquished pool cue, dropped his quarters into the slot, and slammed the lever to drop a fresh set of balls.

"It amazes me how people think they can do this in a town as small as Roslyn," Ryne said. "Doesn't everyone know them?"

"I guess the standards of behavior are a little different up here in the mountains." Lena couldn't stop watching, hoping for some clue that would dispel her suspicions. Tom took off his down vest and handed it to the young blond. He turned up the sleeves of his flannel shirt and waited for his heavily bearded opponent to break the stacked balls. As the game progressed, the young woman stuck close to Tom, moving away only when he maneuvered to line up his shots. After each of his turns at the table, she closed in again to claim possession by proximity.

Tom accidentally sunk the eight ball, truncating the game, and as the spectators shifted to make way for the next twosome of competitors, Lena spied Janet, one of Terry's artist friends mingling between the pool tables. She grimaced as they made eye contact through the crowd and looked away. Lena turned her attention back to Tom's young female friend as she pulled away from him and passed by in a pack of young women on their way to the restrooms in the back of the bar.

Fat thighs, she noticed. Big hair. Too much make-up.

"Big boobs," Ryne added to her silent tally. "Really big boobs." Lena was hoping he didn't mean that as a compliment.

THE TROUBLES LENA WAS HAVING with her friends took a quick back seat to troubles at work. Did other CEOs ever walk into their office after vacation and wish they could walk right back out? she wondered as she unlocked her office door at six o'clock Monday morning. Or did they love the challenge of managing bad news, staff discord, and competitive threats? Was this desire to turn and run proof that she really wasn't cut out to be the big boss?

Lena had checked her e-mails often enough over the past three weeks to know most of what she was going to face before she unlocked her door, brushed the pile of mail and memos off to the side of her desk, and secured a safe spot for her Starbucks latte. But in the spirit of the "work-life balance" she demanded for her staff, she had responded only to what she had to over her vacation. Even when she responded, it was with an admonition that everything could wait until she got back to the office.

She wasn't surprised that her troublesome VC didn't take that well. One of the new e-mails she found in her inbox that morning was "RE: Hacker attack" – a response from Blake to her e-mail informing him and her other VCs about the threat from the credit card hackers. She had sent it late the night before when she got into Seattle.

Her heart rate quickened and her fingers shook on the keyboard when she finally clicked it open, knowing it was going to be a scorching indictment of her decision to take vacation time in the midst of what he would undoubtedly characterize as World War III.

It was. And then some:

I question your judgment in taking time off in this midst of a security crisis like this. But I am even more concerned that you are ill-equipped to handle the hacker situation. You have neither the experience with cybersecurity nor the technical expertise to understand the issue. Further, my understanding is that some of your employees have found your leadership incommensurate with the demands of a fast-growing technology company, and when your lack of leadership has been noted, you have not risen to the occasion, but have found fault in others. Please respond immediately with a specific plan to address each of these issues. I will schedule a meeting with the entire VC team in the next week to discuss these with you.

Lena's head was spinning, and her eyes were blurring by the time she closed the e-mail. She was so stung by the tone Blake had taken that she was tempted to delete it and pretend like she'd never seen it. She suspected that the "employees" Blake referred to were Ken and some of his followers. She believed that the rest of her executive team, at least, had not lost faith in her. But, clearly, if she didn't respond to Blake, she would precipitate her own dismissal, as he would contend that she was not only derelict in her management but disrespectful of him to boot.

She'd have to calm down and write a response, but first, she wanted to check with Taylor to see if they had received any more correspondence from the hackers. And there were other things demanding her attention as well, not the least of which was a letter from the USGA with more bad news.

It wasn't a final, formal response to their petition for approval of the RF golf ball, but the USGA informed Lena and George that the equipment committee of the golf association had voted unanimously to recommend that the USGA decline their application for approval. If the full body did that, not only would pros be prohibited from using the ball in competition – a ruling that they had always expected – but amateurs would be prohibited from using it in their tournaments as well. Basically, the ruling would discourage anyone from playing with the ball, even in friendly rounds with golf buddies.

The letter had come into the office just the previous Friday, which explained why George hadn't tried to contact her yet. He could well have been traveling or on vacation himself, and she expected that he was opening and reading the letter at about the same time as she was.

Her premonition was correct. Amanda buzzed her and announced that George was calling on her second line – the one with the phone number she gave out only to the most important partners and investors.

"George!"

"Lena! How was your time off?"

"Great. I guess you got the letter too?" Lena didn't waste any time getting to the point.

"Yup. We should meet. Can you find time today or are you too busy catching up?"

"Nothing more important than this, George." She saw no upside in bothering him with her big issues of the day — the hackers and Blake's demands. "Are you coming downtown or do you need me to come up there?"

"I'll be downtown for lunch, so how about I swing by about two o'clock?"

"Super. Who needs to come in with us?"

"At this point, let's just talk this over ourselves," George suggested. Lena was relieved. She wasn't ready yet for a big table discussion. She needed to think over their contingency plans and how those plans felt to her now that they had an official, if not final, USGA response.

Lena had way too much to do before she met George. She needed to get updates from her staff about fourth-quarter sales and earnings projections. She needed to meet with her PR and legal counsel to discuss what to do about the hacker incident. Routine business affairs that she had ignored over the three weeks she was on Christmas vacation begged for attention.

And she had to answer Blake's blistering e-mail.

Meanwhile, the regular weekly meeting with her direct reports was only a half-hour away, and she had replied to only half of the e-mails that Amanda had flagged as needing her immediate response.

As if she needed more stress, Ken darkened her office door with his laptop in his hand.

"May I come in?" he asked, walking into her office without waiting for an answer.

"Of course," Lena said, looking up from her overstuffed e-mail box and standing up to greet her systems tech. She felt her jaw stiffen; this was not likely to be a pleasant meeting. Meetings with Ken rarely were anymore, and the look on his face gave away his mood. It was ugly.

"We have a staff meeting in half an hour," Lena said, motioning at the same time for Ken to take a seat at her small conference table. "Are you sure you want to talk now, or do you want to wait? We'll have more time after the meeting."

"We've already waited long enough," Ken said gruffly. He sat down, opened his laptop, and focused on his computer screen as he addressed her. Lena was used to that behavior from her technology staff. They never joined a meeting without first opening their laptops in front of their faces. Lena thought it might be a prop – something those who struggled with interpersonal relationships could hide behind.

"Waited long enough?" Lena repeated Ken's words, forcing a low laugh. "You mean you've been waiting for my return? I didn't think you liked me that much!" She sat down at the table across from Ken with her coffee cup in front of her. The coffee was her prop; it gave her something to do with her hands when she got nervous.

"We have no time left to respond to the vulnerability," Ken answered flatly, rejecting her attempt at humor.

"You mean to the blackmailers."

Ken continued to click away on his computer as if any conversation with Lena – however serious the topic – wasn't taxing enough to adequately occupy his big brain. "Yes. We received five more e-mails over the holidays while you were out on vacation."

"And they still want us to pay them to not reveal the path into our credit card files?" Lena asked.

"Right. They will fix it for $250,000. That's not much money."

Lena looked at Ken, astonished. "Not much money? Do you realize that is pretty much our entire operating profit so far this year? Why would you say that's not much?" Lena shook her head. She put her hand to her forehead and looked at the ceiling, and continued. "Let me get this straight. This is simple blackmail, is it not?"

Lena knew that in Ken's world, Internet trickery was generally celebrated, whatever tack it took — whether breaking into classified government documents, causing big websites like Amazon's to crash, or breaking into corporate files that held customer credit card numbers. To Ken, hackers were just really smart guys who were showing the world who was the smartest of them all. By calling it blackmail, Lena was clearly not in his camp.

But the way he shrugged off a quarter-of-a-million dollars still surprised her. He knew enough about the company P&L to know it was a serious amount of money for the small start-up. Was there something else going on here? Was he thinking of how many ways that money would have to be divided among those involved in the hacking scheme? Maybe he knew more about these hackers than he was letting on.

Ken continued, undeterred by her reaction. "Regardless of what you call it, we haven't responded to them, and very soon, they're going to publish their finding that our credit card files can be breached."

"How soon?" Lena asked.

"Since we have taken so much time to accept their offer to fix the problem, they're ready to go to the bloggers with the story right away. The last e-mail came on Friday, and it wasn't a friendly message."

"Offer!" Lena exclaimed. "You honestly believe that's an offer? It's blackmail, Ken. Let's get that straight. Blackmail!"

"Well, still, the problem is we still haven't responded. You were gone for weeks."

Lena took a deep breath and tried to keep her voice from rising. "Okay, Ken, you have now mentioned my vacation four times," she said, feeling her face turn hot. "Let's get beyond that and talk about the problem."

"It might be too late to get beyond that." Ken finally looked up at her and smirked. "As CEO of this company, I would have thought you would have understood the urgency of this matter."

Lena was stunned. She was accustomed to fairly straight talk — sometimes bordering on insubordination — from her direct reports. In fact, she encouraged them to tell her what they thought. It kept problems, petty and big, from becoming subterranean subtexts that could disrupt smooth corporate operations. But Ken's comments were getting personal, moving well beyond simply questioning her judgment.

He took advantage of her stunned silence.

"Since you know so little about technology, software, cybersecurity … well, really anything, I don't expect you to understand how serious this is," he continued condescendingly. "So, let me -- "

"Stop right there!"

Lena slapped the table in front of her, making Ken jump.

She had let Ken set the agenda in this meeting so far. But Lena knew from her earliest days in business that whoever controlled the agenda controlled the meeting. She had to either get the upper hand, or she would continue to suffer his insults, and they'd get nowhere closer to solving the problem.

"There is no reason for ad hominin comments," she said, holding her hand out to mute him until she had a chance to reset the course of their discussion. He may have outweighed her by sixty pounds; he may be a man; he may be able to yell louder. But she was still the CEO, and she intended for him to respect that.

"I don't think – " Ken jumped in, ignoring her body language, but Lena stopped him again.

"No, I don't really want to know what you think right now," she said sternly. "I want to know what you have done to solve the problem."

"How could I do anything when I didn't know our strategy?"

"You are telling me you did nothing to locate the so-called vulnerability because you were waiting for someone else to tell you what to do?" Lena shook her head as if astonished by his answer.

"You don't understand," Ken retorted. "How could you? This is complicated. We tried -"

Lena cut him off again.

"Tried? Tried?" Lena threw her hands up in exasperation. "You are sitting here insulting me for not knowing as much as you do about code, codex, cyberspace, security

– whatever – and yet you are telling me that a bunch of thugs from outside our company hacked into your financial management system, a system you are supposed to have intimate knowledge of, and found a problem that you can't locate yourself?"

Lena could tell that Ken was surprised at her comeback. Did he expect her to let him continue to insult her without responding?

She took advantage of his silence this time. "You should remember that this company's business is not software development," she said. "We sell golf clothes to women online. Your software and Taylor's code are just tools to getting that done. So, don't give me any more of your condescension."

"The software at this company is key to what we do," Ken answered huffily, sticking his chin out over his laptop screen.

"Yes, Taylor's programs are," Lena agreed. "They are proprietary and they are the secret sauce that makes our site work for our customers. But yours are not. They're standard software packets from PeopleSoft. Your only job is to make sure it all works together and is secure enough to protect our customers. Don't be so full of yourself."

Lena got up from the conference table and walked back to her desk. She could hear Ken breathing through his teeth behind her.

"The real problem here," Lena said, sitting back in her desk chair, "is the damage to our business if news of this weakness in our security gets to our customers. Our attorneys say an actual breach is less likely than a PR attack. These guys will publicize our security issue to punish us for not paying them off.

"So, what we have is a PR problem created by a technology problem," she continued. She watched Ken. His fingers hovered over his keyboard. The clicking and typing had ceased, but he continued to stare at his laptop screen.

"I will work with legal and with Jordan's PR team to figure out what to do about the PR issue. You are responsible for the technology problem," Lena said. "Now, what I want you to do is go back to your office. You are not invited to today's staff meeting. I'm giving you thirty-six hours to find that vulnerability. I don't care how many of your guys have to work all night tonight and all day tomorrow. Figure it out!"

Lena picked up the receiver on her desk phone and punched a number into the keypad. Ken slapped his laptop closed and spun out of his chair. He left her office without a word.

"And Ken!" Lena called after him. "Don't bother calling Blake about this. I'm calling him myself right now."

Bounty

Lena was furious at Ken, and as soon as he was out of earshot, she put the receiver back down. She wasn't ready to call Blake, although she knew that she had to answer his e-mail soon. Ken was certainly going to disregard her admonition, and call his favorite VC. But she hoped he'd at least get his team working on the hacker problem first and give her some time to calm down and reach Blake before he did.

Leaving Ken out of the weekly staff meeting was as much of a punishment for his lack of respect as cutting his salary would have been. Not knowing what was going on with the other departments and not knowing what Lena was going to tell his co-workers about the hacker issue would sting. In a company as small as The Perfect Tee, politics weren't complicated: it was about knowing what was going on and never being surprised by something someone else knew that you didn't.

But now, Lena had another reason to start leaving him out of the loop: she suspected that he knew who the hackers were, and, worse yet, he might even be involved in their blackmail. To prove it would be difficult, and maybe, in the end unnecessary, but she was going to have to keep a very close eye on him. Her entire management team would have to be more circumspect about what corporate strategies and other secrets they shared with him.

Lena figured that however things turned out with the hackers, Ken had to go; he simply had no respect for her. Firing a manager as high on the corporate ladder as Ken was never cheap or easy, even if he didn't have an employment contract. Without proof that he was involved in the hacker scam, they would probably have to pay him a year's salary and benefits. And, if he left angry, it was hard to guess how much damage he could wreak on the company's technical infrastructure before he left – or even after he left, given his knowledge of their systems. But if she could make it uncomfortable for him to stay, he might decide to look for greener pastures at another company, and she wouldn't have the problem of what to do with him.

On the other hand, with Blake on Ken's side, it could be Lena that would be leaving soon. She shook off her anger as she walked to the meeting with the rest of her staff. It would do no good to give more of her senior staff reason to express doubts about her leadership to the VCs.

"Where's Ken?" Taylor asked as soon as Lena closed the conference room door to start her regular meeting with her direct reports.

"I've asked Ken to skip the meeting this morning," she said, sitting down and passing around the one-sheet agenda. "I might as well use that to start our first topic."

Lena briefly described the hacker threat to the group, although Taylor; Jordan; and her general counsel, Jerry, were all already aware of the issue. Lena kept to the facts, offering little opinion or analysis of the issue, hoping to keep the discussion to a minimum so they could move on to discuss the fourth-quarter results and progress on launching the new line of tennis clothes without the meeting stretching into the noon hour.

Luckily, the others were also interested in getting back to their desks and urgent projects rather than tearing apart the potential implications of the hacker. Possibly, they had seen these kinds of threats many times before in their experience at online companies, and knew they usually ended with a whimper, not a bang, for small companies like theirs. For once, it was nice not to be Target or Amazon.

The fourth-quarter news was better than expected, although John cautioned that the numbers were preliminary. Still, Lena looked forward to sharing those results with the VCs once they closed the books.

The rest of the meeting was short and pleasant, and when George showed up to discuss the golf-ball venture, Lena had regained her composure and confidence. She had managed to turn most of her unanswered e-mails over to Amanda, whose quiet competence was proving itself more and more valuable every day. Lena wondered if there was a promotion that would reward her adequately, and then wondered if Amanda even would want one. The best admins weren't necessarily in the role because they lacked skills or smarts to do other things. Many had chosen it because it employed their organizational and multi-tasking talents, and yet allowed them to avoid much of the corporate politics and the time commitment that didn't fit with their lifestyles.

Together, George and Lena called Dan at GTI, and they had a quick and uncomplicated discussion about the USGA letter. While the news wasn't positive, Lena was relieved that it didn't change anyone's position on the project. GTI had already decided that USGA approval had nothing to do with its business strategy. In fact, the official rejection might be helpful. It was consistent with their marketing statement: we're not the company for the pro. It was damn the torpedoes, full speed ahead.

Although the day didn't turn out as badly in the end as it had started, Lena was glad that Ryne was back in New York, working with his editors that evening. She spent the last minutes of her thirteen-hour day writing a short, composed e-mail response to Blake:

1) Ken is now finally on top of his investigation into the hacker findings and the solution to the vulnerability. He has promised a resolution in the next 36 hours.

Lena first had written "that Ken is now on top of" but backspaced over the "now" and changed it to "finally." She meant that after doing nothing, he was finally on the job, but she was sure Blake would think she meant "now that I'm back from goofing off." She edited out "finally." She would have liked to point out that Ken had done nothing for three weeks — at best, waiting around for instructions on the matter, even though he thought she knew nothing about cybersecurity. But that would only look like she was passing the buck, as Blake accused her of doing in his e-mail. It wouldn't help.

2) I am certain that I have the confidence and support of everyone on my senior team with the exception of Ken. If you feel it appropriate, please feel free to contact them and ask them yourself. I can have Amanda send you their direct lines and e-mail addresses.

She decided to acknowledge Ken's role in Blake's assessment up front. Feigning ignorance was not going to add to his confidence in her. She could have written much more, but all the things she thought about including came across as defensive. She closed by welcoming a meeting with the VCs soon.

By the time she turned off her light and locked her office door, she was exhausted, and when she was tired, Lena wasn't good company for anyone but a particularly sympathetic dog.

On the walk home to her condo, Lena stopped at the QFC and picked up a package of sushi for dinner. She tossed it in the refrigerator, changed into rain pants and her rain parka, and wrestled to put the doggie rain poncho over Bounty's shaggy coat. The rain and wind had both picked up before they reached the ground floor in the elevator and slipped out onto the wet street.

Although she wasn't fond of her raincoat, Bounty didn't mind the weather. She'd been cooped up all day in the condo, and happily jaunted down the street, stopping to read the "p-mail" on every light post and stop sign.

They dodged the deepest puddles and sloshed down the street to the park at the south end of Lake Union. They walked up to the big white museum that guarded the southern-most point of the lake, and turned left, abandoning the sidewalks and skirting the lake's steep bank on muddy grass. The ground would be soggy and slippery for at least the next four months. Bounty had grown up in both rainy, messy Seattle winters and dry, sunny Suncadia summers, and other than her dislike for the raincoat, she didn't seem to have a preference. As long as Lena let her wander and sniff as she wanted, Bounty trotted along happily.

They walked across a bridge over an inlet and turned again down the bank toward the lake. Lena let her off her leash, and Bounty trotted along ahead of her, nose-down, tracking ducks, raccoons, squirrels, and rats that made their homes around the lake edge.

Lena was startled by something moving under a sprawling tree above them on the bank, away from the lake. Bounty let out a short warning bark. The dark figure under the branches waved a friendly greeting, and Lena relaxed.

"It's okay, Bounty," she assured her dog, and the mutt moved on, sniffing the ground along the bank.

Backlit by the street lights in the distance, the dark silhouette laid a tarp on the ground and anchored its corners with plastic bags full of his possessions. As Bounty paused for a long investigation of a particularly interesting spot, Lena watched the man put down a layer of cardboard, reach into a big plastic bag for a lumpy sleeping bag and neatly tuck another tarp around it. As he busied himself, preparing his camp in the rainy night, he whistled a jaunty tune. Lena didn't recognize the melody; she guessed it was made up of randomly combined licks of long-remembered songs, if it had any source at all.

He sounded happy. Was he to be pitied for the lack of a roof over his head? Most likely he preferred this freedom and solitude over the noise and stench of one of the city's shelters, Lena guessed. But if it were Lena making that bed, the incessant rain, the cold wind, and the scary dark night alone in the park would add up to a certain hell.

On the other hand, that old man would probably find her day-to-day existence torture: reading logs of customer complaints, arguing with employees, sitting at an indoor desk under fluorescent lights, and taking orders and criticism from VCs who hold the purse strings. Or, as the cliché went: "working for the man."

Maybe she was naïve, or maybe she was evading responsibility for the fate of homeless people by imagining theirs as a choice. She had no way to know if it really was, and probably no one else did either.

Suddenly her mother's old saying – "you make your bed, you sleep in it" – took on a new depth of meaning. She had chosen to be a CEO – no one forced it on her. She had a warm and dry condo, a comfortable home in Suncadia, a smart and handsome boyfriend, a loving and healthy dog, and plenty of food in her refrigerator. Even if The Perfect Tee crashed under the weight of her mismanagement, she and Bounty would survive. Ryne would still love her. She could still play golf. She wouldn't be making her bed on a muddy Seattle lake bank on a rainy night in January.

That night, lulled to sleep by the patter of rain on the roof of her condo and spooning with her damp dog, Lena slept soundly.

THE NEXT MEETING WITH GTI in San Diego was only a week away, and Lena still had to compile the reports from all the teams working on the golf-ball project.. The only report she was waiting for was from Ray, the manufacturing SVP of GTI, who was supposed to be completing a detailed plan for the actual manufacturing of the radio-frequency enhanced ball.

True to her word to the VCs, Lena was working after regular business hours on the summary report for the meeting in San Diego. She had strictly limited the time she was spending on the golf-ball project to weekends and evenings, except for their monthly trip to GTI headquarters. As far as she was concerned, The Perfect Tee was not suffering from her split loyalties, even if her stamina was.

Lena took a break from her summary to compose an e-mail to Ray to beg for the manufacturing report, but when she opened her e-mail, she was surprised by a late-day e-mail from Ken.

"Vulnerability located and mitigated," the subject line read. At first, Lena thought it must be a note on his team's progress on finding and fixing the credit-card vulnerability discovered by the hacker, but then she realized it sounded too final for just a status report.

Why did he choose to send an e-mail rather than call her with the news? Or come down to her office? Everyone knew how late she worked in the office these days. Their relationship had deteriorated beyond repair. It was time for him to leave the company.

As she read through the brief and self-congratulatory e-mail from Ken, she felt relief spreading down her neck and through her shoulders. Of course, she knew the threat might not be entirely over. It was still likely the hackers would try to make news of the weakness in The Perfect Tee's credit card system as retaliation for not paying them to identify and fix it.

Still, whatever the hackers tried to make from the incident, the damage to the company was likely to be minimal, making her next meeting with the VCs much more pleasant. She could now work with the legal and HR teams to find a way to get Ken out of the company.

Changing gears, Lena wrote an e-mail to the VCs announcing Ken's success at patching the vulnerability in their credit card system, and using the occasion to propose a meeting before she left for San Diego the next week. By the time she sent the e-mail, it was nearly nine o'clock, and Lena picked up the phone to see if Ryne was still hanging out at her condo with Bounty. He had returned from New York that afternoon, and promised he'd come over with take out. He was still there with now-lukewarm Thai food.

"I've been waiting because I have something to show you," Ryne said. From the tone of his voice, it was clear that the "something" wasn't especially good.

"What?" Lena asked.

"Better you come home and read it for yourself," he answered. He sounded sober and worried. "I don't want to try to describe it for you."

"I'll be home in twenty minutes," Lena assured him, standing up to gather her purse and briefcase with the phone still at her ear. "And whatever it is, I have good news to tell you. Maybe it will make your news seem less bad. I'll tell you when I get there."

As soon as she let herself into her condo, Ryne handed Lena a beer and a printout of a blog one of his tech reporters had shown him that afternoon.

"CEO's Past May Cloud Golf-ball Venture" was the headline. It was a poorly written regurgitation of Kurt's murder trial, and the writer implied that her former marriage would jeopardize a golf-ball venture that The Perfect Tee, RF Inc. and GTI were pursuing.

As far as she knew, the blogger had not tried to reach

her to get a response, but his article indicated "Bettencourt was not available for comment." What? Had he tried to call her at two in the morning? She was always available for comment. She may have decided not to comment, but she certainly was available.

Obviously, the blog was sloppy journalism at best, and probably didn't even deserve the label "journalism," but in the day of more bloggers than real newspapers, Lena didn't find it terribly surprising.

"What I don't understand is why anyone would even think to write this," she said, sitting down at the breakfast bar.

Ryne shook his head in solidarity. "Honey, I don't – "

Lena interrupted. "Honey? Since when do you call me 'honey?' Don't be patronizing, Ryne. I need to think this through with you, not get your sympathy."

Ryne took a sip of his beer and said nothing. He watched Lena read the blog piece over again and lay it down on the counter.

"Do you know this blogger?" Lena asked. Ryne didn't answer. He looked slightly uncomfortable, as if he were afraid to say anything, and Lena regretted snapping at him.

"I'm not upset with you," she assured him, putting a hand on his knee. "I shouldn't have said that, but I want to think analytically about this. I'm not going to take it personally, because I'm sure it's not about me. It's about the golf-ball deal. Someone wants to taint it, although I think this is a pretty weak way to do it."

"You're right." Ryne nodded. "And no, I don't know the blogger. But I can have Jen look into it."

"Jen?"

"The tech reporter who showed me this," he said, dropping his sympathetic tone and adopting Lena's matter-of-fact one. "Actually, she left it on my desk before I got back from New York, so I didn't get to ask her about it. She follows these bloggers in case they ever come up with something that resembles news."

"So, Jen knows about us?"

"I guess she does," Ryne said. "I don't think anyone else at the paper does though."

Lena wasn't sure that was a good thing. Was he hiding their relationship just in case Kimberly decided to take another run at him? It seemed unlikely, but exhaustion and stress did strange things to the imagination.

Lena picked the article up again and re-read the paragraph about the golf-ball deal. "I don't know how this guy found out about the golf-ball," she mused. "And GTI. Who knew about GTI? Do you think it could have been one of my employees?"

"Or, it could have been one of George's," Ryne offered. "Maybe one of them feels left out of the venture and is getting even by leaking the story."

"Right." But Lena shook her head. "I have a feeling that there's something more nefarious going on here." She set the article down and slipped off the bar stool and walked to the big windows that looked over the blocks of warehouses, Amazon office buildings, restaurants, and bars six stories below.

The streetlights bounced in all directions off the wet streets and sidewalks, and pedestrians jumped over deep puddles along the curbs while dodging the waves of muddy water splashed up by cars and buses. The city had done a poor job of keeping up with the sudden traffic growth brought on by the migration of thousands of Amazon employees into the neighborhood. It would take years of disruptive road and sidewalk construction to catch up with the new reality, and meanwhile, the ugly dance of drivers and pedestrians would provide Lena and her neighbors with hours of mild entertainment.

"Why didn't the city plan ahead for this mess?" Lena wondered aloud, as Ryne stepped over Bounty to stand next to her. They looked out at the busy night scene for minutes, sipping their beer.

"I will see what I can find out tomorrow," Ryne said quietly. After their disagreement over Christmas regarding Kim, she was glad he was finding a way to help her with her stress.

"Thanks, sweetie," she said, turning and putting her arms around his waist.

"Sweetie? Since when do you call me sweetie?" Ryne pushed her back and laughed. Lena smiled and stood up on her tiptoes to kiss him.

"Touché!" she said. "I really don't mind being called honey, by the way. It just seemed so out of context."

"Okay honey," Ryne said, dropping his empty bottle in the recycling bin and picking up the dog leash. "I think we should take Bounty out for her walk and go to bed."

The VCs

The first thing Lena did when she got into the office the next morning was check the morning news summary of the Puget Sound Business Journal.

Lena trusted that the editor who put the summary together would recognize that the blog story about Kurt's murder conviction wasn't news. She had met Ben Miller back when he was a reporter for the paper, covering small business. He had written a story about The Perfect Tee, and they had gotten along well enough to become friends — the kind of hands-off, distant friends that business reporters and their subjects should be.

Luckily, either he hadn't seen the blog item, or he recognized it wasn't news.

Lena had been checking the PSBJ morning summary daily since the hackers had first made their threats back in December. So far, no news about that had surfaced either. She clicked through to the national news summary the Business Journals posted, as she usually did, and was surprised to find a story about Grocery Distributors of Idaho, Larry's company. Larry had sold his company to a national grocery chain, and the brief story quoted him saying he would be leaving day-to-day business management to seek out investments in retail and wholesale companies that could use his expertise.

"I already knew that," Lena mumbled to herself. Their golf-ball venture was apparently one of his first targets.

At ten o'clock, George arrived for their meeting with Lena's VCs. The meeting would be the first real test of the investors' interest in funding the golf-ball venture, but she didn't hold out much hope for a positive outcome. The VCs had turned most of their attention recently to investments in software applications and mobile-phone apps. Manufacturing — even manufacturing that involved a technological innovation like their trackable golf ball — was too old-school and too slow to return the kind of returns they could get investing in what might become the next hot app.

Lena expected the meeting to be difficult from the start, given her e-mail from Blake the week before. But the VCs welcomed George pleasantly. Perhaps, she thought, they wanted to keep the company's dirty laundry out of sight, and were saving their reproach for later in the meeting, after George left.

"What has the USGA said about the technology?" Blake asked, skipping past the possible technological and manufacturing questions he could have asked, and jumping right to the elephant in the room. The other three VCs sat back and allowed Blake, the most avid golfer of their group, to lead the discussion.

"We expect that they won't approve the ball for professional or amateur competitions," George answered, matter-of-factly. There was no reason to try to obfuscate. Lena was glad he didn't try.

"Have they said as much?" Blake continued. Lena wondered who was feeding him information, and once again suspected it might be someone at either George's company or hers.

"Not in final form," George said. "We received a preliminary letter indicating they are unlikely to approve it."

"So where do you go from there?" Blake asked.

Lena jumped in. "We are partnering with a company that believes that there is plenty of room for companies in the market who cater to those golfers who don't care," she said. She saw the other three VCs raise their eyebrows in surprise.

"No, really," she continued. "A vast majority of recreational golfers never even post a score, let alone play by the rules."

"Post?" the oldest VC, Kyle, asked. Apparently, he knew little about golf. Lena wondered how he ever decided to invest in The Perfect Tee in the first place.

"Record an official score and get an official handicap," George replied. Lena liked the way they were showing the VCs their partnership they'd formed.

"Have you heard anything about the concept of bifurcation?" Lena asked. Blake nodded and quickly filled in the other three VCs about the possibility of a separate set equipment rules for professional golfers and amateurs. "The pros are developing skills levels totally unattainable by weekend duffers, so the idea of the two groups playing by the same sets of rules seems ludicrous," he said. "There's even been talk of developing courses with larger holes for the average golfer who can't spend ten hours a week practicing putting."

Lena jumped back in as he finished. "GTI, our manufacturing partner, is developing a new brand of golf equipment and clothing that caters to the recreational golfer," she said. "This golf ball would be an entry in that market."

"Very interesting," Blake said, turning to the other VCs for their thoughts. Lena was pleased that he seemed willing to pursue the idea of a new product when she thought he had only been interested in an IPO and an exit. Maybe the problems he was having with his early IPOs on the East Coast had changed his mind.

"I think we should keep an open mind about it," agreed Doyle. "But I don't think we're in a place to make a commitment at this point."

"Nor do we expect one," George said. "We just wanted to get the conversation started."

George took his leave, and Lena's heart rate picked up. *Now, it gets nasty.* She kept her voice level and suggested they continue directly into the agenda she had distributed, which started with the audited financials for the fourth quarter. Revenues had risen 40 percent year-over-year, and rising marketing costs hadn't eaten up the gains. The VCs reviewed the numbers with few questions and then congratulated her on the good results. She quickly described the progress on the new clothing lines and the customer service upgrades they were building to support them.

Then she turned to the hacker threat. She gestured to Blake, offering him the chance to start the discussion. She wanted to get her beating over with as soon as possible. Blake took her by surprise by passing around a blog article written at the behest of the would-be blackmailers about the vulnerability. Lena hadn't seen it before.

"Where did this come from?" she asked. Bloggers were

becoming the bane of her existence. Didn't they have any real news to write about?

"Off the Internet," Blake answered, unhelpfully.

"How did you find it?"

"I follow many blogs," Blake said. "But actually, a source sent this to me this morning."

"Ken?" Lena postulated. It would be just the kind of thing her IT guy would do — inform the VCs before telling her about the post.

"I can't say." Blake shook his head. But he wouldn't look Lena directly in the eye, and she knew she was right.

"This website is pretty obscure, isn't it?" Lena asked.

"Probably," Blake said. "I expect that it won't garner much publicity for these hackers. I will follow up with my sources and find out who this 'Blackstone Financial Information Group' is. They've copied a pretty hefty financial brand name to cover their lack of substance, and I'm guessing that won't go over well with the real Blackstone."

Lena was surprised. Blake seemed cold, but he was not nearly as confrontational as she expected him to be, given the tenor of his e-mail the week before. She had expected something just short of a burning at the stake: blistering questioning about her leadership abilities, her lack of judgment, her paucity of experience with cybersecurity issues. Blake was not letting her off the hook, but he seemed downright restrained.

"The point I'd like to make is different," Doyle broke in. "We have a lot of expertise around this table about these kinds of things. Why didn't you come to us before this week to get some help with this?"

Here it goes. Lena let the VCs verbally beat up on her

for the next few minutes. There was no way she could excuse herself for not coming to them sooner without admitting that she'd simply avoided the entire hacker incident for three weeks over Christmas so that she could vacation in Palm Springs and Hawaii. Better to just take this one on the chin.

Once the fire had gone out of their discussion, which included much less input by Blake than she expected, Lena handed out copies of the blog post Ryne had discovered the day before. The VCs read it quickly and one-by-one, looked up, each shaking his head in disgust.

"This is incredibly cheap and stupid," summed up Nick.

"Agreed," Blake said, folding his copy of the post into a paper airplane and shooting it into a waste can in the corner of the meeting room. "I'm not even going to comment on it. This kind of stuff is inexcusable. Thanks for bringing it to our attention, but other than that, I think we don't have to spend any more time on this."

Lena sat in the meeting room after they left. She was shaking and relieved but also stunned. What had happened to Blake's crushing criticism? Where had the fire gone? Or was it still there, and he was staying cool before he dropped the bomb? If he were going to dismiss her, it would take more planning and preparation than he could manage in one week. She was too cautious and realistic to allow herself to imagine that her troubles with him were over.

WITH SO MANY ITEMS TAKEN off her list of worries in one day, Lena was feeling pretty good about herself when she packed up her briefcase and left the office early for the Chief Technology Officer of The Year awards reception sponsored by the Business Journal.

As CEO, Lena received hundreds of invitations for local business affairs, as well as hundreds of invitations to go to dinner with vendors and consultants who worked with The Perfect Tee. She disliked schmoozing, and she abhorred the boasting and posturing that constituted conversation at most business events. She turned down all but a handful of events a year. She guessed that this – among other things – made her different from highly successful CEOs, especially those who rose to manage Fortune 500 companies.

Lena made an exception for the CTO awards event because Jordan had nominated Taylor for the award as part of her PR strategy for the year. When Jordan couldn't attend the function, Lena agreed to go.

Of all the events she might have attended, however, this was probably the one where she felt the least comfortable. If you weren't an engineer – software, electrical, computer, network or other – you were in the smallest of minorities in the room. It wasn't just the CTOs who were techies, most of the CEOs who attended also had engineering, computer and technology degrees. Not only that, but 99 percent of them were men and more than three-quarters of them were younger than forty.

Lena stood in the corner of the hotel ballroom that was farthest from the bar so she could watch the crowd, hoping to pick out a familiar face. In the middle of the room, surrounded by men six to twelve inches taller, she wouldn't have been able to see anything.

Absent were CEOs or engineers from Seattle's heavyweight companies – Amazon, Expedia, Microsoft, and Zillow. They didn't need accolades from the local business press. The lesser lights like Blue Nile, RealNetworks, Outerwall, F5, PopCap, and Drugstore were the hot draws for the wannabe CTOs in the crowd. Maybe those young wannabes were creating the next Instagram, Lena thought, but mostly, they were developing apps, not companies. Products, not innovations. And the companies they worked for were more likely to be the next Pets.com than the next Google. Of course, most of those strutting their stuff that evening were too young to remember Pets.com.

Lena knew that the engineers in the crowd had no higher opinion of her than she did of them. Ken wasn't the only one who believed her lack of an engineering degree or code-writing experience amounted to a moral flaw. Her former CEO at TrueWeb had told her she couldn't succeed in management at a technology company without technology credentials. And Blake had belittled her in meeting after meeting with comments about technology issues she "couldn't understand."

Why, Lena wondered as she sipped her glass of cheap California cabernet in the corner, did she put herself in these kinds of uncomfortable settings? Once when she was working as the speech writer for Roger, the TrueWeb CEO, she accompanied him to Boston for an industry conference. One evening in the trip, they met an old family friend of Roger's at a classic seafood restaurant near Copley Square. The two men reminisced through the meal, recalling scrapes they'd had with their parents when they "summered" in the Hamptons, and scrapes they'd had with the law as undergraduates at Harvard. Lena could barely understand the vocabulary the two men used, let alone identify with their childhoods and adolescences.

She had felt as out of place that night as she did at CTO awards.

Lena scanned the audience for Taylor. If he had decided not to come, she could sneak out early and no one would know the difference. She finally recognized him in a clutch of fellow Stanford graduates who had gathered under a school banner along one wall to catch up on gossip and news about their classmates. She stared at him for a couple of minutes, hoping to catch his eye for a quick nod. If he knew she had shown up, he'd probably forgive her for skipping out before the awards were handed out.

"Hey there!" Lena jumped at the sound of Jim's voice. She hadn't seen him approach, a glass of brown liquid and ice in hand.

"Jim," she stated, matter-of-factly and diplomatically, sticking out her hand for a shake. "I didn't know you'd be here. Do you know one of the nominees? Maybe the winner?"

"No," he shook his head. "Do you know who won?"

"Yeah, they published the list on the web this afternoon," Lena said, continuing to try to catch Taylor's eye. She had even more reasons to join him now that Jim had shown up. "It lets the winners know so that they come. Nothing more embarrassing than giving out awards to people who don't show up."

"Makes sense," Jim said. "No, I'm here trolling for investment ideas." Lena looked up at the former banker. He was dressed as if he were trying to look like a techie. Instead of banker attire, he wore a button-down oxford shirt without a tie, pleated khaki pants, and loafers. He still didn't look like he fit in.

"You know," he said, "Larry and I have joined together to form a little angel investing firm."

"No, I didn't know," she lied. Had he forgotten the two men had approached her about a joint investment in the golf-ball venture at her birthday party? Were they going to make another run for the golf-ball project?

Jim answered her thoughts. "We're still interested in your golf ball, you know."

Lena looked away and rolled her eyes. She was never going to get rid of this guy, was she?

"I am guessing," Jim continued, lowering his voice, "that it's going to be harder for you to attract other investors now that the story is out. Maybe it's time to talk with us."

"What?" Lena focused on keeping her voice low when she wanted to scream. "What story?"

"The one about you and Kurt," Jim said, a smirk crawling across his lips.

How could he even know about that? Then, it hit her. He had leaked the story to the blogger. Just how low would this guy go to get even with her for rejecting his pass?

"Did you have something to do with that?" Lena asked. "Did you hire that blogger?"

"Why would you even suggest such a thing?" Jim stepped back, pretending he'd just been literally slapped.

"Well, that writer doesn't have much of a following," Lena pointed out. She hadn't had a chance to find out if Ryne had any new intelligence on the blogger, but she had checked to see that none of her executives had ever heard of him. "I'm surprised you saw it."

"I read everything that mentions you," Jim said smugly.

Lena wondered if he meant that as a threat or if it just felt like one.

"Well, there was nothing new in that article that hasn't been a matter of public record for some time," she said, angrily. "Except for the innuendo, of course."

"Right, but it might change some investors' minds," he said, gesturing with his drink as if pointing out an obvious fact that she had missed. "Might it not?"

You wish, Lena thought. She couldn't stand there and listen to him anymore. Even if it meant diving into the crowd of engineers, she had to get away from him before she lost her temper. She looked back at the gaggle of Stanford alums where Taylor had stood. He had apparently moved on.

"I need to go find my CTO," Lena said, ducking Jim's attempt to shake her hand in parting. She slipped around him and slid into the sea of young men.

The Times

The next day, Lena answered her desk phone to hear a reporter named Mandy introduce herself as a writer for the New York Times.

Executives who have never worked in the media get excited when the New York Times or the Wall Street Journal calls. Free publicity, they think. Finally, someone has noticed how great we are!

But Lena knew better. A front-page story in either paper was more likely to point out a scandal, scam, or business failure than it was to laud a company on its success.

"What is this about?" she asked, cautiously, trying to keep her voice neutral. While she wasn't naïve enough to think the reporter had called to write a puff-piece about The Perfect Tee, neither did she want to convey a reluctance to talk. That could be a signal that she had something to hide or the company had something to worry about. Lena's past as a newspaper reporter sometimes made dealing with the press harder, not easier.

"I'm working on a story about hackers," the reporter said, bluntly. Lena appreciated the fact that the woman wasn't beating around the bush or leading her on. "I saw a blog post about a vulnerability in your credit card system."

"Yes, we have discovered the issue and fixed it," Lena said matter-of-factly, hoping she could cut off the reporter's interest while at the same time knowing that was unlikely.

"Good. Great news," Mandy said. "But I'm trying to get to the bottom of something I've recently heard about, and I wondered if you had experienced it."

"What's that?" Lena asked, now as curious as she was cautious.

"A lot of these hackers appear to discover what they call vulnerabilities and then blackmail the companies into paying them for fixes."

Lena wasn't surprised that the reporter had hit the tactic right on. In her experience, good reporters at the Wall Street Journal, the Washington Post, and the Times figured out what was going on in spite of companies' refusal to talk about things. They picked up on trends by reading anything and everything they could about the industries they covered, including obscure blogs and industry trade rags.

"What makes you think that happened to us?" Lena asked.

"Well, I don't know if it did," Mandy said. "But I'm looking for examples of companies that have experienced this."

"I imagine that it's hard to find anyone who wants to talk about it," Lena said, sympathetically. She had worked as a reporter long enough to know how frustrating it was to get companies to go on the record about things they wanted to sweep under the rug. Airlines didn't want to talk about innovations in flight safety because it only focused attention on the possibility of accidents. Online retailers didn't want to talk about Internet scams because it focused attention on potential security breaches. Credit card companies didn't want to discuss identity theft, and so on.

"Yeah," Mandy said, perhaps sensing a sympathetic ear. "No one wants to piss these hackers off, I'm guessing."

"I'm sure you're right." Lena nodded at the phone. She paused. She needed to balance her sympathy for Mandy's story line with The Perfect Tee's need to stay as far away from being connected to security breaches as possible. No good could come from her customers thinking their identity had ever been jeopardized by her company. Or from re-igniting Blake's anger by making headlines.

"Look," Mandy continued. "I know your instinct is to avoid the subject as much as possible. But I looked you up. I know your background as a reporter. I would like you to think about the good that you could do helping me with this story."

Lena laughed. Mandy was good. It would be easy for Lena to get sucked into cooperating with a reporter like that. She'd suckered others into working with her on stories the same way, back when she was a reporter at the Denver paper. A little flattery. A little helplessness.

But she and Jordan had agreed. The only response they would give to the media about the hacker issue would be "it's fixed," and "no credit card numbers were acquired by hackers."

Still, perhaps this was her opportunity to get even with those blackmailers. And maybe get even with all those techies out there that worshipped them as well. Perhaps she could figure out a way to participate in the story and still keep the company's nose clean. She wanted time to think about it, time to weigh the ramifications of taking such a risk. She wanted to talk with Ryne and Jordan. They'd have totally different perspectives, but they'd both be valuable.

"Look," Lena said, slowly. "I can't say what our experience was, but let me think about this."

"I promise — " Mandy started to respond.

Lena cut her off. "No, don't promise anything. I know your obligation is to your readers, not to me. Don't promise me something you won't be able to keep if the story goes in a direction you don't expect."

"You're right," Mandy said. "I really don't know where this could go."

"Then let me think about it," Lena said. "I'm not saying we have anything to contribute to the story other than to say that we had a vulnerability that we fixed and no credit card information was breached."

"Understood," Mandy said, but Lena could hear the optimism in her voice. "Can I call you back tomorrow?"

LENA WALKED TO JORDAN'S OFFICE right after she hung up with Mandy.

"I don't think this is a good idea," Jordan said, shaking her head vehemently. "You were a reporter long enough to know that there's no good that can come of this."

"I know. I know." Lena slumped in Jordan's visitor's chair. "But I just think there might be some merit in doing this."

"What merit? Tainting the company's reputation in the Times has no merit whatsoever!" Jordan was adamant, and Lena could understand her conviction. No matter how sure you were that a story could be tilted in your favor, the reporter had final control. Lena knew that. Even if you believed you could use the bully pulpit of the Times or the Journal to your advantage, chances are you would become the victim, not the hero of the tale.

"Okay, just stop for a minute and think about this," Lena said, holding up her palms to stop Jordan's expected response. "Imagine that we could do something for the entire industry by showing what jerks these hackers are."

"Unlikely," Jordan said. "You know that. Unlikely."

"Right. But I wonder," Lena said, staring into space past Jordan as she thought about a possible strategy. "I don't know this reporter very well. She covers banking, not online retail. But I had a good feeling about her. Let's look into her background and see what she's written before we decide."

"I'll have someone start on that," Jordan acquiesced. "But I still don't think this is a good idea. Whatever we find."

Lena sat back. Be honest with yourself, she thought. Are you motivated more by doing good or by bringing someone down? Are you interested in making online retail safe or do you want to get even with these software guys who demean you for your lack of technology credentials? Are you seeing this as a way to get even with Ken — and maybe even Blake — for doubting your leadership?

Yes, she admitted. All the above. Why couldn't she accomplish them all? If she had made the world safe for democracy and raised America's stature at the same time, she's Woodrow Wilson in 1921, right? But, at stake would be her job, not just her reputation. If this didn't work, she would certainly be fired.

"What I'm thinking is this," she said, shifting her focus from the horizon to Jordan. "I'm thinking we could not only 'out' these blackmailers, but we could enhance The Perfect Tee's reputation as a forward-looking place to work, a confident company. And given the change I'm anticipating in our IT leadership, I think that would help us recruit some great talent."

Slowly, Jordan relented.

Now that the hackers had posted their news of the "vulnerability" on the blog, Lena had something she didn't have before: some information that could help to identify the blackmailers, however difficult it may be to track the evidence down. They had to trust that Mandy would use the resources of the Times to figure out who these people were and what other threats they'd made in the past. Ken might have been able to use his connections to help Mandy identify the culprits, but she didn't trust him.

"The biggest risk, I think, is that the hacker community at large will be so pissed at us that we'll be attacked again," Lena said, thinking out loud as they concluded their strategizing. "What if they launch a denial of service attack?"

"Possible," Jordan said. "I suppose we'd better plan ahead for that, too."

IT WAS THE END OF February, and Lena hadn't been up to Roslyn since she returned from Hawaii after Christmas. The hacker threat, the fourth-quarter reporting, the golf-ball venture, Bounty, Ryne, and the blogger stories had all soaked up whatever time she had left after managing the day-to-day business at The Perfect Tee.

Besides, it was one of those winters when getting up and over Snoqualmie Pass to Suncadia was risky. It seemed to snow every Friday, and even when the pass was open, there was no assurance it would be open on Sunday night when she had to get back to Seattle. And golf at Suncadia was still months away.

As a result, Lena felt estranged from Terry. Their weekly phone calls seemed superficial, in part because Lena and Ryne had decided not to tell Terry that they'd seen Tom with another woman at the Brick.

Finally, the two friends talked on a Sunday afternoon.

"I'm going to try again," Terry said. "I really do want to make this marriage work."

Lena paused. It was hard to put much credence in any of Terry's vacillating decisions about Tom. But if she really did want to save her marriage, it would be more difficult to tell Terry about Tom's behavior at the Brick. Harder, but perhaps necessary.

"What happened? Why the change in heart?" Lena didn't want to discourage, but neither did she want her friend to spend another six months in a futile battle with a philanderer.

"Maybe it's winter," Terry conceded. "I hate these cold, snowed-in days. It would be so much better to have someone else here warming up the cabin nine months of the year."

"What about the other three months?" Lena laughed. "I don't know if you can just send him away when the weather warms up."

Terry agreed and laughed, too. "But you know what I mean. It's just damn lonely around here. Especially without Rex."

Maybe getting another dog would be easier, Lena wanted to suggest. But she decided to skip the cynicism and be supportive. It sounded like Terry really needed it.

"I hope you can make it happen," Lena said, sincerely.

The conversation, coming as it did on another rainy, dark weekend in Seattle, was anything but inspirational. The dark, dreary winter months stretched longer than usual for Lena, as she found little time to get away from the office, and even when she did, she didn't get away from its worries. Hackers, bloggers, Blake, Ken, Jim, Larry – they all added up to one big pain in the ass. On top of that, she hadn't heard from Carly and Brandt for more than a month, and she was afraid that the accident in Hawaii had cemented Brandt's opinion of her as a klutz, a jabbermouth, and a pain in the ass.

Lena wanted to escape to Palm Springs again – at least for a weekend, but it wasn't possible. Many nights, sleeping alone because she hadn't managed to get home in time to be with Ryne or Bounty, Lena considered the high cost of her decision to take the CEO job and her quest to prove that she was capable in a way that so many people – mostly men – had doubted. The rare nights when Bounty was there, her angel-dog exhibited the stress of her long absences and the lack of escapes to the woods of Suncadia. She was anxious and gaining weight. After their infrequent walks in the neighborhood, instead of sitting down and napping, Bounty paced and whined.

"Hey!" Ryne interrupted their walk one night with a phone call. "I have found out who that blogger was. You won't believe it."

"Oh, I don't know," Lena said wearily. "I would probably believe anything these days, especially if it's bad news."

"Well, it is, and it isn't," Ryne said. "It depends on what you want to do with the information."

"So?"

"So, he was a low-level banking reporter at the Post Intelligencer," Ryne said. "He was laid off when the paper quit printing."

"Yeah, lots of them were."

Ryne snorted. "Horrid profession I'm in, isn't it? Who knows when I'm next?" He continued. "I had our librarian see if there was a connection between the blogger and that fellow Jim by looking through old Intelligencer articles in the archives. This guy quoted Jim a lot. It isn't much of a stretch to conclude that Jim tipped the guy off to the story."

"Right," Lena said. The news didn't surprise her at all. "I'll bet he even paid the blogger to write it."

Lena thought for days about what to do with that information. She talked with Ryne about it again. She talked with Jordan. Finally, she decided she had nothing to lose by making a phone call.

"Lena! I'm so happy to hear from you," Larry said as he answered the phone. Apparently, he had her phone number in his cell phone, and caller ID had identified her as the caller.

Calling Larry had its risks, but in retrospect, she decided that Larry's come-on on the plane was less creepy than Jim's apparently vindictive pursuit. And he was at least a nominally religious man, she reasoned. Certainly, he had the scruples to keep his business dealings honest and above board.

"Have you decided to talk to us about the golf-ball venture?" Larry asked, expectantly.

"No, that's not why I'm calling, Larry," Lena said, trying to sound as sober and serious as possible. "I want to talk about Jim."

Larry said nothing. She could imagine that he was trying to figure out where Lena was headed.

Lena waited. Finally, she continued. "I am worried about his intentions, Larry," she said. By repeating his name, she hoped to communicate the confidence she had in him.

"What do you mean?"

Lena explained the blog post and the connection between Jim and the former banking reporter. She relayed the number of times she'd run into Jim since he had made a pass at her three years ago, and how he never seemed to get beyond her rejection.

"You, however, were a gentleman," Lena said, softening her take on the story of their first meeting. "I never felt any inappropriate intentions, any inappropriate behavior from you when I told you we couldn't have a relationship. I appreciated that."

Lena waited for Larry to process that new version of their meeting on the plane. He would either believe that she was, indeed, sanguine with their interaction, or he would believe that she was willing to let the past be the past. Either way, he might think that she would drop her opposition to his investment in the golf ball measure if she was no longer upset by it.

"Well, of course," he said, after a long pause. "I am not a Neanderthal. I know that no means no, these days."

"But, apparently, Jim can't let things go. At least, that's why I think he's tried to smear my reputation with this blog post."

"You really believe that was his doing?"

"I can't prove it, but I do believe it."

"What do you want me to do?"

"I am hoping that perhaps you can find out for me," Lena said. "Can you help him see that this is not helping any possible future of us all working together?" Of course, what she hoped to accomplish was that never having to work with Jim at all.

"Can you send me a link to the blog?" Larry asked. "I haven't seen it myself. And then, I'll think about this. I really don't want us to be a thorn in your side. I really want to see if we can help you make this golf ball work."

Lena didn't know whether she could trust Larry completely, but she was convinced she could trust him more than she could trust Jim. She thanked him, and hung up.

It wasn't but a minute before her phone rang again. She looked at the caller ID panel to be sure it wasn't Larry. She wanted him to think things over before they talked again. She didn't want him to have a chance to change his mind about talking with Jim.

But the caller was Terry, not Larry, and Lena picked up the phone, relieved.

"Hey girlfriend!" she greeted Terry.

Silence.

"Terry, are you there?" Finally, Lena heard her friend sob. "Are you okay?"

"How could you?" Terry blurted. "Why didn't you tell me?"

Lena immediately knew what Terry meant, but she pretended not to.

"What? Not tell you what?"

"I know about Tom and that slut he's been hanging out with, and now I find out that you were there at the Brick that night when everyone else in town found out."

"What are you talking about?"

"Janet told me. She told me yesterday." Terry was crying. She sniffled and continued. "She said you were there. She didn't know why you didn't tell me. Me either. Why didn't you tell me?"

Lena leaned forward and rested her forehead on her desk. Why did these girl-boy problems always revert to high-school-like blow-ups? At fifty, weren't they beyond this? And, if Janet knew, why didn't she tell Terry earlier? Why was Lena the one to blame?

"You betrayed me, Lena," Terry sniffed. "I thought I could trust you. I don't know why you always cover for him. I'm beginning to think that staying together with him means more to you than it does to me."

Terry rambled on for a few more minutes and then abruptly hung up. She was drinking her way through this break-up in the same way she had so many others, Lena realized. Still, it bothered her that one more friendship she considered precious was endangered. Brandt and Carly were no longer talking with her. Kim had not called since he left her condo the night he ran into Ryne. Other than Ryne, who did she have left?

Well, Bounty. Thank god for Bounty.

Golf Again

Finally, the golf season at Suncadia started, but with a whimper. Golf in the middle of April was always a bit dicey on the east side of the Cascades. But Tina had called in the middle of the week to propose that they play the first weekend Rope Rider was open, getting a head start on George, who was in New York on a business trip.

After a stressful winter and a rainy, dreary start to spring in Seattle, Lena was willing to make the effort to christen spring with a round of golf on Rope Rider. She still preferred Prospector, but it would be another three weeks before that course would open, and Tina was as eager to get out and swing the club on an actual course as Lena was.

Lena hadn't played with Tina for months, not since October. The last time they'd teed up at Tumble Creek, Tina was rusty, even though her game showed promise. But over the winter, she'd taken lessons and spent hours on the driving range at Interbay in Seattle, a golf facility more known for its instructional staff than for its par-three course. She'd improved and it was clear that she was excited to show Lena the results of her hard work.

Lena had hoped that they would have Ryne's company for what turned out to be a soggy round, but he was back in New York as well, combing over the final galley proofs of his novel at Knopf. Terry was still sulking about Lena's failure to tell her about Tom's infidelity. She was a fair-weather golfer anyway, and on the Saturday that Rope Rider opened, the wind blew freezing rain sideways from the northwest, keeping Carly and Brandt at home in Seattle.

Lena and Tina gave up after nine holes, and decided to toast the new golf season in warmth with a glass of wine. Sitting on the hearth in front of the big fireplace in the living room of the winery, they warmed their backsides and drew their fingers through their hair to encourage the wet strands to dry.

"Nasty out there," Tina summed up the half-round. "Why do we do these things?"

"Still beats the best day at work," Lena mused. "At least it has seemed that way this spring."

"Yeah, George has told me about some of your battles," Tina said, sympathetically. "I think you are very strong to do what you do. I couldn't begin to manage it all."

Lena lifted her glass to acknowledge the compliment. "Well, it's not curing cancer," she said. "I am still just selling golf clothes."

Tina bumped shoulders with Lena. She leaned forward, elbows on her knees and stared into her glass of wine. She sighed deeply.

"What's the matter?" Lena asked, leaning forward as well to look over at her friend.

"I'm sorry, but I'm wondering how things are going with you and Ryne. George never mentions anything about your personal life." Tina looked sad.

Lena suddenly suspected that she needed quickly to

protect her heterosexual credentials. Tina's clingy behavior last fall flashed before her eyes.

"Well. Really well. It's probably the best relationship I've ever had in my life," Lena said enthusiastically.

Tina continued to stare at her wine glass, but her face dropped. She could only look so forlorn for one reason, thought Lena. It was flattering that Tina was attracted to her, but, even more, it was unsettling. God, friendships were complicated. And why did so many of them get tangled up with sexual tension? She and Jim? She and Larry? She and Kim? Was the Marquis de Sade right that all relationships were sexual?

Given the problems she had with Brandt, Carly, Kim, Jim, Larry, and Terry, Lena hoped that George wasn't next on the list. What if he got a hint that Tina was interested in Lena?

"Look," Lena said. "I don't want to mislead you or jeopardize our friendship."

"No, I get it," Tina said, interrupting her. "You don't have to spell it out for me."

Lena looked over and they locked eyes. "Thanks," Lena said. "I appreciate that. I have had so much stress in my life in the past year, I really could use a friend without complications."

"It's not your fault," Tina said, straightening up and looking over the big stone-lined room. Lena followed her gaze. Couples lounged in the leather loveseats, heads together and arms lazily draped over each other's shoulders. The bar stools in the corner were similarly populated with couples, engrossed in conversation.

"Is this something new for you?" Lena asked. She

wasn't sure if Tina would want to talk about her feelings with someone who just rebuffed her.

"No." Tina sighed. She sat her wine glass down on the hearth beside her, and fingered her wedding ring. "George was actually my first heterosexual relationship. I met him skiing right before I turned thirty. I thought it was time to grow up and act like a normal adult. But it's been a struggle ever since."

"God, I'm sorry," Lena said, and then immediately wondered if she had said the wrong thing. She meant she was sorry that things were a struggle, not that George was the anomaly in Tina's love life. She didn't mean to say she was sorry that Tina had feelings for women.

Here it was, well into the twenty-first century, and these conversations were still awkward. Perhaps Lena was limiting her social group too much. Maybe this was easier for most people; certainly it was easier for younger generations who grew up with more overt diversity.

"Well, it's not your issue," Tina said, faking a chuckle. "It's mine. But I'm still glad I told you. And, really, I am glad that you and Ryne are doing well. If I were attracted to men, he'd be near the top of my list too."

Lena smiled. Perhaps this friendship was salvageable after all. Perhaps all of them were. It just took a little understanding, a little empathy, and patience.

"Another glass of wine?" she asked, and she was pleased when Tina said yes.

LENA RETURNED TO WORK ON Monday feeling like she was staring into an abyss. Nice weather at Suncadia was still two months away, at least, and her next golf vacation was likely at least a year away. What stretched out before her was work, work, work.

Sitting at her desk, putting off opening her inbox and looking at her calendar for the day's meetings, she tried to cheer herself up by looking at the big picture. The big picture was not the day-to-day hassles of HR issues, legal issues, and meddling would-be investors. It wasn't the long days and spoiled weekends. It wasn't canceled dinner dates and truncated walks with Bounty.

The big picture was still pretty compelling. The way GTI wanted to approach the product presented a fascinating marketing challenge — how to create an entirely new niche, a category of golf products aimed only at the weekend duffer. The big picture was turning The Perfect Tee into a powerhouse of a women's athletic wear retailer, not just a golf clothing site. The big picture was looking back in two, three, or four years and seeing that they'd made something happen.

Rise above it! Lena commanded herself, sitting up straight in her chair and pounding both fists on her desk.

This was the kind of perseverance and fortitude that made for successful CEOs. If she wanted to be able to walk away, to spend her days playing golf, to travel to Europe and New Zealand with Ryne, to walk for unfettered hours in the woods with Bounty, she needed first to succeed at this job.

Now, how to do it?

Unfortunately, Lena realized, slumping a bit, it started by opening her inbox and getting through her e-mails. Unfortunately, it meant being sharp at the six meetings she had scheduled with her staff that day.

She pulled her laptop out of her messenger bag, snapped it into her docking station and pushed the "on" button.

Two hours later, Blake called unexpectedly. "Can you meet?" he asked. "I'm in the neighborhood."

Lena cringed. "What's this about, Blake?" she asked. "I have a really busy day."

"It won't take long," he assured her. "But I do think it would be good for us to talk before you guys head to San Diego next week to talk with GTI."

To relieve a bit of the potential tension, Lena suggested a neutral location, the Starbucks in her office building. She was encouraged that Blake didn't argue; whatever he wanted to talk about, it couldn't be horrible if he was willing to talk about it in a public setting like that. She probably wasn't going to get fired in Starbucks.

When Lena pushed through the Starbucks door and looked around, she didn't see Blake. She stood in the short afternoon line and ordered a decaf-double-tall-non-fat-extra-hot-no-foam latte, a drink that might have tied the tongue of the uninitiated, but didn't come close to intimidating the barista. Living in Seattle mandated learning the coffee vernacular, even if you were anti-Starbucks. Every coffee shop knew the language, whether Starbucks, Peet's, Tully's, Cherry Street, or no-name.

Blake burst through the door just as she was sitting down at a window seat with her latte.

"Hey, am I late?" he asked. "I'll be right back." He headed toward the counter to get a drink. He returned only seconds later with a plain drip coffee. She was jealous. She couldn't drink coffee in the afternoon without losing an entire night's sleep.

"Lena, I think we have some patching up to do," Blake started before even sitting down. It was certainly not the start she had expected. She had expected that it would probably start with some announcement that he was "again" "disappointed" with "something" he'd "found out about" — most likely from Ken.

Lena waited to hear more.

"This is the bottom line," Blake said, fairly rushing into his narrative. "I've been pretty harsh with you, and I think part of that has had to do with some issues I've had with other investments."

Lena started to wave off his apology, as she had learned to do over decades of working for jerks who resented having to say they were sorry about anything, but Blake held up his hand to stop her.

"Also, I was too eager to respond to a group of your employees who were itching for an IPO, and who came to me last fall to see if I would support that," Blake said. "Bottom line: it was a mistake."

"Why are you telling me this?" Lena asked, failing to mask the suspicion in her voice. Not only was his apology unexpected, it was unbelievable that Blake was being this straightforward and diffident. "What's going on?"

"Okay, let me explain," Blake said, slowing down and settling into the pillows on the window seat like he knew it might take some time to say what he wanted to say.

"I know Ken has been causing you plenty of headaches," Blake continued. "He was working hard to get me to accept an early public offering, and I know you knew that. He also was agitating inside and had quite a following."

"I knew that," Lena concurred. Actually, she knew he

and Blake had talked about pushing for an early IPO, but she didn't know he'd gathered a group of employees who were aligned with them. Was this another failure of hers — being clueless about employee cliques?

"Well, I've learned a lesson, an important one," Blake said. "I no longer support an IPO for a company with less than about $300 million in revenue. I've seen what happens when such tiny companies try to attract Wall Street interest. I've learned that patience is a virtue."

"Good," Lena said. "I'm 100 percent in agreement."

"Well, that's not all." Blake stopped, and took a long sip of coffee. He looked sad, like he didn't want to continue, but like he felt that he had to finish what he started.

"I know you don't have the contacts I and the other VCs have in this community," he said.

"Community? You mean Seattle?"

"No, I mean tech."

"Oh. No, you're right. I don't." Lena couldn't imagine where he was going with his story. Another examination of her tech short-comings?

"Well, I've held that against you at times, your lack of technology skills, expertise."

"Yes, I know. I feel it every day. But not just from you."

"We are a pretty cliquish lot." Blake finally smiled. "You'd think after being bullied as nerds our whole lives, we'd be better at empathy."

"Yeah. Maybe." Lena couldn't deny her assent.

"You don't have to be so quick to agree!" Blake laughed. Lena had never seen him like this before. He seemed positively human!

"So, what is this about?"

Blake paused again, and Lena watched him take in the Starbucks ambiance. He was strikingly handsome, she realized. Perhaps she hadn't noticed it before because their relationship had been so tense. Maybe his new, more human demeanor softened his jaw and allowed his better attributes to show through.

She followed his gaze. The lucky homeless man in the far corner, who had somehow gathered enough dimes on the street that day to enjoy a cup of joe and a warm corner. The Hispanic nanny at the table with the baby in the stroller, speaking Spanish to her charge, reveling in the attention and innocence of the infant. The disaffected, cynical frowns of the pre-teen girls sitting together at the high bar in the middle of the store, ignoring each other in their lace tops and quilted down jackets, heads down, texting.

Was this money man, this egotistical, self-aggrandizing elitist looking around and seeing something universal in the human experience as she watched?

Probably not. But for the first time, she saw him as a fellow earthling, not as a cyborg waiting for input from his algorithms and flow charts. It was the first time she saw him in the real world, outside of his engineered environment, sitting in a coffee shop and seeing — actually seeing — people who weren't controlled, couldn't be programmed, shouldn't be calibrated. Maybe she had been a little judgmental too. But then, he'd given her plenty of sleepless nights.

"So, I had to be the one to tell you," Blake finally continued. "I've been your hardest critic, at least on the VC team, and so I owe this to you."

"What?" Enough prologue, already. This was a man

who always cut to the chase, always said what he thought without a filter. Now he was beating around the bush.

"Ken. He was working with the hackers who tried to blackmail us."

Lena blinked and sat her latte down so hard that some foam popped out of the hole in the lid. She was stunned.

It wasn't that she hadn't suspected Ken. But it still came as a shock. How could he betray the very people he worked with, day in and day out? The very people who put their faith in his talents and his leadership?

"Are you sure?" Lena closed her eyes and cupped her face in her hands.

"Yes. Ken will be gone when you get back to the office. That's why I had to meet with you right away," Blake said. "I worked with Jerry on it over the weekend."

Lena hadn't seen Jerry, her general counsel, for about a week. She had no idea he had been working on this with Blake. She started to get pissed that she'd been left out of this very important decision about a key employee. But, she was too tired of Ken and the problems he had caused to not approve of Blake's actions, even if it seemed that he had gone over her head to do it. She paused to let her relief catch up with her anger and then extinguish it.

"How did you find out?" Lena finally asked.

"Once the hackers issued the press release, I noticed a lot of coincidences. Three of those in the group that purported to be 'helping' protect consumers" – Blake made air quotes around "helping" – "were classmates in Ken's UW graduating class. They were all consumer science majors, and they all stood up for each other in their weddings."

Blake stopped a minute to chuckle at a private joke. He

shook his head. "How any of those guys ever got married is still a mystery to me."

"You knew them?"

"Yes, I was the teaching assistant for a couple of the math classes they took. That's why I supported Ken when he applied for the job at The Perfect Tee."

Blake scrunched up his empty coffee cup. "It's sad about Ken, you know. He was truly talented. The other three" – he shook his head again – "well, they could write code, but they always seemed to be looking for a way to make something out of nothing. Hit the jackpot. Get somewhere without really working for it. HP without the garage. Bezos without the old door for a desk."

"But how did you know Ken was involved?" she asked. "Surely, those other guys know lots of other people."

"Yes, but the connection to The Perfect Tee led to only Ken. No one else."

"True. But are these always inside jobs?"

"Not always. But often," Blake explained. "It's a dirty little secret. Sometimes entry is made through a vendor who has network access, like an Internet-based climate-control system. But many of these hackers have insiders who help open doors for them. Sure, hacking is not brain surgery, but it's a lot easier if you have a few helpful hints to use as short cuts. Like passwords."

"I thought they just by-passed passwords."

"Yes, they can. But again, it's a lot faster if you can just get some help from the inside."

"So, how did you confirm this? Can you prove it?"

"Unfortunately, yes," Blake said. "And it wasn't very hard. I called Ken and asked him to meet me at my office.

He showed up with a guy he introduced as his brother. They didn't even look alike."

"Who was it?"

"His attorney. One of my assistants recognized him from an intellectual property case he'd won. Once we knew who he was, we were able to get him to convince Ken it was better to hang up his stirrups and vacate the corral without the gunfight."

"Wow! An Old West metaphor." Lena smiled. "Where did you come up with that?"

"Oh, there are a lot of things you don't know about me," Blake said. "Maybe now that this is over, we can start over. Maybe you'll even play that round of golf with me."

Sorry

As she took the elevator back up to The Perfect Tee, Lena imagined that things with Blake were going to be different from then on. What most amazed her was how simply he had apologized. He had simply said he was sorry. He didn't follow that up with an excuse, starting with "But I was just …" like so many people did.

As soon as she reached her office, Lena called out to Amanda.

"Can you cancel the rest of my meetings for today and schedule a meeting with my execs — everyone but Ken — for first thing in the morning?" She owed them an explanation of what had happened, although she expected everyone would have heard the news by then. She still wanted to give them her version.

Then, she packed her briefcase and walked home to retrieve Bounty, who was surprised to see her and then ecstatic when she realized that they were going somewhere in the car. Lena drove straight out of Seattle and over the pass to Roslyn.

Lena opened the passenger door and Bounty jumped out onto the sidewalk in front of Terry's wine bar. It had been weeks since Bounty had been able to hang out on the floor of the tasting room and wait for tastings of summer sausage and cheese. She bounded through the door as Lena held it open.

"Bounty! Sweetie!" Terry fell to her knees to meet the big dog who slid on the wood planks into her. "I haven't seen you in so long!"

Lena watched them exchange kisses and hugs. Bounty couldn't stop wiggling, and Terry couldn't stop giggling. They had really missed each other.

"You probably aren't so happy to see me," Lena said as things calmed down.

Terry stood up and brushed the dog hair off her jeans. She looked at Lena, expressionless, and turned, walked behind the bar, and opened a case of wine. She yanked the bottles out of the box and lined them up on the back bar against the wall, releasing each one heavily on the granite surface.

Lena had lots of excuses for not telling Terry that she had seen Tom. She wasn't sure that it was fair to interpret the chumminess of Tom and his blonde friend as proof of anything. She hadn't seen them kiss, and she and Ryne hadn't stayed at the Brick late enough to know if they left together. Terry had professed a hope that she and Tom would get back together. And, because Lena and Terry had spent so little time together over the past couple of months, Lena thought it was a bad idea to storm into Terry's life with bad news.

But her reasons didn't matter. What mattered was that she was sorry.

So, she said so.

"I'm sorry, Terry. I'm sorry I didn't tell you."

Terry sniffed, and Lena realized she was crying.

"Oh, honey, I'm so sorry. I'm a horrible friend!" Lena started crying, too, as she ran behind the bar and threw her arms around Terry from behind. "Please, please forgive me!"

But, even as she did it, Lena felt silly. She was doing exactly what was expected from her as a friend — a female friend. It was a kind of stereotypical, emotional circus act. What compelled her to act like a thirteen-year-old, sobbing, hugging, and professing guilt she didn't really own?

"Oh, get off of me!" Terry yelled through her snotty sobs. "This is not some fifth-grade slumber party!"

Relieved that Terry's sentiment was pretty much the same as her own, Lena stepped back and rounded the bar, grabbing a napkin to wipe away her stingy tears. She sat at a stool and commanded Bounty to lie down at her feet. She watched as Terry finished unpacking another half-dozen wine bottles and storing them in their rightful places behind and under the bar.

Finally, Terry finished her work — it looked like make-work, really — and stood up behind the big bar counter to face Lena.

"What do you want, Lena?" she asked, sincerely. "What do you want me to say? That it's all fine? That it is Tom who is the schmuck, not you?"

Lena paused for a moment and thought. What was her real sin here? What did she really have to confess to or be sorry for? All she had done was give all parties the benefit of the doubt, and not pretend like she knew more than she did.

"Yeah, maybe," Lena said. "Right after 'you're forgiven?'"

Terry stopped. She put her elbows on the bar between them, bent at the waist with her forearms stretched forward, and for a long silent minute, she stared at her hands. Lena waited.

Finally, Terry took a deep breath and slowly released it through a small "o" she formed with her lips. She looked up at Lena with wide, wet eyes.

"Tom is the schmuck, not you," Terry said. "And I forgive you. It's not easy, but I do."

"Thank you," Lena said quietly, and waited for Terry to continue. Her friend stood up and walked around the bar and pulled out a stool next to Lena. She pushed herself up and plopped her small frame in the middle of the seat with practiced ease.

"I've been so sad lately." Terry shook her head and stared at her reflection in the mirror behind the bar, pulling at the crow's feet at the corners of her eyes. "Do you think I've aged? I feel like I've aged a hundred years. Of course, it's probably only been twenty or thirty." She gave out a half-hearted chuckle.

"You've probably aged a couple of months over the past couple of months," Lena answered. "Me too. But tell me about the sad part."

Terry raised her eyebrows. She looked like she didn't know if she was ready. But, after another long pause, she obliged.

"A month ago, I just wanted to get back together. I told you that," she started. "But he had clearly moved on already. So, no go.

"Since then …," Terry paused and swallowed a sob. "Since then, I've been trying to tell myself I don't care about Tom, I don't need him, blah, blah, that I'm just fine by my own, just me and my good friends."

"But then, I didn't seem like such a good friend?" Lena interjected.

"Yeah," Terry agreed. "You and Janet and everyone else. I started to realize that I really didn't have such good friends after all. At least that's what I thought. I felt crazy lonely. I knew I didn't want Tom back. I'm so mad at him, I don't think I'd ever let him come back. But I didn't want to be alone either."

She looked over at Lena. "Do you think I will always be alone?"

Lena shook her head slowly. "No, I don't think you have to be," she answered, trying not to be a Pollyanna but also searching for the right way to say what she thought: that it was going to be hard to find a good partner, and the older you are and the smaller the pool of candidates, the harder it was going to be. And that wasn't just true for Terry. It was true for everyone.

"I don't know if Tom is a good man or not," Lena said. "And I don't know if the two of you will or should ever get back together. But this much I do know: you did love each other once, and that's pretty hard to find once you're over fifty. It seems you can fall in love over and over when you're young, but it gets harder and harder to be charmed by someone the older and smarter you get."

Terry snorted her agreement.

Lena took the encouragement and continued. "But your life isn't a lottery, and you can't start making decisions about love based on odds. You have to decide only one thing: do you love Tom enough to try to make it work, in spite of all you know now."

Terry looked at her friend and frowned. "You know what? I don't think that made any sense at all."

Lena laughed. "No, it didn't."

"Well, kind of it did," Terry said. "You were right about one thing – the only question here is whether I want Tom to come back or not, and you know what? I really don't. And just because it's hard to find a husband or partner or boyfriend or whatever, that's no reason to put up with something that isn't working."

Lena nodded. "I think that's the bottom line."

Now it was Terry's turn to laugh. She slapped Lena's arm with the back of her hand. "Bottom line? I can't believe you said that! This isn't an accounting problem, Lena!"

Lena jumped off her stool and hugged her friend. "Watch Bounty for a minute. I drove up here in a hurry and I really have to pee."

When Lena returned to her bar stool, Terry was behind the bar, opening a bottle of wine. "Here," she said, pouring a glass of white wine and pushing it across to Lena. "Tell me what you think of this."

Lena smiled and took a sip. "It's interesting. A viognier?"

"Right!" Terry said. "You're so good. And now I want to change the subject. What kind of a dog do you think I should get?"

HER RELATIONSHIP WITH TERRY BACK on the mend, Lena slept well in her condo in Suncadia, and then rose early the next morning to get to work in Seattle. She had to take Bounty for a walk in the dark, drive over the pass, and then drop her dog off at her condo in Seattle before going into the office. It was a push, but she walked into The Perfect Tee just a little after eight o'clock.

That gave her an hour before her meeting with her direct reports — minus Ken — to plan how to discuss Ken's dismissal with the rest of her top executives. She closed her eyes and threaded her fingers together in a kind of meditation.

"Knock, knock."

Lena looked up to see Jordan standing at her door.

"Hey!" Lena greeted her, smiling. "Come in. What's up?"

"News," Jordan said, reaching out to offer Lena a newspaper. "I wanted to show you before we went into the meeting."

Lena took the copy of the New York Times that Jordan proffered. Her marketing VP had folded it open to a technology column in the business section, and Lena recognized the byline: Mandy English. And, nestled in the middle of the column was The Perfect Tee's logo. So, this was it.

Lena looked up at Jordan, hoping to get some indication of whether her gamble paid off before she had to read the column for herself. Jordan stood with the stoicism of a Buddhist monk and looked away.

The headline didn't give much away: Small online retailer takes on hackers.

Lena sat down and took a deep breath. She did her best to read the article the way it was meant to be read — word by word, sentence by sentence. But her eyes wouldn't hold, and her impatience won out. She skipped to the last paragraph.

It could have turned out to be foolish, and it could have turned out to be brave. When Bettencourt decided to take on the hackers, she didn't know how it would end. But all online retailers — indeed, all consumers who buy online with their credit cards — may end up owing her a favor. She proved they can be beat. They aren't the masters of the universe they have come to believe they were for far, far too long.

Lena looked up at Jordan, whose poker face had shattered into a huge smile.

"Pretty terrific, huh!" Jordan exclaimed. "Pretty fucking terrific!"

"I can't focus right now," Lena admitted. "I just skipped to the last paragraph. Is this really her take? We've saved the world?"

Jordan laughed. "Well, we haven't cured cancer, but Mandy seems to think we took a stand that was risky and long overdue. I think we come out smelling like roses. Or, I mean, you do. I'm not trying to take anything away from you!"

"Oh, Christ! Don't be silly," Lena chided her. "This isn't about me, and you know it. I get the credit because I also get the blame if things go bad. But we agreed on this strategy. It's about all of us."

She looked back down at the paper, and then called out to Amanda. "Please make a dozen copies of this for me, could you, Amanda?" she asked, handing the paper to her assistant. "I need them for the meeting in five minutes."

She turned back to Jordan, who was still smiling wide. "You know, this could have gone either way," Lena said. "We could have gotten a different reporter. It could have turned out very, very bad. We are lucky."

"The outcome of every gamble depends partly on luck." Jordan nodded. "But even poker players have skills they fall back on. The cards will fall, but it takes a good player to understand the odds." Clearly, Jordan remembered she had tried to talk Lena out of taking with Mandy and taking on the hackers.

Once her meeting with her executives was over, Lena sat down and read the article carefully. Mandy hadn't known about Ken's involvement in the hackers' attack, and Lena was glad that development had come too late to be part of the column. It wouldn't have been as positive if Mandy had known that the hackers had inside help.

What the column did was expose the tactic of blackmail, which other articles on credit card breaches had not discussed, at least not as far as Lena knew. It turned the tables on the hackers — blaming them, not the companies who were hacked — for the identity theft threats and vulnerabilities of online purchases. Lena thought Mandy may have gone a little overboard absolving most companies — but not all — of guilt in allowing these breaches. But who was she to argue with the article's basic conclusion?

Congratulatory calls and e-mails poured in throughout the day, including one from a most unlikely source: Lena's old CEO at TrueWeb, Roger, the very man who said she didn't have the technical savvy or leadership ability to be in top management. His e-mail fell far short of admitting his poor judgment of her character, if he even remembered it, and when Lena read it, she snickered. She didn't feel vindicated. But she did feel a bit more powerful. She immediately deleted the e-mail. It would be one of the few she didn't reply to with humble thanks.

Europe

That night, Lena and Ryne celebrated her PR victory with an expensive bottle of French wine Ryne had shipped home from his year in Provence and a pizza from Pagliacci's. They stayed at her condo rather than going out to eat so they could share the good fortune with Bounty and get to bed early.

After dinner, they walked Bounty down to the lake, bringing unfinished wine and their wine glasses with them. They sat on the wide wood dock at the south end of the lake and finished the bottle in the moonlight. Bounty lay in front of them and kept watch for dangerous ducks and other potential threats.

"You know, like Mandy wrote, that could have gone either way," Lena said, picking up on where their dinner discussion about the Times column had left. "I can't believe how well it turned out. Jordan says it wasn't all luck, but I think most of it was. I just can't figure out how we got so lucky."

"Luck doesn't have a why," Ryne said, softly. "It isn't rational. It's chance. There isn't any why."

Lena looked at him and smiled. His logic was impeccable, as always. That was one of the things she loved about him: his ability to be absolutely systematic in his thinking, while retaining his romantic side when logic wasn't necessary.

"You're right," she mused. "But what I worry about now is that hackers all over the world will be trying to get even with us. We could get hurt a lot worse."

"Did you talk with Sarah about it?" Ryne asked.

Lena had shared her plan with the company founder before she ever answered any of Mandy's questions, and Sarah had fully backed her decision. Sarah had been the first person Lena called after her morning meeting.

"Yeah," Lena said. "Sarah had already seen the article and would have called me, but her phone was busy with calls of congratulations, too."

"What did she say?" Ryne asked.

"Say about what? About the hackers?"

Lena was puzzled. Sarah had indeed started The Perfect Tee, and therefore had some credibility as a businessperson, but as far as Lena knew, Ryne had no reason to suspect she had greater PR expertise than Lena did.

"I was just thinking that as long as you have her support, you will be okay," Ryne said. For the first time, Lena realized how naïve he was about the way her world worked. It wasn't the founder of the company who held the cards, it was the guys who had funded the start-up – the VCs. But then, Ryne had always worked on the city desk at the newspaper, not the business desk, and in politics things were different. In business, it wasn't one man, one vote. It was one dollar, one vote. Her VCs had all the dollars. And all the votes.

"The VCs will decide if I'm okay, not Sarah," Lena said,

and let it drop. She didn't want to sound like she was lecturing Ryne on the ways of the business world. "But Sarah did say that she thought that, in the future, the hackers would rather target someone who didn't have the ability to pick up the phone and talk with a sympathetic New York Times reporter."

"Yeah, the Times has quite the cachet, doesn't it?" Ryne said, sounding a little hurt. He hadn't said anything to indicate that his bosses at the Seattle Times were pissed that she had worked with a reporter in New York instead of the home-town paper to expose the blackmail. Maybe they still didn't know about Ryne and her. If so, why was he so reluctant to reveal their relationship? Was he holding back because he wasn't sure about it yet?

But Lena suspected Ryne's lament was about something else. The center of Lena's media universe had shifted. It was no longer Ryne, who had let her know about Jim's connection with the blogger. Now it was a New York reporter who thought that Lena was the cat's pajamas and who had just helped her out of a jam.

"Ryne! You know I couldn't work with you on this," Lena whined. "It wouldn't have looked objective."

"No, you're right," Ryne said, nodding. He took another sip of wine from his glass. She watched his face in the soft lights of the small harbor.

There was a time, Lena recalled, when any sign of vulnerability like this in Ryne turned her off. She didn't want him to be defeated by a waif of a girlfriend who once played with him like a puppeteer. She didn't want him to be jealous of Kim; she wanted him to be confident, strong, courageous. Somewhat surprised, she realized she didn't need him to be perfectly solid anymore. His humility and faults didn't chip away at her love or respect anymore.

Ryne rinsed his wine glass out with some of the water they had brought for Bounty and sat back. He looked like he wanted to say something else, but he hesitated.

"What? What are you thinking?" she asked.

Ryne turned to look in her eyes. He took her chin in his free hand and kissed her gently. "I have something to tell you that I've been holding back."

"Holding back? Why?" Lena frowned.

"I'm quitting," Ryne said.

"Quitting? Quitting what? Us?"

"No, silly! I'm quitting my job."

Lena stared back at him for a long moment. She didn't know what to say. Work had seemed so important to Ryne that quitting was nothing short of astonishing.

Lena blinked and shook her head to clear the shock. Her opinion of him wasn't going to change if he quit. She'd still love him even if he decided to become a bum. But his job was such a big part of his identity – how she saw him – it would take a while for her to adjust to the change.

"Why?" she finally managed to ask.

"I'm going to write another novel," Ryne said, "and my bosses aren't willing to give me another leave."

"Another novel?"

"Yes, I just got a contract from Knopf for a novel I proposed at our last meeting in New York."

"Well, shoot! I think that's great! But why did you not want to tell me?"

"It seemed that you had so much stress, so many things to deal with that weren't fun. I didn't want to brag while you were struggling so hard to keep everything on an even keel."

"Brag? That isn't bragging," she said, leaning into his shoulder. "That's just good news."

"And ..." Ryne stopped.

Lena sat back up straight. Here comes the bad news, she thought.

"And, what?"

"And, I have to go to Europe for six months to do some research."

"Oh." Now it made sense. No wonder he hesitated telling her.

But then Ryne redrew the universe. "As long as Sarah is happy with you right now, do you think you could come with me?"

Lena was stunned again. Going to Europe wasn't just a matter of getting on a plane and schlepping around the continent for a few months of leisure. That would be easy to say yes to. But it would also mean stepping away from The Perfect Tee. It would mean putting friendships on hold, and maybe golf as well, for months – the kind of time period that could do serious damage to both. And it would mean leaving Bounty for an insufferably long time.

Perhaps most frightening, it would also mean making a kind of commitment to Ryne she hadn't really considered up to this point. Apparently, he hadn't been the only one holding back in ways; up to now she didn't realize she had been holding back too.

As if she read her mind, Bounty pushed her big head under Lena's elbow, tipping her wine glass and spilling a few drops of dark red onto Lena's khaki pants. Lena shifted her glass to her other hand. She hugged Bounty's big head and kissed her on the forehead.

"I don't know, Ryne," she finally answered. "I think this is something that Bounty and I have to talk over."

THE MEETING AT GTI HEADQUARTERS served as a warm-up for George's and Lena's presentation to her VCs early the next week.

At the meeting at GTI headquarters earlier that week, she, Dan, and George sat down with their CFOs and the business development team from Dan's staff to talk about financing the project.

George was apparently getting along much better with his new CFO, Chan, although George confided in her that he wasn't betting on a long-term, rosy relationship with any CFO anymore. Lena had brought her CFO, John, along for an extra ear that she knew was loyal to The Perfect Tee and her VCs, whose interests she was there to protect. But on the financial side, the GTI CFO, Bruce, had done most of the heavy lifting to get ready for the meeting.

Mergers and acquisitions were slim to none in GTI's history, but Bruce assured her that he'd recently hired a top-notch guy who had worked on the Acushnet deal that sold Titleist and Footjoy to Fila and a South Korean private equity firm.

Walking into the usual conference room in La Jolla, Lena was surprised how young this new M&A "star" looked. Miles looked half her age - literally. And in spite of some immature behavior — slumping in his chair, toying with his iPhone while others talked — he carried himself with confidence, and the hand-outs stacked in front of him for the meeting were impressively thick.

The meeting quickly dragged to an eye-drooping pace, as the three CFOs in the room debated the details of the discounted cash flow analyses – all six of them! – that Miles had developed to explore different funding options.

Two hours into the afternoon, Miles was still at it. "On the one hand, this might be the perfect time to lever up and get a higher operating margin on the entire company via this venture," he droned. Lena winced at "lever" – she hated it when people used nouns or transitive verbs as intransitive verbs, but she'd learned long ago to leave finance jargon alone. It didn't help to argue about it.

"The difference in DCF over seven years would be about…" the young M&A man continued his droll analysis and Lena tuned out. She was afraid she'd fall asleep. She couldn't sustain her interest in minute financial details beyond two hours. Finally, she excused herself for a "restroom break" and walked out to stretch her legs.

When she returned ten minutes later, Miles's financing discussion had finally ended. Marlena and Jacob, RF's and GTI's marketing vice presidents, walked into the meeting room with her to hone marketing strategies.

"What did you guys decide about financing?" Lena whispered to George as she sat back down next to him.

"Nothing. Everyone wants to spend more time with the numbers," George said. "But it seems like an equity partner makes more sense than debt."

"To you or to everyone else?"

"Both."

Now she had good news to bring to her investors: they would at least be given a chance to make an offer to buy into the deal.

The tenor of the VC meeting was much different from those earlier in the year. The success of the hacker strategy and the great sales results were obviously a factor. But Blake's new attitude probably had the greatest impact. He seemed downright friendly, not to mention supportive.

Using the three most popular financial models Miles had presented at the meeting, Lena and George gave the team a quick picture of the investment needed to start golf-ball production and marketing, and the kinds of returns they might expect given different sales assumptions.

"Where are you guys on the USGA approval?" Kyle asked.

"Nowhere," Lena said flatly. "We don't expect it, and we don't need it. If the golf industry is experimenting with "hack golf" and a twelve-inch hole, I think even the officials recognize that making everyone play the same game the pros play isn't going to grow the sport."

"Hack golf?" Kyle apparently hadn't heard about it.

"Like soccer on a golf course," Blake answered.

"Why don't you spin off the project and take it to the public?" Doyle asked, suggesting they do an IPO of the venture instead of keeping it inside GTI.

Lena started to respond, but Blake cut in.

"I've had some recent experience with small IPOs," he said, "and it hasn't been benign. I now believe revenue needs to be upwards of $300 million before a public company makes sense."

Lena was glad to have Blake carry that message for her. Finally, they had come to the same place on that issue, and she felt no need to say "I told you so."

After some discussion, the VCs agreed: they would like

to have the opportunity to talk with GTI's M&A guy and see whether an investment made sense. Blake said he'd set up the meeting on Lena's introduction.

"One more thing," Blake said, as the other three VCs started to pack up to leave. They sat back down.

"I heard from Jim Treacher's partner, Larry, the other day," he said. Lena was surprised. She hadn't heard from either Larry or Jim since she had talked to Larry about the leak of her personal history to the blogger.

"Apparently, their equity partnership didn't last too long," he said. "I'm not sure what happened, but Larry is now out on his own."

"Is he still interested in the golf-ball venture?" Doyle asked.

"He didn't say," Blake said. "But I thought it was only fair to let you all — especially you, Lena — know that Jim has burned one too many bridges. I don't think we'll be hearing from him again."

Approval

Lena hadn't seen Ken since Blake had effected his dismissal with the help of Jerry, The Perfect Tee's legal counsel. Jerry and HR had worked out a severance deal that paid Ken nothing, but let him off the hook more than she would have preferred. Jerry had convinced her it would be expensive to pursue him for his theft of company assets, including passwords and code, and there would be no financial recovery for the company.

Saying it was against his better judgment, Jerry let her meet with Ken when he came into the office to sign the agreement. Lena was intent on having a chance to finally put the arrogant IT guy in his place, regardless how uncomfortable it was likely to be.

Lena arranged for them to talk in a stuffy telephone room, where staffers who worked in the company's open office space could make phone calls in private. It was only about eight feet long and five feet wide and had no art on the bland, beige walls — a far more appropriate place to have their final face-off than the comfortable, elegant conference room they used for executive staff meetings.

Ken walked in, escorted by building security, but when he saw Lena waiting, he turned to leave.

"You can leave now, but if you do, you won't have an opportunity to sign the agreement HR worked out for you," she said. "If you don't sign today, I will pursue prosecution."

Ken reluctantly turned back into the room, sat down, and hunched forward. He folded his hands and focused a steely gaze out the small window at the brick wall of the building next door, appearing stoic in the face of the criticism he had to know was coming. Lena closed the door.

"Do you have anything to say for yourself?" Lena asked, enjoying the opportunity to stretch out his discomfort. She'd never realized how vindictive she could be. But then, she'd rarely had this much reason.

Ken looked Lena in the eye, his jaw set. "I've known since the beginning that you were a little person," he said, obviously not looking to curry her favor. "You have a chip on your shoulder about who knows what and you hate engineers."

"What does any of that have to do with what you tried to do to this company?" Lena asked. "This isn't about me. It's about you."

"I just think you should know what your employees think of you," Ken said, sneering up at her and then returning his gaze out the window at the blank wall next door.

"I'm not falling for that," Lena said. "I'm totally comfortable with my relationship with our employees." She lied — she still had some work to do to repair the damage that Ken had done there. But she wasn't about to discuss that with him.

"But it's true." Ken said.

"That I have a chip on my shoulder? Yes," Lena said.

"And all I have to do to get rid of it is succeed at running this company. Then it won't matter where I came from. But you didn't want that to happen."

Ken didn't answer. Was that all he had?

"And, let me tell you: I don't hate engineers," Lena continued. "I have the utmost respect for those NASA engineers working on sending a probe to Mars. I have extreme regard for the engineers who are exploring planets in other solar systems and dark matter with nothing but mathematical models and metallurgy. And the bio-chem engineers working on cures for cancer and Alzheimer's, and the mechanical and electrical engineers designing better medical laser scalpels and better radiation treatments. Even the programmers and analysts who built the government health care website."

She paused. Ken sat mute, unmoved.

"I just don't have that much respect for guys who think they're masters of the universe because they build apps that enable people to tell me they're tired or hungry or sick of homework or what they ate for dinner. You guys write code. You administer networks. But come on, Ken. You're not curing cancer!"

"Do your other engineers know how you feel?" Ken finally responded. "Does Taylor know you hold him in such low esteem?"

"I don't hold him in low esteem," Lena said, shaking her head. "He does a great job, and I respect him for that. But I don't think he believes he's god's gift to the universe — at least he doesn't act like he does. That's what people who think they can get by with theft and deceit think. People like you."

"You may have won this little battle, but your lack of software experience will bring you down eventually," Ken said, snickering.

"That again?" Lena held up her hands in frustration. "That business about my not knowing anything about software or programming? Haven't we already crossed that bridge? Didn't we already figure out that your expertise and my expertise were supposed to be complementary, not redundant?"

"I think that you've been awfully lucky, considering how little you know," Ken said, "how little knowledge you have about the real intellectual property here."

Lena was furious. He wanted this conversation about her weaknesses and prejudices instead of about his crime. What kind of leader was she if she couldn't even fire someone well?

"I think you're wrong," Lena steered the conversation back on the right track. "I've been lucky, yes. But let's not forget what the real subject is here. I didn't sell my soul to some scammer for a few bucks." Lena moved a little closer and looked down at Ken. "I would never have done what you did, and it doesn't take a computer science degree to know better."

Ken looked up, hatred seeping from every pore. "Now that you have Blake on your side, you think you've mastered this thing, don't you?"

"What thing?"

"You think you're now the boss, that you won't have to answer to anyone or prove yourself again," he stated, menacingly. "But let me tell you, you will always have a boss. It will be a VC like Blake, or an investor, or maybe even a lowly IT guy like me who knows a lot more than you do about what makes your company tick. But you will never be on top, Lena. Never."

"I don't expect to be," Lena answered. She stood and walked to the door. As she closed it behind her, she was shaking. Not only had he usurped her intent to humiliate him, his last point had unnerved her. Regardless of his internal bias or motivation, he was right. She had won this battle against him, but as long as she needed the approval others, just like everyone else, she'd never be in control. She knew that. She really did. But, for the first time, she realized she now believed it.

She just hated the fact that it had to be Ken who brought it to her attention.

LENA LEFT THE MEETING KNOWING that Ken didn't care what she thought of him. He had no respect for her, and that was never going to change. The only thing that tipped the balance in her favor was that no one would ever hire him again for a position that gave him access to a company's network. He'd pay for his subterfuge for the rest of his career. Everyone would know. Tech might have been a very broad industry, but in some ways it was also a very small world.

As Lena walked home over the hill that separated the piers on Puget Sound from her South Lake Union neighborhood, she stopped at the Space Needle and looked up. She'd been to the top once, but that was before the 2001 Nisqually earthquake. Once she had felt terror in that earthquake – and she was only on the fourth floor of her office building at the time – she had refused to go back up.

Friends who came to visit Seattle had to go up to take in the magnificent views from the observation deck without her.

Leaning back to look up at the big disc in the sky, Lena swayed slightly and grabbed the railing of the crowd-control chicane that wound up a concrete ramp to the ticket booth. It wasn't the needle that was moving, Lena laughed, even though her unsteady stance made it look that way. She was the one who was shaky, although standing on perfectly solid ground.

On weekdays in spring, before the big summer tourist crowds descended on Seattle, no one stood in line waiting for a ticket to ride to the top. But it was a gorgeous, clear day — the perfect setting for a grand view of Seattle's iconic Mount Rainier, the Cascades and the Olympics. Why not? She had slain bigger dragons than this lately. Put your reason to the test, she told herself. What are the chances of an earthquake happening the minute you go up there?

All the logic and reason that Lena considered didn't keep her heart from pounding as she rose with two tourists to the top. When she stepped out onto the metal platform, she focused on breathing slowly and regularly. Still, it took about five minutes before she steadied herself enough that she could walk all the way up to the railing and peer down.

Looking out at the stupendous view of the snow-capped mountain ranges; the volcanoes of Mount Rainier and Mount Baker; the green urban forest; and the sparkling water of the sound, Lena realized how little she was taking advantage of the wonderful place where she lived. Other than trips up and back to Suncadia, had she spent any time enjoying the Pacific Northwest in the past five years?

How narrow had her world become? Seattle, Roslyn, Suncadia and occasional trips to San Diego and Palm Springs. A narrow slice of the business world, surrounded by a few executives not much different from herself. A little bit of golf and a few friends — fewer friends than she had last year before the disaster with Brandt and Carly in Hawaii, for that matter.

She never got out on the Sound anymore, not on the jazz cruises put on by the local public radio station; not on the Victoria Clipper to the San Juan Islands. She hadn't been to Portland for ten years, which was the last time, she drove down with a friend to visit the city's famous bookstore and hang out in the hip Pearl District. She hadn't even visited any of the half-dozen great golf courses on the Kitsap Peninsula — only thirty minutes from Seattle by ferry — since she'd won her amateur title.

Lena studied the view below her as it deepened with the growing shadows of spring's long evenings. Maybe it was time to break out of the narrow rut of business and golf that she had allowed to define her. Maybe she'd accomplished as much in her business career as she wanted to. Maybe it was time to do something different. Perhaps going to Europe with Ryne was a good idea. At this point, even playing golf in Europe would be something different.

It was just an idea, just a thought. She couldn't decide until they had determined what was going to happen with the golf-ball venture, or who would pick up her role at The Perfect Tee. If she was going to abandon ship, she owed it to Sarah to make sure there was a new captain who was capable of keeping the company on course. Sarah's friendship was too important to lose.

Before taking the elevator back to terra firma, Lena stopped at the rotating restaurant on the level below the observation deck. If she could handle the deck, she could handle a spot a little bit lower. She had a celebratory glass of wine, toasting herself and the end to her troubles with Ken, her new relationship with Blake, and the likely start-up of RF Golf. And the fact that she was finally back on the top of the Space Needle. It was a lot to accomplish in a couple of years.

AT THEIR SECOND MEETING ABOUT the golf-ball deal, Blake reported to George and Lena on the VCs' meeting with GTI's business development team in San Diego.

"It went very well," Blake said, once the salutations and preliminary small-talk were done. The group spent the next few minutes detailing for Lena and George what their major concerns and questions were about the deal. Apparently, the USGA approval – or lack of it – wasn't an issue for them. The issue that generated the most discussion was whether consumers would be willing to pay for the technology that allowed them to find their balls, or if they'd rather just take a drop with another cheap ball. Lena wasn't sure that would be the deciding factor in the VCs' decision, but it provided for a significant amount of entertaining speculation. The meeting was the most fun she'd ever had with the VCs.

"What are you guys thinking?" Lena said, finally, trying to wrap up the discussion in time for lunch. "Are you going to submit a proposal? Or do you need more time to look at the deal?"

Doyle answered for them. "I believe we're going to

look at it," he said. "It isn't complicated, though. It shouldn't take too long."

"But," interjected Blake, who looked first at Lena and then at George with a sparkle in his eye, "I have one big hurdle I have to get over before I can commit, whatever the deal looks like."

"What's that?" asked George.

"I think there's one thing we need to know about the woman who has been leading the organization of this venture," Blake said, swinging his head around from George to wiggle his eyebrows at Lena.

"What?" Lena laughed.

"Can you really play golf, or were all of those other women pushovers?"

"How are you planning to decide that?" Lena asked, amused but also a bit concerned about where the conversation was headed.

"Well ..." Blake started, teasingly. "I asked you to play golf with me four years ago when we hired you as CEO of The Perfect Tee, and you have resisted ever since. I think I finally can make the case that this is the time you should take one for the team. Are you willing to play for this deal?"

Lena blanched. She certainly couldn't risk the possibility of losing a potential investor – her VC group – by losing a golf match to Blake. Her game was rusty – she played only a couple of times a month these days, and when she did, she didn't work very hard at it.

"I understand that you aren't taking golf as seriously these days," Blake said, as if reading her mind. Was she really that transparent? "But neither am I."

"Are you suggesting that your decision would depend

on a golf game? Really?" George interjected, sounding flab-
bergasted.

Blake waved him off, and continued to look at Lena.

"I'm not saying that you have to win to get my vote,"
Blake said. "I'm just saying that you have to play with me
to get me to vote. And, of course, we could put something
else on the line to make it interesting."

"What are you suggesting?" Lena said, starting to take
the competitive bait that Blake was reeling out to her. She
couldn't immediately think of what she owned or had access to that Blake would find interesting enough to compete for.

"Maybe the next invitation you get to a PGA tournament could be passed along to someone as lowly as me," he
proposed.

Lena laughed. She would have given him that if he'd
just asked anytime in the past three years. Then, she realized: he really didn't want to win anything. He just wanted her to finally relent and play a round of golf with him,
something she'd always resisted as likely to interfere with
their delicate balance of power.

"Okay!" she said. "You are on. Now you make vote to
make a bid for RF Golf, and I will meet you to play wherever you choose. Just pick a nice day because I am a very,
very fair weather golfer."'

Drive for Dough

Lena was pleased with Blake's choice for the venue for their much-anticipated round of golf. She had wanted to play the new Salish Cliffs course north of Olympia on the Kitsap Peninsula across the Sound from Tacoma since it opened in 2012. But playing new golf courses was one of many things she had put off in order to focus on The Perfect Tee and the golf-ball venture.

On the other hand, competing on a course she'd never seen before posed its challenges. It was very easy to be mis-led by the distances on a scorecard or even on a good GPS system. Uneven lies, thick rough, wet fairways, elevated greens – they were all unknown the first time you played any course.

Still, Blake said he'd never played it either, so at least they were in the same boat.

The June day chosen for the match was spectacularly clear and warm. That was a good sign, Lena thought; it was unusual to find nice weather in June anywhere along the West Coast it seemed, from San Diego all of the way past Vancouver, B.C. Then she realized that if it were a good sign for her, it was for Blake as well. She was going to have to look for a good omen that pointed only to her.

Lena had stayed overnight at the Little Creek Casino near the golf course with Ryne. George, Tina, and Terry had come over that evening from Seattle as well and had joined them for dinner and a few cranks of the one-armed bandits. Kim, on a break from the PGA Tour for a couple of weeks, drove over that morning. He had called her a week before, and over dinner, they apologized to each other for whatever sins they could think of that explained the demise of their relationship. When she told him that she had a match with Blake, he insisted on caddying for her.

Lena was feeling a little guilty for having such a partisan crowd when they pulled into the parking lot and unloaded her clubs. Blake stood alone, chatting with the starter at the bag drop.

Blake had reserved two hours' worth of tee-times, which allowed everyone to take a cart out on the course and watch the match.

"This must have cost a pretty penny," Lena observed as she shook Blake's hand.

"Well worth it," Blake said, smiling broadly. "I've been waiting four years to play golf with a USGA champion!"

Lena wasn't sure whether to take him seriously; their friendly relationship was still too new for her to be able to read between the lines.

"Well, I hope I can make it worth the wait," she said, and introduced Blake to Ryne, Terry, and Kim. "I hope you don't mind I have a little bigger gallery than you do."

"Oh, Doyle, Kyle, and Nick are on their way. VCs are never late for meetings, are they?" he teased. "And my wife is in the pro shop looking for a souvenir. She's my caddie for the day."

"Nice!" Lena laughed. "I brought a professional. Kim has been working the PGA tour for most of the past year."

If Blake was bothered by her advantage, he didn't show it. "Let's go warm up!" he shouted to the small crowd with a big inclusive arm wave, and hopped into his golf cart and spun away toward the driving range. "What a great day!"

Lena looked at Kim and Ryne with a raised eyebrow. "Should I be worried?" she asked them under her breath. "He seems terribly happy."

Lena started warming up on the range while both Kim and Ryne looked on, chatting like long-time friends. She was amazed at how easily they had gotten past their competition over her. Maybe it was because they really were grown-ups.

Once she felt loose, she and Kim headed for the putting green, and Ryne and Terry headed to the clubhouse to stock up on beer for the spectators. Lena and Kim were just walking off the practice green when she looked up and saw Brandt and Carly walking toward them. "Oh, look!" she shouted at no one in particular and ran to hug them both at once. "I can't believe you're here! Who told you?"

"Terry," Brandt answered, matter-of-factly.

"So, you're not mad at me anymore?"

"No, of course not," Carly answered for both of them. "We never were. It was an accident. And he's healed just fine. The winter's a terrible time to play golf in Seattle anyway." Carly put her arm around Lena and walked her back to her cart where everyone was waiting for the round to begin.

"Well, you are my good omen," Lena said, smiling through tears, and looking around at her little crowd of friends. Kim had forgiven her for abandoning him for Ryne, and had returned Cali to Lena's care whenever he was out on tour with Lionel. Terry had forgiven her for not telling her about Tom. Brandt was able to walk without crutches again and had apparently forgiven her, too. Even Tina seemed to have accepted Lena's rejection, and she and George looked happy together.

Apparently, a romantic rejection, a surprise love triangle, a betrayal of trust, and a broken knee were not sufficient reasons for anyone to abandon a friend. Friendship was more resilient than she knew.

"What?" Carly asked. "What are you getting all weepy about?"

"Never mind." Lena laughed. "Not important. I'll explain later."

Salish Cliffs was highly awarded as a top golf course in the state as soon as it opened, and it didn't disappoint Lena and Blake or their little crowd of spectators. Many of the tee boxes were elevated, offering views of one hundred eighty degrees or more of the surrounding wooded hills or peekaboo views of the sound. Each hole felt secluded, like it was the only one on the course. Hawks and bald eagles soared overhead, enjoying the free ride of rising thermal air currents, and deer hopped across the fairways in front of them in twos and threes.

Lena and Blake played from the same white tees, but he had to give her six strokes to even out the men's and women's ratings. Since they were playing match play, that meant he had to give her an extra stroke on the six hardest holes. With that advantage, she came to the eighth tee box ahead by one hole.

At a daunting 550 yards from the white tees, the hole would require three long shots. Considering how far they had to carry their first two shots in order to play a short iron shot into the green, the fairway looked dangerously narrow. The longer the shot, the higher the risk of it fading right or drawing left into the trees.

"So, this is why it's the hardest hole on the course," Lena said out loud to no one in particular.

"Afraid, chica?" Blake teased her as she watched Kim pull her driver out of her bag.

"Nah," Lena said, holding up her had to refuse the driver. "Give me the three-wood, Kim."

"You're crazy, it's 550 yards!" Blake said, surprised.

"I'm not crazy enough to blow a one-stroke lead being macho about my drives," she answered. "Remember: 'drive for show, putt for dough.'"

Lena played it safe, and finished the hole with a bogey, while Blake carded a seven, thanks to a nasty slice and a lost ball on his drive.

"Probably could use that RF technology to find that ball." It was Lena's turn to tease.

But the tenth hole — another narrow, long par-five challenge — proved her nemesis. Lena abandoned her caution and pulled her driver on the tee box. She drove into a sand trap on the right, escaped to the center of the fairway with a sand wedge, but then sent her third shot into a sand trap on the left. She over-clubbed trying to get out of the sand, and her fourth shot landed on the far side of the green, and rolled off into a messy tangle of rough. Discouraged and angry at herself for ignoring her own advice, she conceded the hole.

Still up by one hole, Lena stood on the tee on number fourteen, and conferred with Kim. It wasn't a terribly long par-four, but the approach shot had to clear a nasty ravine, and there was no room between the heavily-vegetated hazard and the green. They decided she would lay up on the second shot, and hope a wedge on the approach would put the ball within one-putt range.

Luckily, her drive was longer than Blake's, and he didn't have the chance to take advantage of Kim's good advice by example. Blake tried to reach the green with his second shot, and his ball ended up lost in the ravine. Lena safely landed in the middle of the green with her approach, and even though she two-putted, she still won the hole with a bogey.

The two players tied on the next three holes, and the match was over on seventeen. Lena was up two holes with only one to play. They played the eighteenth hole for the fun of it.

As they drove the short distance to the club house, Blake skidded to a stop right in front of her cart. Kim hit the brake and barely avoided hitting him.

"Are you crazy?" he yelled at Blake.

Blake turned around and addressed Lena. "You know, I think that if I hadn't given you those six shots, you wouldn't have won. I think we should fashion a play-off."

"But I only needed four of those six," she protested. "Are you a sore loser?"

"Yeah, maybe, but let's do something that puts us both on equal footing. How about a long-drive contest?"

"Seriously? I out-drove you at least half of the time," she said, shaking her head.

"The winner will have to buy dinner."

Lena sat back against the seat of the golf cart and contemplated the situation. If she won, there'd be absolutely no questioning her total victory for the day. If she lost, the worst it could mean would be a tie of sorts – she won the round, he won the long-drive contest. At this point in her improving relationship with Blake, an even score didn't sound like such a bad idea.

"Okay," she finally said. "Three shots at it, and if you take a second or a third, you can't go back and claim the earlier attempt."

"Deal!" Blake said, turning and squealing his tires. He led the way to the driving range. Their small entourage followed.

Lena had honors. For the first time of the day, she felt nervous setting her ball on the tee. She took a deep breath, stood back to eye her shot. The range was wide enough to accept just about any hook or slice, but anything spinning right would lose distance.

She stepped up and swung. In the middle of her down swing, she realized she hadn't relaxed her shoulders, and the drive flew a disappointing 200 yards.

Chuckling, Blake set up and hit his first drive. His ball carried twenty yards farther, and he turned to Lena and smiled. "I guess you'll need to try again. Or are you ready to concede?"

"Of course not!" she laughed. "Get ready to curtsy!"

Lena's next drive was her best of the day, landing at least 245 yards down the range. Kim measured it with his range finder, and announced the yardage to their audience.

"Now, I guess you have no choice," she told Blake, turning to stand back to watch his second attempt. "Go for it!"

Blake laughed. "That was pretty amazing. But watch this."

The competitive juices were apparently flowing in his veins as well, and Blake hit his best drive of the day, just dribbling past Lena's drive.

"Your turn," he said.

"Now I guess I have no choice." She laughed and stepped up to the teeing area. She turned around and looked at all of her friends watching behind her. "Remember this day," she announced to them. "And Blake, remember and weep."

That evening, she had one of the best meals of her life, and what made it so good was that she didn't have to pay for it.

Drive for show? How about drive for dough? she thought as she fell asleep next to Ryne that night.

"Larry," Lena answered the phone. "I'm surprised to hear from you. What's up?"

Back in the office the next afternoon, Lena decided Larry's call would be the first of a dozen phone messages she needed to attend to. She hadn't heard from him since she had called him to talk about Jim's nefarious leak to the blogger. While she hadn't thought much about it since then, her call had apparently had an effect. Jim had disappeared.

"I heard that congratulations are in order," he said. "I understand you beat Blake two ways to Sunday."

"Yeah, it was a pretty good day for me," she said. "I'm surprised, though, that news travels so fast."

"I heard it from George."

"You talked to him?"

"Yes, and now you. I have news for you both."

Lena caught her breath. It seemed that these kinds of "news announcements" usually were a mixed bag at best — some good and some bad. Often, they were just bad.

"I have made an offer for GTI."

Lena sat up straight in her chair. "What? Really?"

"Yes," he laughed, hearing the surprise in her voice. "I put a deal together with some of the investors who got shut out of the Acushnet deal. We're offering a 50 percent premium to the market, and I wanted you to know that the golf-ball deal was part of the reason we're so excited about it."

Lena sat silently for a moment, turning the news over in her mind. So, they wouldn't need her VC's money after all. Other than that, she wasn't sure how this news would affect her, but mostly, she worried that it would mean she would have to deal with Jim.

"What about Jim? Is he involved?" she asked.

"No, our partnership ended a short time after I talked with you last."

Lena was relieved. She took an audibly deep breath into the receiver. However creepy Larry had seemed at first, he'd turned out to be a pretty good guy.

"Well, congratulations, Larry," she finally responded. "I'm happy for you. I hope this all works out. But what about Dan?"

"Dan can stay if he wants," Larry said. "We aren't managers, we're investors."

"Great," she said, relieved about that too. "I've been impressed with him and his team."

"But how about you?" Larry asked.

"What do you mean?"

"Would you be willing to come to work for us, running the golf-ball venture?"

"Oh, my!" Lena was surprised.

"Is that a yes?"

"Definitely not!" she replied, immediately embarrassed at the volume of her own voice.

"That's a no?"

"No," she backtracked quickly. "I mean it's not a yes, at least not yet." In her surprise, Lena babbled on. "Wow, I don't know what to say. I need to think about this. I have a job, and I need to think about whether I'm ready to leave it, and if I do, what that means for The Perfect Tee."

"Of course." Larry laughed. "I didn't mean to spring that on you. I'd like to come to Seattle and talk with you next week."

Lena hung up the phone and realized she was shaking. It was a lot of news to absorb at once. The golf-ball venture was going to move forward. She was being offered a chance to run it for a new set of investors. All of this meant she would have to make a lot of decisions, very fast.

She was torn. If she took the golf-ball job, she'd have another opportunity to succeed at running a venture, and if she did, her success at The Perfect Tee couldn't be seen as a fluke.

But on the other hand, she'd been running a company for nearly four years. And for those four years, she'd had little time for anything else. She wasn't playing much golf even though that hadn't kept her from beating Blake. She hadn't been spending enough time with Bounty, and she was facing the possibility that Ryne would be taking off for Europe early the next year without her.

And worse than all of that, she wasn't ready to take on a whole new set of bosses that she'd have to prove herself to, a new set of adversaries, and a whole new set of engineers and CFOs she'd have to win over. She wasn't interested in more of those battles. She had enough money to retire and no desire to accumulate more wealth for the sake of it — or for the sake of a bigger house or a fancier car. None of that appealed to her.

What did appeal to her was traveling to Europe for a while with Ryne. She could leave Bounty with Terry for six months. She could take a barge down the Rhine, play some golf in Andalusia, and tour the wineries of the Côtes du Rhone. She'd never seen Tuscany or walked the Cinque Terre. She'd never played golf in Scotland, or hiked the West Highland Trail. She wanted to bike in Amsterdam and walk the Camino de Santiago in Spain.

Of course, she couldn't do it all in six months. But suddenly, spending another three or four years in the corporate world seemed even more impossible.

That night, she told Ryne she would come with him to Europe. She called Terry and asked her to keep Bounty, a request that her friend enthusiastically granted. Then, she called Sarah.

The Dedication

Sarah promoted Jordan to CEO at The Perfect Tee, and Lena spent the rest of the summer helping her get up to speed on those parts of the business she'd not been involved in before. By the middle of August, Lena was free. She and Ryne wouldn't leave for Europe until spring. Until then, they'd spend some time in Palm Springs and go to New York for Christmas. She'd work on her golf game, and he'd work on his next novel.

At the end of August, Ryne treated Lena with a birthday trip: four days at Bandon Dunes Golf Resort. They left Bounty with Terry, who was looking forward to introducing them to her two new Corgis, Heidi and Tristan, and reveling in a crowded houseful of loving canines.

Ryne and Carly drove down the coast of Washington and Oregon, enjoying the scenery, a nearly forgettable minor opening act compared with the blissful experience of four rounds of links-style golf at Bandon. Neither Ryne nor Lena had ever played at the resort before, even though it was considered one of the top golf destination in the country.

Ryne surprised her by inviting Carly and Brandt to join them, all paid for out of his advance from the first novel, which had just left the printer. The two couples stayed at the Inn at Bandon, and mixed with the other guests in the evenings at the bar in the Library, a perfect setting for happy discussions about wind, rain, great holes, horrific triple-bogeys, and personable caddies. It was all golf, all the time, and Lena couldn't imagine better way to celebrate both the end of her fifty-fourth year and the end to her tenure at The Perfect Tee.

After drinks at the bar the last night of their stay in Bandon, Lena and Ryne had dinner alone in the lodge. As they finished a shared dessert, Ryne reached into his messenger bag and handed Lena a package. She knew it was his book — fresh off the press. She tore the comic-paper wrapping off, and stared at the cover.

The illustration was of a woman golfer, standing far off in the distance on a tree-lined golf course. The woman didn't necessarily look like Lena, but she was relieved that it didn't look like Kimberly either. She smiled and looked up at Ryne.

"Open it!" he demanded.

She opened the cover and was disappointed to see that the first page was not autographed. But then, she turned to the next page and read the dedication, phrased as a question.

She looked up and met Ryne's waiting eyes.

"Yes," she answered them. "Yes, I will."

9 79899 1 496766